JET VII

Sanctuary

Russell Blake

BOONE COUNTY PUBLIC LIBRARY
BURLINGTON, KY 41005
www.bcpl.org

Published by

Reprobatio Limited

CHAPTER 1

Medellín, Colombia

Amber veins of light trickled down the surrounding slopes, giving the metropolis a festive aura even at eleven on a moonless night. The cool mountain air huffed benignly, a welcome deliverance after a passing cloudburst had rinsed the city clean, leaving behind an essence of ozone, jungle, and wet earth mingled with the smell of wood-fired barbecues and exhaust. The downtown nightclub area had just found its stride, and young lovers ambled along in time as they toured the car-clogged boulevards, the atmosphere crackling with excitement and possibility.

In a working-class neighborhood near the clubs, a blue neon toucan clutching a whiskey bottle and waving an AK-47 blinked over the doorway of a colonial façade nestled at the bottom of a deserted side street. The faded lettering on the frontage promised cold beer and air-conditioning. Strains of plaintive music drifted from the entry, a salsa ballad equal parts heart-wrenching lament and diatribe against love gone wrong. A collection of rusting sedans and battered trucks lined the curb for the entire block. Roving stray dogs loped along in the shadows in search of scraps or better booty, their occasional warning growls competing with the mélange of ambient music.

Inside the gloomy watering hole, a pall of smoke hung over the customers like a cloud of mosquitoes. A wiry bartender with heavy acne scars and a thick black mustache stood behind a dark wood bar polishing a glass, one eye on a television silently blaring out Shakira's greatest hits as the feisty singer's hips ground with rhythmic veracity. The clientele was awash with middle-aged men, alone and serious about drinking, doing so in muted tones and with the steady efficiency of automatons. Blind by now to the image of the gun-toting warrior toucan – an unfortunate theme on the dingy walls – they had long since stopped feeding the half-century-old red jukebox that glowed in the far corner, and conversation was muted. The smattering of ladies among them were professional companions for hire who'd been plying their trade there for so many summers they now played the jukebox out of habit.

Five men sat near the back of the room at a circular wooden table, a small pile of American money in the center – tens and twenties. Bottles of half-drunk beer sat sweating as wooly tendrils of gray smoke streamed upward from two oversized ashtrays.

Four of the players were obviously local, faces hard, skin the color of burnished brass – men who spent their lives outdoors, the sun's toll a badge of honor. The fifth man had light-brown hair, a goatee and a fair complexion. His face was unremarkable except for the eyes, which were grayer than sharkskin beneath their hooded lids. He reached for his nearly empty rum and Coke and drained it, then set the glass back on the table and laid his cards face down in front of him.

The other men suppressed their disapproval as he leaned back and fished a cigarette from the pack beside his cocktail, every movement slow, as if the alcohol had caught up with him and the simple act was exhausting. He flipped open a steel Zippo lighter and thumbed it alight. Once his Marlboro was glowing, he blew a long stream of smoke at the ceiling.

"Come on. What's it going to be?" a player snarled in Spanish, his patience at an end.

"Why, Jaime – that's right, isn't it – Jaime? It's rude to intrude on another man's thoughts when he's considering how to play his winning hand to maximum effect." The American could have been chiding a child – in acceptable Spanish.

"We don't have all night," Jaime's companion complained from beside him. "Enough of the big talk. All night with the big talk. Put up or shut up."

"See? That's the thing. I took the time to remember your friend's name. Yours too, César. And yet I'd win a side bet you didn't do the same for mine, which is just plain rude." The American supplemented his declaration with a cold stare.

As César leaned forward, the lines of hardship on his face deepened under the glare of the lamp suspended over the table. "I don't care. I'm not here for a date. What are you going to do?" he demanded, nodding at the American's cards and the pile of dollars.

"Are you always in such a hurry to lose your money?"

Jaime slammed his hand down on the table. "Enough with the talk. Let's see what you've got."

The American shook his head. "That's not how poker is played, gentlemen. A man has to have time to make a decision."

The snub nose of a Smith & Wesson revolver glinted in the light as César placed it on the table. He glowered at the American, and when he spoke, it came out as a rasp. "This is how we play it here."

"Well, if we're going to do it that way, we might as well play for it all, your gun included. Looks like it might be worth a couple hundred." The American pushed in everything in front of him. "Raise. All in."

César nodded. "Call. The pistol too." He pushed his remaining few bills into the pot. "Showdown, *puta*."

The thickset man eyed the gun without blinking. "I'll show when you do," he said, stretching poker etiquette to the breaking point.

"Don't be an old woman," César scolded and fanned his cards out with a triumphant smile. "Three aces." He gave the American a dark look. "Time to go home broke, *puta*."

The thickset man rolled his cards onto the table and snorted. "*Mierda*. Beats my two pair."

Jaime tossed his cards into the muck. "I'm out."

The American hesitated, the tension building as he lifted the edge of his cards and looked at them. He drew a long pull from his cigarette and flipped over the pasteboards, revealing queens full of sevens.

César's left eye twitched once. His gaze locked on the American's, and then he was groping for his gun as the thickset man pushed away from the table.

The American reacted in a blur. Cigarettes flew everywhere as the heavy glass ashtray caught César across the bridge of his nose. Blood erupted onto his shirt, and he howled in rage as Jaime clumsily drew a Ruger 9mm pistol. The American rounded the table with a lunge, and his beer bottle caught Jaime in the temple. The bottle shattered, leaving the American holding the jagged neck, which he twisted across César's throat before grabbing the revolver from the tabletop and slamming the butt into Jaime's jaw. Bone cracked with an audible snap. Jaime's cry of anguish was cut short by another blow to his skull. His eyes rolled into his head, and he slumped to the floor with a groan. César clutched his traumatized neck, trying to stop the spurting river of blood with his splay of wooden fingers.

The American stooped down, retrieved the Ruger from the floor, and pocketed it. The thickset man stood, transfixed by the sudden violence, his eyes wide with fear, his breathing heavy. The rest of the bar had gone quiet, nobody daring to say a word. The American held up the revolver so everyone could see it.

"I won this pot fair and square. Right?" he said, his voice soft.

Thickset man nodded. "Absolutely."

"And everyone saw César there go for his gun, and his buddy Jaime pull his – on an unarmed man, *sí*? This was self-defense."

"Of course."

The American scooped up the cash, stuffed it into his jacket pocket and then moved to the door. At the threshold he turned to face the room, holding the revolver aloft. "It would be smart if nobody was still here in five minutes. I might come back to check. You" – he waved at the bartender with the gun – "give the police an accurate description of me. A short laborer from the coast – dark skin, black hair. If anyone says different, I'll hear about it, and you don't want to invite that into your life." He stared at the assembled drinkers and then reached into his pocket, tossing a hundred-dollar bill onto the floor. "That's for the drinks. I mean it about coming back to check," he said as he tucked the revolver into his waistband. "Five minutes."

Once on the deserted sidewalk he broke into a jog. When he reached the main drag, he turned the corner and blended into the flow of late-night revelers, confident the bar would be empty by the time the police arrived. Nobody wanted trouble, and the cops in Medellín were as notorious as anywhere in Latin America for extortion and corruption. Being caught up in an investigation would lead nowhere good, especially for the working girls, who'd probably vanished within sixty seconds of his exit, followed closely by anyone with a brain.

That left the bartender who would, if he was smart, claim he didn't remember anything specific…and César and Jaime. César would be dead within minutes from blood loss, and Jaime wouldn't be talking to anyone for a long time – eating through a straw tended to dampen the enthusiasm of even the most garrulous – and the American was confident that the police would have better things to do than try to run down a hazy and conflicting description weeks or months after the fact.

Two blocks up he cut over onto another small street, and then he was gone, the echo of his footsteps fading into the night.

CHAPTER 2

Los Andes, Chile

Jet's vision was beginning to blur after driving for hours. The change of altitude from the summit and the constant vigilance demanded by the treacherous road were finally taking their toll. The infinite twists and turns had required all her attention, and now, as two a.m. neared, she was fading and knew it. Hannah snoozed cozily in her car seat in the back while Matt did his best to provide quiet moral support from the passenger side, watching the mountain terrain blur by as he fought to keep his eyes open. They needed to get off the road for a while.

They continued toward the town of Los Andes, at the base of the jutting mountains, and then took the exit and entered the city limits. Theirs was the only car on the empty main street, but Jet watched her speed, wary of attracting the attention of any bored or enterprising police eager to shake down tourists.

"How you holding up?" Matt asked.

"Good, although I'm ready for some sleep. How's the arm?" she asked, eyeing his cast.

"A twinge every now and then. Remind me not to dive off balconies anymore, would you?"

"I didn't tell you to show off."

"True. You want to find a motel here?"

She glanced at him. "Too close to the pass. I think I'd rather keep going to San Felipe."

"How far?"

"Fifteen minutes."

"You're the boss."

They rolled through Los Andes and entered an alluvial valley framed by farmland on either side of the two-lane highway, the snowcapped outline of the mountains glowing behind them. The damp breeze was thick with the scent of vineyards, the vista of grapevines a parade of rigid lines stretching to the horizon under a wash of ghostly moonlight. After more or less forever, San Felipe appeared from the darkness like a blatant mirage. One moment they were surrounded by endless farmland, bugs splattering against the windshield, and the next, multistory buildings were rising out of the gloom.

Jet drove slowly along the main road until she saw a small sign with "Hotel" painted on it in red. An unsteady arrow below pointed down a side street. She swung the SUV right and found herself facing a long building constructed of variegated brick, only a few cars in the lot, all with Chilean plates. She pulled to a stop near the office, which was dark except for the soft glow of a low-wattage bulb somewhere in its depths.

"Wait here. I'll get us a room."

Matt looked at her. "You sure? I can handle it."

"You're a little more memorable with the broken wing and the barbecued head than I am."

"Not really, but I know better than to argue."

Inside, she rang a bell on the chipped counter and waited as rustling emanated from the back room. Moments later an ancient man with a prune face shuffled through a doorway and, after a brief discussion, gladly took her American dollars and handed her a key, uninterested in details pertaining to her identity or nationality.

She returned to the car and pulled it around to a spot near the room door before hoisting the still-dozing Hannah and ferrying her as Matt secured their entry.

The room was no worse than countless others she'd laid her head in. She placed Hannah on one of the two twin beds and spent a long moment gazing at her before catching Matt's eye.

"I'll be back in a second with the bags," she said.

"I can help."

"I don't need it. Just get ready for bed."

Jet drove the Explorer off the motel grounds and parked in front of a modest house on a side street. She glanced around, looking for evidence of potential problems. Confident she was alone, Jet popped the glove compartment and removed the Explorer's owner's manual. After reading a few pages, she felt around under the dash and quickly located the fuse box, removed the fuel pump relay, and then slipped it into her pocket, ensuring the car wouldn't be driven off without her during the night. Satisfied that any thieves would be frustrated by her precaution, she retrieved her bags and the various parts of the Glock and headed back to the motel.

Matt was coming out of the bathroom when Jet returned to the room. Jet sat wordlessly at the table near the window and quickly reassembled the pistol to functional order. She chambered a round, set it on the nightstand, unzipped her bag and removed a T-shirt and her hygiene kit.

Matt was already asleep when she emerged from the bathroom, and she only hesitated a second before climbing onto the bed with Hannah, who snuggled next to her with a low mewl and then resumed sleeping, breath soft and moist and sweet against her mother's neck.

Jet's last thought as her eyes fluttered shut was that they'd made it, leaving their pursuers with nothing. She smiled at the thought and drifted off to sleep, one of the longest days of her life now drawn to a close.

CHAPTER 3

Langley, Virginia

The early morning rush hour was just getting underway as Carson Santell entered the cavernous warehouse three miles from CIA headquarters. He'd parked his black Lexus on the far side of the lot well away from the security cameras that monitored the front and rear entrances, and made his way to the side door, where he knew from long experience the feed would have been turned off several minutes earlier.

He strode across the scuffed concrete floor, wending around pallets of oversized wooden crates, a polystyrene cup of coffee in his left hand and a waxed paper bag of donuts in his right. He ducked around a forklift, reached the door to the administrative office, and stepped inside, reassured when he entered that there was only one other person there – Jason McDougal, one of his partners in the international drug trafficking empire Santell operated as a profitable sideline to his day job as a section head with the CIA.

Santell sat across from McDougal, who was studying a computer monitor on his desk, and tossed the donuts to him.

"How long do we have?" Santell asked as he removed the plastic lid from his coffee.

"Half an hour till the first workers show up, but call it fifteen minutes if you want to be safe. What's up?"

"I've been thinking about the Buenos Aires incident – Tara's remarkable failure and the loss of not only the target, but also the stones."

"And the entire team. Let's not forget that." McDougal had been with the agency for two decades before retiring early and opening an import-export business, the better to facilitate his trips to the heroin production centers in Afghanistan and the Golden Triangle as well as to Colombia, Bolivia, and Peru, where cocaine was the big export.

"How could I? What a disaster. I've been running interference for the last two days."

McDougal checked his watch. "What do you want to talk about? That op's dead, isn't it? Time to cut our losses and move on."

"The bastard still probably has a bunch of our diamonds," Santell seethed. He took a cautious sip of coffee and winced as he burned the tip of his tongue. "Damn. They superheat this stuff every time."

McDougal opened the bag and extracted a glistening chocolate-glazed donut. He regarded his paunch with rueful eyes and then took a massive bite out of it. "He might. Or might not. You said Tara was unclear."

Santell nodded. "I want to send someone in. A freelancer. I can't have any more agency personnel involved. It's left too large a trail." Santell caught the bag McDougal tossed him and removed a cinnamon roll. "Who do you have in that neck of the woods?"

McDougal sighed. "South America? Boy, it's not like the good old days. Most of the best are long dead. And the newbies are lazy and sloppy. Butchers. If Tara couldn't pull this off, sending any of them in is a waste of time."

"I'm not asking you what won't work. I'd say I already have a pretty clear idea of what not to do," Santell snapped.

"The best freelancer on that continent is a name you're not going to like. We decided to never use him again after the slaughter in Honduras, remember?"

Santell's face fell. "You don't mean…"

McDougal nodded. "I do. Drago."

Santell stared at the cinnamon roll like it had turned into feces, and set it on the table, his expression pained. "Shit. Who else is there?"

"Who's reliable and won't just disappear if they locate the stones? Nobody. If he's still got some, we're talking millions. Tens of millions." McDougal paused and munched on another chunk of doughnut. "Drago's the best, and he's rigorous."

"Drago's a walking wrecking machine. He's got all the subtlety of a bulldozer. And he enjoys carnage a little too much for my liking."

"Hey, you asked. I'd just as soon let it go. Like I said, that's already played."

Santell shook his head. "It's more than just the money. Matt knows too much. And he's just the kind who'll surface a year from now, or five, and pull a Snowden."

"Nobody would believe him."

"We have no idea how much he knows."

"Pretty fair bet he's got the Laos details at the very least."

"Of course." Santell's eyes locked on a calendar mounted on the wall behind McDougal that featured colorful hot air balloons soaring over Albuquerque, New Mexico, at dawn. He took another pull on his coffee, ignoring the pain as his tongue protested the scalding.

McDougal folded his hands and leaned forward. "If it's not the money, what's really eating at you? We're almost out of time. Spit it out."

Santell's attention returned to McDougal. "The Russians. If Matt approached them with all the data he's carrying around in his head, they could prove we're responsible for the huge upturn in heroin consumption in Russia as well as most of Europe. Let's just say that if a nation with that many nukes starts rattling its saber, any story they tell will get a whole different kind of scrutiny from the Justice Department. We don't need that kind of heat."

McDougal stuffed the remainder of his doughnut into his mouth and chewed appreciatively, lost in thought. He glanced at his watch again and stood. "Come on. I'll walk you out."

The pair moved unhurriedly through the warehouse. When they reached the side door, Santell paused and turned to McDougal. "How much do you think Drago would want to do this?"

"Probably half a mil before it was done. He'll need travel expenses, documents, spread it around money…it could go north of that depending on what he finds."

Santell scowled and then nodded. "Budget a mil. But don't let on how much is in the kitty. No point in being foolish with our cash."

"Of course. How much do you want me to tell him?"

"You really trust him?"

"As much as any of these freelancers."

"Tell him the minimum he needs to know. Don't let on about any agency connection. And don't get too specific about the amount of diamonds we're looking for."

A flock of seagulls screeched overhead, wings stretched wide against the cold gray sky, wheeling over the industrial park on their way to the Potomac as Santell plodded back to his car. He tried to ignore the nagging feeling of dread that had lingered just beneath the surface of his every waking moment since he'd gotten the news about Tara, but it was no use. He slipped behind the wheel of the car and shook a small white oval pill from a prescription bottle with a trembling hand and dry swallowed it.

The motor started with a purr, and Santell took several deep breaths before putting the transmission in gear. He was one of the most powerful men in the American intelligence community – a veteran of countless black ops and deniable missions, even if he'd largely directed them from the safety of a corner office. He didn't run scared. Santell was one of the predators in the clandestine jungle, one of the hunters. Matt was a nuisance, an irritant, nothing more. He'd be squashed like a bug eventually – and while Santell didn't like the idea of unleashing a psychopath like the contract killer known as Drago into the world, he was out of options. McDougal had been around long enough to know how to launder the funds and avoid any trail leading back to them, a prudent step. Drago's MO was to leave a trail of bodies in his wake, drawing too much attention for Santell's professional liking.

Then again, after an aircraft had been shot down in Argentina's capital city and gun battles waged in front of one of the nation's most prestigious banks, being low profile was hardly an issue. He just hoped the killer would accept the assignment and succeed in tracking Matt down, diamonds or no diamonds, and punch his ticket once and for all.

CHAPTER 4

Rio de Janeiro, Brazil

The Rio de Janeiro state secretary of security stood at the base of the infamous Favela do Cantagalo only a few short blocks from the sparkling blue water and white sand of world-renowned Copacabana beach. Several television news trucks were parked nearby, their crews nervously looking up the hill at the myriad red-brick tenements that clung to the side of the mountain like cancerous lesions as the huddle of bureaucrats prepared to address the press. The sun had risen from the eastern expanse of ocean like an angry god, its rays spangling the surface of the nearby surf in a dazzling display of luminous pyrotechnics, all gold and yellow and orange.

At first light, a retinue of heavily armed police in blue combat gear and bulletproof vests had emptied from a line of vans and taken up positions along the lower perimeter of the slum – one of the dangerous neighborhoods under the full control of the drug warlords who ruled whole tracts of the city and whose enforcers were often better outfitted than their law-enforcement counterparts. Illegal power lines draped from utility poles like black tentacles, hundreds of cables bootlegging electricity in plain view; no utility employees were willing to risk their lives trying to disconnect them.

Gun battles were a daily, sometimes hourly, occurrence in the larger favelas like Vila Cruzeiro, Manguinhos, and Jacarezinho, the latter two known to the locals as "Gaza" and considered a war zone by the authorities and residents alike. Favela Cantagalo was positively peaceful by those standards – the last shootout on the hill had been thirty-six hours earlier, a lifetime by Rio slum standards.

One of the TV reporters took up a position with the favela in the background to get her establishing shot of the location before the functionaries began their hopefully brief speeches. The event was to commemorate a major offensive by the police to reclaim the lawless ghettos, where drug dealing was endemic. The favelas rivaled war zones for mortality rates and were a constant source of embarrassment for Rio, which had spent considerable sums to attract high-profile events like the World Cup and the Olympics.

Traversing high-risk corridors of open warfare to get from the international airport to the soccer stadium or downtown was a considerable blemish on the city's public face, so the latest of endless attempts to clean up the worst of the favelas was to begin shortly, which would cut into the drug warlords' profits while underway, as well as open up costly territorial disputes in the vacuum left by armed troops and tanks.

The cameraman peered through the lens at the comely anchorwoman and then zoomed out to frame her against the backdrop of the slum. Narrow alleys and walkways cut into the side of the mountain's steep slope, the squalid dwellings defying gravity, perched one atop the other in rows of brick shanties that snaked up toward the summit. Graffiti marred many of the surfaces rival gangs had tagged, and the barred windows that stretched up the reach were filled with the dark faces of curious inhabitants watching the display of force below.

~ ~ ~

Fernanda swept the tense countenances of the police with the Schmidt & Bender PM II telescopic sight. Their jaws were set in determination as their eyes roved over the favela, including her invisible position inside the darkened interior of one of the dwellings near the top of the hill. She'd chosen the location carefully – the maximum distance she could put between herself and the gathering given the layout of the slum. Her laser rangefinder showed the distance as three hundred meters, which was an easy shot for her, all things considered.

She inched forward until the crosshairs of the scope were aligned on the back of the secretary of security's skull, noting the ridges and indentations on his balding pate. She made a small adjustment to the scope, compensating for the ten-knot breeze, and returned her attention to the man's head, which was the size of a breadbox in the scope.

The SAKO TRG sniper rifle felt warm in her hands, like an old friend, and she hated that she'd have to abandon it once it had done its job. She'd already wiped it down, as well as the five .338 Lapua Magnum cartridges she'd loaded, and now wore latex gloves to avoid leaving any prints. Her lush ebony hair was pulled into a ponytail beneath a black baseball cap, and she brushed an errant smudge of loose dirt from her chocolate long-sleeved man's shirt, her jeans loose to enable maximum ease of movement.

The quiet putter of a motorcycle engine greeted her through the empty doorway. The tenement was abandoned; piles of debris and garbage littered the interior along with broken syringes and used condoms. Music rose from somewhere below, a tinny radio blaring funk carioca. The infectious beat echoed off the rooftops, and Fernanda hummed along as she watched her target begin what would be his most memorable public appearance.

~ ~ ~

Gustavo Ferreira cleared his throat and raised the microphone to his lips, noting with satisfaction that there were nine cameramen filming – an auspicious sign for his media profile. He hesitated, waiting for the small crowd of supporters that had gathered to quiet, and began speaking with a polished cadence.

"For too many years, our beautiful city has been the victim of criminal gangs that terrorize the residents and spread misery wherever they go. The favelas are not playgrounds for miscreants, nor should they be havens for drug peddlers and pimps. People –

hardworking common people lacking options – live in them, children grow up in them, and those people deserve to be safe."

The crowd gave a halfhearted round of obligatory applause.

"In the past, we've tried a number of things, but the only one that has worked is to go in with the army, take possession of the favela, and then set up police outposts so we can respond swiftly and decisively when the gangs return and try to restart their criminal enterprises. While that is our least appealing choice, we will be going in with our colleagues in the armed forces and cleaning out the rats that have infested our city for too long."

Ferreira smiled for the cameras and pointed over his shoulder at the slum.

"But we need the public's help. Too many believe that the drug lords are like Robin Hood, robbing the rich and distributing to the poor. They aren't. They're parasites, preying on the weak, spreading misery wherever they go. And like all parasites, they must be stamped out, not glorified!"

The top of Ferreira's skull vaporized, and his brains blew onto the street in front of him as he tumbled forward, dead even as the microphone raced his body to the pavement. The sharp crack of a rifle shot reverberated off the buildings a split second later, and a kit of pigeons alighted from the hillside, startled into flight by the gunshot. The officers opened fire with their automatic weapons as the residents of the favela took cover, and the commander pointed at the shamble of brick high above where he thought the shot had originated as he screamed orders. His lieutenant barked into his handheld radio as the shooting from the police continued. The commander drew his pistol and stood by the fallen bureaucrat, facing the cameras, yelling for everyone to stay back as two officers knelt by Ferreira's fallen form.

One of the men looked up at his superior and shook his head. The remaining dignitaries had scrambled for cover behind cars, and the commander instructed several of his men to protect them, a sinking feeling in his stomach as he did so. Whoever had assassinated the secretary of security had done so for maximum effect, on live television, and the message was obvious: take on the drug lords and no matter who you were, you weren't safe. He seriously doubted, given the single shot to the head at considerable distance, that the execution had been entrusted to a sixteen-year-old. This had all the earmarks of one of Rio's professional hits, and he had slim hope that his men would find the shooter once they made it to the top of the hill.

The lieutenant approached, radio to his ear. "Helicopter's on its way. Three minutes," he said.

"Get the press out of here along with the suits. Prepare the men to move. I want to set a record for climbing that hill."

~ ~ ~

By the time the shooting from the police started, Fernanda had dropped the rifle and was almost to the doorway on the far side of the little room. With any luck, one of the enterprising residents would abscond with the rifle before the police got there, and it would have been sold five times by sunset.

Her husband, Igor, was waiting astride a Suzuki DR-Z400S motorcycle, a black helmet with darkened visor in place. As she stuffed the baseball cap in her back pocket, he tossed her a dark blue helmet. She pulled it on, swung a long leg over the seat, and then put her arms around his waist.

"Let's get out of here."

Igor twisted the throttle, and they roared off down the three-foot-wide unpaved passageway in a spray of dirt. The motorcycle bounced over a rut where sewage had carved an indentation in the trail and zipped horizontally before he rolled to a stop by a concrete stairway.

"Hang on. Going down."

The bike's shocks cushioned only part of the impact as they rattled to the next level, where Igor veered south down a narrow alley. A startled woman dumping a pail of cloudy water jumped back as they brushed past, her face radiating the fear that all the inhabitants felt when a motorcycle raced down one of the connecting paths. The drug gangs favored motorbikes for their maneuverability and their ability to disappear into the favelas – which meant any motorized conveyance could be transporting death just as easily as a neighbor returning home from a menial job.

The pair reached the southernmost reaches of the slum, and Igor killed the engine. They dismounted and tossed their helmets down the hill onto a small pile of accumulated trash. The stink of the garbage was almost overpowering, but they ignored it and were halfway down the hillside when Fernanda paused.

"Listen. You hear that?"

Igor nodded. "Helicopter. But too late."

They resumed their descent, ignoring the two teenagers with pistols at the bottom of the hill, and made their way to the street forty meters away, the keening of sirens from the far side of the mountain as distant as the Caribbean as far as they were concerned.

That night, the news programs were filled with the horrifying image of Ferreira losing his head for the cameras, and Igor toasted Fernanda with an icy-cold beer in their contemporary Ipanema loft as they watched the coverage.

"Another long day at the office over," he said, a smile on his handsome face.

"Who do you think contracted for the hit?" she asked, taking an appreciative sip.

"Probably the Red Command. But we're better off not knowing," Igor said, naming one of the largest and most violent of Rio's numerous drug gangs.

They'd received the sanction from their agent, who handled the money and acted as a buffer between the contractor and the client – a prudent setup that had served them well for the six years they'd been Brazil's most expensive hit team.

"Well, let's hope that the police pacification program continues. So far it's been one of our best years, and we're not done yet."

"Nice to be in a growth industry, that's for sure."

Fernanda slid closer to Igor and put a hand on his bare chest, noting his washboard abs with approval. Their eyes met, he set his beer down, and they silently made their way upstairs to their bedroom, pleasure their only earthly concern for the rest of the evening.

CHAPTER 5

San Felipe, Chile

Jet started awake, groggy for a second before she remembered where she was. Sunlight streamed between the curtains as she rolled toward where Hannah lay next to her, still asleep.

Jet froze when she saw a black form scuttling along her daughter's bare arm, its eight legs moving with mechanical precision. Her breath caught in her throat as she reached over and flicked the spider onto the floor with her finger. She leapt to her feet and smashed the arachnid with the sole of her shoe as Hannah opened her eyes. The little girl stared at her mother, shoe in hand, and then closed her eyes again and rolled over.

Matt came out of the bathroom and, seeing Jet awake, rounded the beds and kissed her. Jet whispered to him about the spider, and he shook his head.

"Well, we sort of got what we paid for, didn't we?" he said. "Maybe you two should wash up, and we can figure out what we're going to do next over a late breakfast?"

"What time is it? I'm starved."

He looked at his watch. "Almost eleven. Maybe an early lunch..."

Jet got Hannah into the shower with her, and they scrubbed away. When they'd toweled off, Jet inspected the scab on her cheek from her fight with Tara – it would come off in another day or so. Hannah struggled with the hairbrush until Jet took it from her and pulled it through her tangles after running it across her own head.

By the time their ablutions were done, a half hour had gone by. Matt was sitting at the table, a good-natured smile on his face. "I killed two more you-know-whats while you bathing beauties were splashing around."

"That's reassuring. I hope they've got better restaurants in this town than hotels."

"Call it a hunch, but I wouldn't expect gourmet cuisine."

"That's fine. I'd settle for some coffee."

"Then I think we can accommodate you."

They debated leaving their things in the room, and Matt voted to do so. Checkout wasn't until one o'clock, so they had plenty of time and no clear destination or schedule. They drove around town until they found a clean-looking restaurant with a number of locals dining at tables on the sidewalk, and then parked around the corner before making their way inside.

Once they'd ordered, Hannah busied herself drawing on the paper placemat with the crayons Jet carried in her purse.

"We can't take a flight out of Chile. If there's any sort of an alert, the computers at international immigrations will be linked, and we'd never make it onto the plane," Matt said.

"Do you really think that's likely?"

"It's a risk, and after the last little adventure, I'm feeling risk-averse." Matt adjusted his baseball cap, his burned head itching.

"Fair enough. That leaves us with three options: We can stay in Chile, drive for a couple of days and cross into Bolivia or Peru, or take a boat north."

"I hear nice things about Chile."

"Like massive earthquakes…"

"Well, there's that. But the wine's pretty decent, and they say the people are friendly."

"Call me crazy, but it's still way too close to Argentina for my liking. I mean, we managed to lose whoever set up the roadblock, but it won't take them forever to figure out that one of the places we could have escaped to was Chile. I mean, there aren't a million destinations close to Mendoza."

The waitress arrived with their food. They dug in, even Hannah shedding her normal reticence and attacking her food with gusto. When they'd finished, Jet ordered another coffee and sat back as Matt looked through the window at the few cars on the main street.

"Two days of hard driving isn't that appealing. If memory serves, there's only one road north, and it's two lane most of the way, isn't it?" Matt asked.

"It is. And there will be border crossings to contend with. Probably not linked to the central computers headed into Bolivia, but there's no telling. My greater fear's that they might have photos of us from the casino circulating. Depending on how much clout they have and who they are, that's a real issue."

"We have to assume it's the CIA. They sent Tara, and there's more where she came from."

"Then how do we do this?" Jet asked.

"I'm thinking boat. That will have the laxest immigrations and customs. Probably nonexistent leaving the country."

"Fine. But it's not like we can just go down to the dock in Valparaíso and hitch a ride."

"What about that guy Sofia's dad gave you? The fixer?" The burner cell phone Sofia's father had handed her contained two numbers – his and that of a man named Alfredo, who he'd told her was relatively trustworthy and could arrange for anything, anywhere. For a price.

Jet nodded. "I suppose I could see if he's got the contacts to pull it off."

"No time like the present."

They returned to the hotel, and Jet dug the cheap little phone from her bag, slipped the battery into place, and then pressed Alfredo's speed dial number. The man who answered on the fourth ring sounded surly and old.

"What?" the gruff male voice demanded in Argentine-accented Spanish.

"Alfredo?"

"Who wants to know?"

"I'm a friend of a friend. I was told you were the man to call if I needed anything."

The voice turned cautious. "Yeah? What friend?"

She mentioned Sofia's father. A silence stretched on the line. When Alfredo spoke again, his tone was alert and businesslike.

"What can I do for you?"

"I'm looking for a discreet boat that can take three people out of Chile."

"I see. Are any of the travelers wanted by the Chileans?"

"No."

"Then why not just book passage on the first cargo ship headed north? They'll usually have space."

"I have my reasons."

Alfredo sighed. "Very well. What's your timing?"

"I'd like to be gone as of yesterday."

"I see. It won't be cheap."

"I didn't expect it would be."

Alfredo seemed to like that. "Where are you?"

"Why?"

"I need to make some calls. See what I can arrange. Your number's blocked."

"In Chile. San Felipe."

"Call me in half an hour." The line went dead. Jet stared at the phone before powering it off.

Matt eyed her. "And?"

"I'm to call back."

"Did he seem capable of helping?"

"He got happy when I said I wasn't price-sensitive."

"Always a big favorite."

They busied themselves with packing their bags and taking a last spin through the bathroom. When they'd fit everything into the Explorer, Jet called Alfredo back.

Alfredo was now all efficiency. "All right. Here's what you need to do. Do you have something to write with?"

She answered in the affirmative.

"It's called the Hotel Olivier. It's on the outskirts of town, secluded enough that you won't be bothered. Get a room, and a gentleman who can handle your request will be there tomorrow morning, no later than eight. Here's his number. Call him at eight, and he'll meet you in the lobby restaurant." Alfredo rattled off a Chilean number. She repeated it back to him as Matt scribbled it down. "I have a connection at the hotel, so they won't require identification. In whose name should I make the reservation?"

"Naomi."

Alfredo paused. "No last name?"

"Naomi Alfredo."

He chuckled. "Very well, Naomi. Feel free to call if you require anything else. Any friend of the great man is one of mine, too."

"How do you get paid?"

"My associate will take care of that. Safe travels."

Jet explained the rendezvous to Matt, and they agreed it would be good to get out of the roach motel, although she had some misgivings about staying at the Olivier, given that Alfredo knew where she was.

"Either he's trustworthy or he isn't. Do you have any reason to believe otherwise?" Matt asked.

"No. Just force of habit."

"We can stay nearby if you want. I'm okay either way. Let's take a gander at the place, and if it looks decent, we can decide then, okay?"

Jet took a final look at the dilapidated motel and turned to Hannah, who was sitting in the car seat, gazing through the window, engrossed in the thoughts of a toddler. A momentary vision of the spider on her arm flashed through Jet's awareness, and she shuddered.

"Okay."

Chapter 6

Santiago, Chile

A black Mercedes pulled to the curb in front of L'École Français for the restaurant's grand opening. Two tuxedoed valets scrambled to get the doors and held them open for a well-groomed couple in their forties, he in a navy blue double-breasted blazer with a maroon cravat around his neck, she in a slinky black evening dress that looked like a year's salary for either of the parking attendants. A photographer took the couple's photo as they stood outside the oversized mahogany and glass entry doors. A limousine rolled forward, and an older couple emerged from its cavernous depths as the handsome, tanned host, also attired in a tuxedo, beamed a white smile at the new arrivals and greeted them with the deference of a diplomat.

Gaspar Soto watched from his position near the kitchen and nodded, taking in the packed bar area, where the city's privileged were rubbing shoulders and drinking Pisco Sours and expensive Scotch. Imported champagne was flowing like water, and a jazz trio played standards, the buzz of excited conversation nearly drowning out the music.

The restaurant was the latest masterstroke in a long career of them for Soto, the head of the most powerful crime family in Chile, and would go a long way toward solving his money-laundering problem – a result of the success he'd had with cocaine trafficking into Argentina as well as north through the busiest port on the Pacific coast of South America. It was a relatively new enterprise for him, only five years old, but the earnings had already eclipsed his other revenue streams, surpassing gambling, prostitution, kidnapping, and loan-sharking combined.

He'd struck a deal with a producer in Peru and his associates in Bolivia, at first shipping only a few dozen kilos from the border and distributing them in Santiago. That had blossomed over time into its current scope, where he transshipped tons into Argentina and Brazil, as well as into Mexico through Manzanillo, where his counterparts in the Mexican cartels took over.

The restaurant was a terrific front: a pricey nightspot with a top chef and two stories of dining rooms through which he could legitimize millions each year even if not a soul came through the door – which was unlikely, given the number of people he knew in Santiago society. Even if Soto was a pariah who lived on the wrong side of the law, money talked, and he was the legitimate owner of an airport supply company, a string of gift shops, several bars and nightclubs, and a shipping company, and as such he had the respect of the elite who owned and operated the country.

His bodyguards stood nearby, wearing dark suits tailored to conceal the bulges of their shoulder-holstered weapons – six seasoned veterans of the ongoing turf war he'd been fighting with his rivals for a decade. Soto claimed most of Santiago and several of the northern cities, and the Verdugos had Valparaíso, a small section of the poorest reaches of Santiago's slums, and several of the inconsequential rural towns. It was a delicate equilibrium, but one that both groups had settled into, preferring to take a large slice of a generous pie rather than fight a war of attrition for territory against an unbeatable adversary. Both Soto and the Verdugos had their pet government contacts, so neither could eliminate the other, and they'd settled into a cautious truce that was in its fourth year – although Soto had been hearing rumblings that the Verdugos had cast their eye on the cocaine business, which he had no intention of ceding even a small part to keep the peace.

A bejeweled woman easily Soto's age, in her mid-sixties if a day, her plastic surgery insufficient to mute the ravages of time's passing, approached wearing a peach sequined formal evening gown and thousand-dollar shoes. She was trailed by a shorter paunchy man with the unhappy demeanor of a basset hound, whose tux looked like he'd been shoehorned into it.

"Gaspar, it's a triumph. An absolute triumph!" the woman said, her voice cultured and modulated with the studied grace of royalty. "You must be so proud."

Soto kissed her on the cheek. "Vivienne. An honor, as always. You look astonishing," he lied. "What's your secret?" He stole a glance at her husband, who nodded and mumbled something unintelligible. The gleam of her diamond necklace was almost blinding in the light from the chandeliers, and Soto looked away, not wanting to gawk. He then caught a flash of movement at the front door and froze when he saw at least a dozen rifle-brandishing police push into the foyer, where the host was doing his best to face them down.

Soto took in the shocked expressions of the nearby guests and leaned into the woman, the better to hide his face from the police. "Will you excuse me?" he asked and, without waiting for her response, spun and climbed the nearby stairs two at a time, followed by his bodyguards. He was already fishing for his cell phone when he reached the top step.

The second-floor dining room had been closed off because the gala opening was limited to the ground floor, and he strode purposefully to the rear of the expansive room, where bare tables were collected next to stacks of chairs. His head bodyguard stood by his side, waiting for instruction, while Soto called his top contact in the police department – the number two official in Chilean law enforcement. By the fifth ring, when the call went to voice mail, Soto knew he had a problem. His contact always picked up. Always, whatever the hour.

Something had happened. What, he didn't know, but whatever it was, for a small army of armed men to disrupt his opening signaled it was no longer safe there for him. This wasn't the way things worked – if he'd been charged with something, a polite and apologetic detective should come to his office after making an appointment. There was no precedent for anyone to send in a SWAT team.

Whatever it was, he'd figure it out from afar, surrounded by a swarm of attorneys.

"Delay them. I'm going down the fire escape. Give me your weapon," Soto snapped at his bodyguard, who handed him his SIG Sauer pistol without comment. Soto tested the weight of the weapon in his hand as he held the man's gaze. "I'll call once I'm clear."

The bodyguard nodded and returned to his men by the dining room entry. Soto slipped the gun into his jacket pocket and moved through a service exit, furious that he was being rousted at a time like this. It had to be the Verdugos. Only they would have the audacity to attempt to turn Soto's moment of victory into a rout. But if they thought he could be overturned this easily, they'd badly misjudged him, and he would get his revenge.

Soto pushed the outer door open and stepped out onto the iron fire escape. The back alley was quiet. A flare of moonlight reflected off a puddle of black water that had collected from a late afternoon cloudburst. After doing a quick scan of his surroundings, he lowered the ladder to the street and descended the creaky steps, muttering an oath with each rung.

His feet had just touched the cobblestones when he heard a squawk of static from the mouth of the alley, and then a distorted voice. A radio. Soto retrieved his pistol and hurried in the opposite direction, hoping to lose his pursuers before they were aware he'd left the building. He slipped into the gloom, his black tuxedo a fortunate choice under the circumstances. He tiptoed along the wall, anxious to avoid making any noise with his dress heels, and was twenty steps from the ladder when a deep voice called out behind him.

"Soto. We know you're back here. Don't make us come after you, or it won't go well."

Soto's finger moved to the pistol trigger, and he pressed himself against the filthy wall behind an overflowing dumpster, bile rising in his throat at the rancid aroma. Something squished beneath his handmade shoes, and he winced at the possibilities. His gaze moved to the alley mouth, where three police stood backlit by the streetlight, rifles at the ready. Hidden in the gloom, he realized they couldn't see him. There was still a chance.

He edged along the wall, pistol pointed at the sky, and had put several meters between himself and the dumpster when the impossible happened – the alley filled with the shrill sound of salsa music emanating from his jacket pocket. Someone was calling his cell phone.

The officers entered the alley, weapons pointed at his position, and this time there was no hesitation in the lead policeman's voice.

"Soto, I see you by the wall. And I can make out what looks like a gun. Please. Give me a single reason to shoot you. Just one."

Soto tossed the pistol onto the uneven surface of the cobblestones and stepped to the center of the alley with his hands raised. "You're making the worst mistake of your life, young man. I'm unarmed. My bodyguard's weapon is on the ground – he has a permit for it. We thought you might be kidnappers."

Soto could see the man's tense face as he neared.

"Get on your knees," the policeman ordered.

"That won't be necessary, officer," Soto protested.

"On your knees. Now. Hands behind your head."

Something about the man's voice bothered Soto. The tone. A sense of menace that was over and above the call of duty. Soto reluctantly complied, the damp pavement soaking through the knees of his trousers as the police neared with their assault rifles trained on him. He was about to speak again when the leader slammed his rifle stock into Soto's face, breaking his nose and splitting his lip. A shriek of pain tore through his skull as blood splattered onto his starched white shirt and the night sky spun above him. His vision was fading to black as he heard the man's mocking words, as if from the end of a long tunnel, taunting him as he crumpled to the ground.

"You shouldn't have resisted arrest. Right, boys?"

CHAPTER 7

Leonid waited impatiently in the lobby of the Grand Hyatt Hotel in Santiago, glancing at his watch every few minutes as he watched the cool staff glide back and forth across the expansive floor like skaters on a rink of polished granite slabs. He'd come to Chile to broaden his chances of locating his quarry. After the debacle south of Mendoza, there had been no sign of the woman, and between his contact with the intelligence service there and his men still on the ground in Mendoza, he felt he had western Argentina covered.

The border-crossing stations had been put on alert following the incident at the roadblock, so he was confident she couldn't make it to Paraguay or Chile now. But there had been latency between the order and its implementation, which left a few hours when she could have slipped through. He thought it unlikely, but he wasn't in the business to play the odds – he would only see his millions if he performed.

His Argentine contact had given him information on the two largest crime organizations in Chile, which between the two of them controlled the entire country. He'd tried to get in touch with the Soto group but so far hadn't heard back, and now he waited for the representative of the Verdugos to appear. His associate in the GRU had put him in touch with the *Agencia Nacional de Inteligencia de Chile*, Chile's equivalent of the CIA, and he'd been able to circulate the image of the woman with the promise that it would make it to all immigration checkpoints. But, as with most things in South America, his confidence level wasn't high that anyone would follow through, so he'd decided to enlist the help of the criminal syndicates in order to increase his chances of a hit.

Antonio Verdugo was the number two man in his family's organization, with his father, Franco, the head. Franco apparently stuck to Valparaíso, leaving Santiago to his son, and it was the son who was running late. Leonid forced himself to relax and told himself that the pace here was different, that even a half hour late was still considered on time, and that he shouldn't draw any conclusions from the crime lord's tardiness.

A tall young man neared him carrying a small leather-bound book. Leonid's pulse quickened.

"Would you like to see the cocktail menu, sir?" the man asked, first in Spanish and then in English.

"No." Leonid waved him away, teeth grinding at the false alarm.

A fleshy man wearing a black windbreaker, his head shaped like a bulldog's, approached.

"*Señor* Ross?" he asked, his voice a smoky rasp.

"Yes," Leonid said. He was using a fake name as he always did when on a mission. He'd picked Ross at random.

"Please. You come with me, *sí?*"

Leonid stood. "Lead the way," he said, his English about as good as the thug's.

"*Bueno.*"

They pushed through the hotel entrance to where a white Lincoln Navigator sat at the curb. His escort swung the rear door open, and Leonid found himself facing a man in his early thirties, his black hair slicked straight back, the two-hundred-dollar silk shirt and ten-thousand-dollar watch out of place given his ratty torn jeans and scuffed combat boots.

The bulldog nodded at Leonid. "Raise your hands."

Leonid debated whether to comply, and shrugged. The search was perfunctory. Leonid wasn't armed or wired.

The young man nodded. "Sorry about that. Purely precautionary, I assure you. Come. Sit. I understand you want to see me?" he said, his English quite good.

Leonid climbed in next to the man. The vehicle was moving before Leonid had his seatbelt on. "Yes. I understand you control the port and a large piece of Santiago."

"I'm working on all of Chile. But for your purposes, sure, that's right. What do you need?"

"I'm looking for someone."

"Ah. Do you have a photo?"

"Of course." Leonid slid a glossy from his jacket pocket and handed it to Antonio, who studied it for several seconds before placing it on the seat between them.

"Girlfriend? Wife?"

"Hardly. Someone who has made my life difficult. I need to find her. I have reason to believe she's in Chile."

Antonio leaned forward and said something in Spanish to the driver, who grunted assent. Antonio sat back and fixed Leonid with a hard stare. "Chile is a big place."

"I know. That's why I'm willing to pay handsomely for her head."

"Her head, huh? Sounds personal. What's handsomely?"

"Half a million dollars."

That got Antonio's attention. His expression softened, and he raised an eyebrow. "That's a lot of money."

"I know. Dead or alive."

"That's an intriguing proposition. One I'm interested in. Do you mind if I circulate this to my organization?" he asked, tapping the photograph.

"Not at all. That's why I brought it."

"What do I need to know about her?"

"She's extremely dangerous. Lethal, with or without weapons. Your men should not engage if at all possible. Rather, they should keep her in sight, and you should call me, any time of the day or night."

"How will the funds be transferred?"

"Wire. I'll do it from your bank's offices once we've got her."

Antonio smiled, reminding Leonid of a Komodo dragon. "How about a retainer?"

"It's all or nothing. If you aren't interested in a half million for a phone call, no hard feelings."

"I'm just saying that spreading a little seed money around tends to heighten everyone's motivation."

"The terms aren't negotiable."

"I see. Fine. How do I reach you?"

Leonid handed him a slip of paper with an Argentine cell number on it. "I'll be in town for several days. There is some urgency to this situation."

Antonio slipped the number into his shirt pocket, and Leonid noted that his fingernails were manicured and coated with a veneer of clear polish. Antonio barked instructions to the driver, and they swung around at the next light, returning to the hotel.

"What else can you tell me about her besides that she's dangerous?" Antonio asked.

"That's all you need to know. I don't have anything else that would be helpful."

"Does she have a name?"

"She's pro, so she won't be using the same one any two days in a row."

"Interesting. What did she do?"

Leonid considered a dozen answers before offering a scowl.

"Crossed the wrong person."

~ ~ ~

Jet reached across the table and took Matt's hand after dinner was cleared by the waiter, who'd promised them the bill shortly. Hannah's lids were heavy as the hour grew late, and she looked ready to pass out after a bowl of buttered noodles and two glasses of lemonade. The hotel restaurant was small but clean, and they were one of only four tables that had been served since their arrival an hour and a half earlier – the pace was typically South American, which Jet was used to from living in Mendoza.

"So far this hasn't been awful," Jet said as she brushed a lock of hair out of Hannah's eyes.

"Not a spider in sight," Matt agreed.

"It seems like a relatively quiet town. A shame we can't stay for a few days, although the hotel leaves something to be desired." The building was older, two stories built around a central courtyard with a pool in the center and a parking lot in front. As far as she could tell, there were precious few guests staying the night, so they had the place almost to themselves.

"There's nothing stopping us, although prudence would say the farther we are from Mendoza, the better. Have you given any thought to where you want to go next?" They'd spent the day discussing possible destinations. Matt had floated Costa Rica or Panama City, and Jet had whiled away several hours on the hotel lobby computer reading about their various high and low points.

"Panama City looks nice enough. Super developed. Like New York or Hong Kong. I don't know why, but I was expecting jungle."

"Costa Rica's got all the jungle you could handle. Monkeys, toucans, snakes, the whole shooting match." Matt ignored the dark look she shot him. "I'm good with either. It's not like I haven't done my jungle time in Laos…"

"The good news is they're close to each other. So if we don't like one, we can be in the other in a matter of hours."

"And they're both thousands of miles from anywhere."

"Always a big plus when everyone on the planet's out to get you."

He smiled. "Out to get *me*. Which, again…" Matt had raised the possibility of separating from Jet, at least for a while – since Tara had been after him, not her. Jet had shot that option down and refused to discuss it further. She'd almost lost him twice now and wasn't going to allow him out of her sight.

"We cut the head off that snake. The stones are gone – or at least, yours are, and they don't know about mine – so if they keep after you, it will be out of spite," she pointed out.

"I don't see that happening. These guys are criminals. It isn't personal. They wanted their money back. The chances of that happening got scattered all over the streets of Buenos Aires, so now there's no reason to allocate resources to a global manhunt. I mean, don't get me wrong, they'd put a bullet in me in a second if they thought it convenient…"

"So you need to make it inconvenient. Very inconvenient."

"I'm certain that any heat will die down. They took their best shot and got body bags in return. I just need to be careful from here on out."

Jet nodded as the check arrived. "*We. We* need to be careful," she corrected.

"Never argue with a lady."

CHAPTER 8

Los Andes, Chile

A booming cumbia beat thumped from overhead speakers as dancers bumped and ground on the floor, multicolored lights washing over them. The young women wore skintight jeans that hugged every contour, and the men were decked out in their weekend best. A DJ worked the booth, exhorting the crowd to more lascivious moves between sips of champagne and yips when he spotted a particularly noteworthy example of the female form to admire.

One wall had a floor-to-ceiling glittering mural featuring ponies in disco apparel toasting and dancing, the mares bashful or coquettish and the stallions universally debonair. The club was the largest night spot in Los Andes, a rural town that owed its fortunes to agriculture, and El Caballo Loco was always jammed with the region's young and celebratory. Tonight was no exception, although it was still early and the floor was only a third full. That would change as the clock struck midnight, and the party would continue until the wee hours, fueled by alcohol and hope as well as the cocaine and methamphetamines the Sotos marketed to the locals.

Rodrigo Soto led his brother, Alejandro, to a booth near the DJ station. After high-fiving the MC, he flipped the reserved sign flat on the table and sat down hard on the burgundy cushions. Alejandro followed suit, and a hostess hurried over to take their order. The Sotos owned the club, and while Gaspar's two sons usually stayed in Santiago for their partying, whenever they were in town they stopped in and expected to be treated like royalty.

Rodrigo ordered a bottle of Gray Goose in a bucket of ice and a pitcher of orange juice. Alejandro eyed the talent with a bored ennui;

the country girls weren't as interesting to him as those from the nation's capital, who were more worldly in every way. Rodrigo elbowed him to call his attention to a pair of stunning brunettes, to whom he offered a dazzling smile as he ran his fingers through his long, thick black hair. One of the women, no more than twenty, returned his smile, and when the server appeared with the bottle, he held it up and motioned for them to come over. Alejandro rolled his eyes but played along with his younger brother's flirtation, their two years of age difference barely discernible in their early-thirties faces.

Rodrigo fumbled a pack of cigarettes from his jacket and lit one with a gold lighter as the girls approached, all cinnamon skin and neon smiles, swaying hips and endless legs. After introductions were made and drinks were poured, Rodrigo toasted with his three fingers of vodka on the rocks, head bobbing to the beat. Two barrel-chested bodyguards with stub necks stood like stone lions near the door, eyes roving over the crowd, hands folded in front of them, their suits incongruent with the simpler garb of the young crowd. The larger of the pair sauntered over and took up position next to the sound booth.

Alejandro stood three inches taller than his brother and was the older of the siblings. His combed-back wavy hair, aquiline nose, and regal bearing together with his immaculate Armani black silk blazer and polar-white shirt lent him the air of a diplomat. Rodrigo's profile was chiseled, but his chin was weaker than Alejandro's, and his look radiated more arrogance than justified superiority. His charcoal jacket was expensive but formless, the sleeves pushed up on his forearms to better display his gym-toned physique and tribal tattoos. The women seemed suitably impressed with them both, though. Rodrigo downed his drink in moments before pouring himself and his new friends another. Alejandro declined a second, his screwdriver only half finished.

The DJ changed songs, and the new beat pulsed on the floor with fresh urgency. The throng squealed with glee as the hypnotic groove hit its stride. Half the dancers were singing along with the gangsta lyrics; the town was about as far from the Brooklyn hood as you could get, and yet the words were familiar to everyone. Rodrigo knocked back his second drink as he finished another cigarette and leaned into his brother, one eye on the ladies, who were fluffing their hair and smiling for all they were worth.

"I'm going to hit the can. Keep them entertained for me, will you?"

Alejandro nodded. "I'll do my best."

Rodrigo stood and, after whispering something in the ear of one of the girls, weaved to the restrooms in the rear of the club like a seaman on a pitching deck. Alejandro grinned at the girls, who were becoming more alluring with each swallow of his high-octane drink. The nearest girl was bouncing on the cushions to the beat, and after another swig of liquid courage, she reached over and took Alejandro's hand to pull him onto the dance floor. He wasn't in the dancing mood, but his resolve melted when he saw the look in her eye.

A half-dozen men burst through the entry, knocking the bouncers aside. The bodyguard by the DJ booth responded like lightning and had his Glock pistol out within a second of seeing the distinctive shape of guns in the hands of the intruders.

Gunfire erupted. The girl who'd been trying to coax Alejandro onto the dance floor jerked as slugs thudded into her. Screams rang through the club from the panicked crowd, and the DJ jerked the volume down and dove for the floor. Alejandro whipped out his Desert Eagle .45 from beneath his jacket as he overturned the table for cover and fired four shots, hitting two of the gunmen. The nearby bodyguard also fired rapidly at the shooters, but a round slammed into his chest, and he tumbled backward, still squeezing the trigger, hitting random dancers running for cover. A hail of bullets smacked into the heavy wooden table, sending chunks of wood flying. Thankfully none penetrated it, and Alejandro loosed another four shots at the doorway.

The bodyguard by the entry blew off the back of the nearest assailant's head. With four of the six gunmen down, the remaining two hesitated as more shooters forced their way through the club doors. Pandemonium reigned inside, the partygoers now cringing wherever they could hide. Bodies littered the dance floor, which was slick with fresh blood.

The club lights went dark, the only illumination muzzle flashes. Alejandro edged along the booth and ducked into the corridor that led to the bathrooms – and the rear exit. Two bodies bumped into him, jostling him as they stumbled along in search of cover, but Alejandro ignored them as his eyes adjusted to the pitch black of the hallway. The shooting receded behind him, and then he reached the heavy steel exit door. He manhandled it open, pistol clutched in front of him, ready for anything. There in the dark was Rodrigo in his silver Land Rover, his face drawn, his eyes startled.

Alejandro pulled open the passenger door and screamed as he climbed in. "Get out of here. Now."

Rodrigo mashed the accelerator and the powerful vehicle lunged forward with a roar. "What the hell happened? What was that?" he demanded, visibly shaken.

"Has to be the Verdugos. Bastards. It's a bloodbath."

"Are you hit?"

"No. But it's a miracle. How about you?"

"I heard the shooting as I was coming out of the john. Didn't seem to be a good idea to go back in."

"You're lucky. They were loaded for bear." Alejandro described the scene in the club. Rodrigo took a hard left and watched the rearview mirror for any signs of pursuit. "Let me have your cell," Alejandro said. "Mine was on the table. It's history now."

Rodrigo dug his phone out of his pocket and handed it to his brother, who called their father, Gaspar. His heart sank when the call went to voice mail. "Shit."

He dialed another number, and the same thing happened. When he got lucky on the third ring, Hector, Gaspar's most trusted lieutenant, sounded worried. "We've been getting reports that your dad was arrested at the restaurant, but we haven't been able to confirm it. None of our contacts with the police are answering their phones. Not a good sign."

Alejandro explained what had happened.

Hector cursed. "With whatever's going on in Santiago, I'm not sure it's going to be safe here for you. Sounds like the Verdugos are trying to stage a takeover. And there are only two ways back to the city from where you are. If they've got the cops working with them, you could be stopped at a roadblock, and that would be it."

"What are you doing?" Alejandro asked.

"Digging in. I left headquarters with some of my best men and went to one of the safe houses. I don't want to take any action until I understand what we're facing."

"Probably a good idea. Do you have the attorneys working on locating my dad?"

"Of course. But it's late, and you know how the wheels of justice roll here. It'll probably be tomorrow before anything happens."

"Damn. You're right, but it's still a tough one to swallow. I'll call you later."

Alejandro terminated the call, lost in thought, and then handed the phone back to his brother. "Make a right up here."

"Where are we going?"

"Hector says Santiago's out, and he's right. We need someplace where we can regroup until we know what's happening."

"What's happening is a hit squad blew our nightclub apart."

"Right, but we can't just drive around all night. That's asking for it. We need to get off the road. Only we can't check into a hotel – if our names are on a watch list, we're screwed." Alejandro scowled. "So we're getting the hell out of here. We'll go to the Olivier hotel in San Felipe. We own a large enough stake in it that they won't ask any questions."

"Are you sure?"

"Absolutely. Nobody else knows we've got a piece of the hotel. It should be safe, at least for one night. It'll buy us breathing room. Which we need right now." Alejandro felt in his pocket for his spare pistol magazine, ejected the almost empty one, and slammed the full one home. "Stick to back roads. We're in no hurry, and I don't want to attract any attention."

"What a disaster."

Alejandro nodded, his face grim. "Tell me about it. But they missed us, so now they have a whole different level of pain coming their way." Alejandro eyed Rodrigo's taut expression. "You okay? You want me to drive?"

Rodrigo shook his head. "I'm fine. Nothing like a gunfight to sober you up."

"That's the truth."

CHAPTER 9

Valparaíso, Chile

A thick bank of fog hung over the Pacific port city like a leaden blanket, slowing the late night traffic to a crawl. A buoy bell tolled somewhere in the harbor, its muffled pealing a steady beat over the sonorous drone of big trucks working the waterfront, their jobs never done. The blaze of megawattage work lights on the wharf did little to penetrate the haze. A row of pelicans stood like guards along the barnacle-encrusted pilings, their somber countenances turned toward the city like disapproving clerics.

Four blocks from the bustling docks, Franco Verdugo sat on a vintage leather sofa the color of dried blood, a glass of Scotch in his hand. Colonel José Campos sat across from him with the drink's twin. Smoke drifted from a pair of Cuban cigars in a silver ashtray on a coffee table fashioned from a centuries-old sea chest. The dark wood-paneled office was decorated in a nautical theme, vintage sextants and barometers and compasses mounted to the wall next to oil paintings of tall ships at anchor in the port's long-passed heyday. Colonel Campos, the head of the armed contingent responsible for the port's security, leaned forward and raised his cigar to his lips and puffed at it before studying the cylinder of ash on the end with satisfaction.

"Nobody does it quite like the Cubans, eh, my friend?" Franco asked and then took another long sip of Johnnie Walker Blue.

"They may not have much of a country, but damned if they don't know how to make a cigar," Colonel Campos agreed. "Thank you for another marvelous dinner. Your man outdid himself."

Franco had a private chef who prepared his lunch and dinner, one of the top talents in Chile, who'd formally trained in Paris before returning to his homeland. The evening's repast of poached salmon in an herb beurre blanc sauce, washed down with a bottle of local chardonnay, had been extraordinary, the fish so fresh it had practically flopped off the plate.

"Yes, he's worth every penny of the ridiculous sum I pay him. You'd think he was my mistress the way he drains my coffers."

Campos laughed good-naturedly.

A cell phone trilled in Franco's shirt pocket. He rose from the couch as he retrieved it, held it to his ear, and walked to the window overlooking the harbor.

"What?" he barked, gazing out into the gray fog, the lights of the neighboring buildings barely visible. He listened intently, his face darkening, and Campos busied himself with his drink, suddenly fascinated by the swirl of amber nectar in the crystal tumbler. "What do you mean, they escaped? How is that possible?"

Bastian Romirez, Franco's capo, spoke in a hushed voice. "A fluke. We went in with enough firepower to start a war, but they managed to slip by when the lights went out. And it gets worse. We lost five men in the process," he said, dreading the outburst he knew would follow.

Instead, Franco's voice grew glacial. "The father is in custody. Everything on the Santiago end is going according to plan. How in the name of God could something as simple as a nightclub execution turn into a disaster?"

"I honestly don't know. But that's not important. We know where they're headed."

Franco set his drink on his desk and poured himself two more fingers of Scotch as he digested the information. "I don't need to tell you to finish this quickly, do I? You know what's in the balance."

"I have men en route. It will be over in an hour or two, and then you can begin the mop-up operation."

"We can't afford for Alejandro to rally his father's men. Rodrigo's a hothead and an idiot, but Alejandro has leadership ability. This entire move depends on a decisive victory, not months of trench warfare. We need a fast win."

"And you'll have it."

Franco terminated the call and continued staring into the fog as though it concealed more than the surrounding buildings. Eventually he returned to his seat, shaking his head.

"As you heard, we had a glitch. But Bastian assures me it will be taken care of."

"Yes, I couldn't help but overhear."

"My problem is that if Alejandro, the eldest son, survives, the war chest the Sotos have accumulated could cause serious problems for us. They could afford to bring in mercenaries, buy off whoever they need…the entire coup depends on eliminating the leadership in one swoop. As long as Alejandro's alive, he poses a threat."

"He's well thought of. One hears things."

"The father has been grooming both sons for a decade. But Alejandro is the clear successor. The younger…well, he's rash and lacks his men's respect. Not a leader."

"You have a contingency plan to eliminate him?" Campos asked nervously. Had he backed the wrong horse on this one? He routinely played both sides – the Sotos controlled some shipments moving through the port, though the Verdugos ran the majority. When Franco had taken him into his confidence, it had seemed like a no-lose proposition, and he'd pulled strings and used his considerable influence to arrange for officers loyal to the Verdugos to take the elder Soto into custody, with his allies in the force sidetracked. But that would only last so long, and if there wasn't a decisive outcome by morning, it could unravel on them – and when Soto dug to find out who had been responsible for his detainment, there would be swift and absolute reprisals. Only hours ago, the outcome had seemed predestined. But now…

Franco lifted his glass and waved his cigar with studied nonchalance. "Of course. Come. Let's not have such a long face. By the end of the night there will be only one organization controlling everything." He paused and regarded Campos with a confident stare. "And I remember who my friends are."

CHAPTER 10

San Felipe, Chile

Jet rose from the bed in the darkened room, unable to sleep, and then went to the dresser and pulled her shirt and pants on. Matt stirred on his bed, checked his watch, and then squinted at her.

"What's up?" he whispered, not wanting to wake Hannah.

"I can't sleep. Might be dinner. I'm going to get a soda and walk around a little."

"At this hour?"

"I'd rather be sleeping, but my body isn't accommodating. You want anything?"

He shook his head and lay back against the pillow. "No, thanks."

"I'll be back in a few minutes," she said. He waved a tired hand.

Jet moved to the door and, after hesitating, retrieved the Glock from the night table and slipped it into her waistband at the small of her back, and then pulled her top over the grip so it wasn't visible – a habit that was going to be automatic with her for the foreseeable future, as it had been for so many years in her covert life. She pocketed the key and opened the door and, after taking a cautious look down both directions of the second-story concrete walkway, pulled it closed behind her.

Her running shoes made no noise as she padded to the stairwell. There was only one light on in a nearby room; the rest were dark, either empty or with their occupants blissfully asleep even as Jet's stomach roiled and her thoughts raced. The roadblock in Argentina had been an ominous sign that Tara's group hadn't given up, but they'd been left with nothing to go on, so hopefully they'd eventually tire of their assignment and be recalled to whatever hole they'd crawled out of. But she understood that she and Matt could no longer be complacent – that false sense of security had nearly gotten them killed. Whether she liked it or not, they had to return to their former state of constant vigilance, leaving nothing to chance and expecting the worst.

That was part of what was eating at her. What kind of life would that be for Hannah? Would they be doomed to having to move every few months? Right now it was manageable, but what about when her daughter was older? When she was school age? They couldn't keep flitting around the globe forever. Eventually they would have to settle down – perhaps somewhere rural where there were few people and even less technology. Reality dictated that even in this day and age, outside of first world countries it was practically impossible to find someone who was determined to stay hidden and who had decent field craft.

She resolved to shake off the self-doubt, the nagging questions – they weren't helping and were a masochistic luxury she couldn't afford, a dangerous distraction. At one point on the drive she'd even wondered if she'd made a terrible mistake taking Hannah from her adoptive family. That had been her lowest moment, when she'd been forced to choose whether to leave the child – her baby, who'd been stolen from her – with strangers. In the end she couldn't do it. Hannah was her flesh and blood, and David had had no right to kidnap her. Jet had been fortunate that Hannah had adjusted quickly, seeming to sense that Jet was her real mother, but even so it had been a gamble, and a part of Jet wondered how much had been pure selfishness and how much maternal instinct. All she'd known when she'd seen Hannah for the first time was that they belonged together, and she'd done everything she could to ensure nothing would come between them…but now, running from God knew what, the wisdom of her decision seemed questionable.

Jet was preoccupied as she took the stairs down to the vending area. The grounds were quiet, the dim moonlight silvering the dimpled surface of the pool, the only sound an occasional motor from the distant road and the rustle of the surrounding treetops in the mountain wind. She emerged from the stairwell and felt in her pockets for change – the restaurant had exchanged their dollars, and she'd taken care to save Chilean coins for the machines.

Movement from the lit lobby across the courtyard caught her eye. Six men wearing dark clothes entered from the parking lot, knit caps pulled low over their brows and pistols clutched in their hands as the oblivious clerk emerged from the office. Her stomach knotted, and her breath caught in her throat. She watched his hands go over his head, an expression of panic on his face. After a strained exchange she could almost hear, he pointed at the rooms in an unmistakable pantomime of fear. The lead gunman raised his sound-suppressed handgun and fired it point blank into the clerk's face. A crimson splash spackled the window, and the clerk collapsed behind the counter.

Jet already had her Glock free when the men pushed through the doors and moved deliberately across the pool area toward the stairwell – on a beeline to where she was flattened against the wall behind the vending machine…and the stairs that led to her room.

Damn. The Argentine fixer must have tipped off Tara's team – that was the only explanation. She watched the men approach, waiting as they closed the distance, cursing silently when they spread out professionally in order to present more difficult targets. When the first gunman was ten meters away, she leaned forward and opened fire, squeezing off shots with deliberate precision, the bark of the 9mm deafening in the confined space.

Her first shot caught the lead gunman in the head, and he tumbled backward into the pool, dropping his weapon as he fell. Blood seeped through the water like a cloud of ruby ink as he flailed, and she instantaneously dismissed him as a threat and drew a bead on his companion. The second gunman tried to dodge left, but two of her rounds punched into his chest, and he dropped like a sack of wet dirt. Sound-suppressed slugs whistled by her and punched into the soda machine, and she ducked as she fired again and hit another attacker in the stomach. He sat down heavily as though taking a rest, a look of surprise on his face, and she finished him with another shot as the remaining three men threw themselves behind whatever cover they could find.

More shots tore into the vending machine, and soda exploded from it in a hissing spray. Jet ignored it and fired three times at one of the gunmen who had sought refuge behind a stone fountain. Two of her bullets went wide, but the third hit him in the thigh, and she was rewarded with a grunt of pain as another volley of silenced shots blew divots out of the mortar near her head. One of the shooters fired twice, and the overhead lamp shattered in a shower of glass and sparks. The rest of the lights followed in rapid succession, plunging the courtyard in darkness.

She peered around the vending machine, gun steady, trying to make out anything as her eyes adjusted. The only illumination came from the watery glow of the pool and the moon. She saw movement but held her fire – she'd used eight rounds, leaving ten in the magazine. More than enough to take on two live ones and one wounded, but she would make every shot count.

Another burst of fire hit the machine and the concrete next to where she crouched, ricocheting with a whine. There was almost no muzzle flash to fire at – a negative effect of the suppressors. This put her at a decided disadvantage: they knew where she was, but she couldn't be sure where they were.

There. A man running in a crouch.

Four shots hammered from the Glock, and two hit him. He went down hard near the pool pump shed, and she quietly waited for the remaining intact shooter to make a move. Her eyes had adjusted to the darkness enough that she could see the man she'd hit behind the fountain, his wound leaking into a bloody pool at its base – she must have nicked an artery, which was fortunate for her as it meant that it was just a matter of time until he lost consciousness. Until then, however, he was still dangerous, although not the biggest threat.

Where is the other gunman? Seconds ticked by, and she began to get a sinking feeling. Had he made it to the far stairwell by the lobby while she was ducking their fire?

If so, Matt was unarmed. A sitting duck.

And Hannah was in the room.

She scanned the courtyard, weapon clenched in a two-handed grip, and backed away from the vending machine, feeling with her feet, eyes locked on the pool area, alert for any movement.

Nothing.

She was almost to the stairs when a hail of shooting peppered the walls. She threw herself onto the ground, rounds sizzling by her head. The wounded man from the fountain was limping forward, his belt cinched around his upper thigh, pinning her down with his fire as a dark form ran toward her in a crouch from the periphery. She couldn't get off a shot, and she crawled to the side, trying to shield herself from the rain of bullets.

Jet tried to get up, but her foot slipped on the soda, and her leg went out from under her. She was bringing her weapon to bear, ready for the running shooter to present himself, when a loud series of explosive shots blasted from the dark stairwell behind her. She turned and swung her gun to face the new attacker and found herself drawing a bead on a young man holding the unmistakable form of a Desert Eagle, pointed beyond her at the pool area. He fired again, and the wounded attacker cried out as a .45 round shredded through his chest, and then her mystery ally raced past her into the courtyard. Another shot sounded from near the pool, the Desert Eagle's low boom – the wounded man had been taken down.

She lowered her weapon as he returned and stood motionless, noting in the moonlight that his gun pointed slightly down in a professional ready position, although it could be brought into play in a split second. He approached until he was two meters away and studied her as though surprised she was a woman.

"Who are you?" he asked in Spanish, keeping his voice low.

"Who are *you?*" she volleyed, but kept her weapon by her side.

"That's of no matter," he said. "Now answer me. What are you doing with a gun, shooting it out with these men?"

"I didn't have much of a choice, did I? They killed the clerk, and they were coming for me next." She stopped as their gaze connected.

Her eyes narrowed with realization. "Or were they? No. That's not right, is it? They were after you, weren't they?"

"At any rate, thank you. Your gun alerted my brother and me that we were under attack."

"Let's try this again. Since you won't tell me who you are, who are – were – they?"

"Criminals. Rivals. Murderers. We were attacked earlier in another town. I thought we'd be safe here…"

"I'd say not."

He took a step toward her and hesitated. "I need to get out of here. There may be more on their way."

"Sounds like a good idea," she agreed. They watched each other for several beats, and then he returned his pistol to its shoulder holster. She slipped hers back into place at the small of her back as he strode past her, confident, betraying not a trace of fear that she might whip out her gun and shoot him. Then again, there was a courtyard full of reasons for him to believe she wasn't a threat.

Jet followed him up the stairs. She stopped at her room, where he turned to her and spoke. "Good night, and thanks again. That was extraordinary – I counted six gunmen, five of which you got." He paused. "If you ever want a job…"

"I need to take care of my family."

He nodded and moved to a door four down from hers – the room that had had a light on when she'd gone for her soda. Matt swung the door open, and she pushed past him, nervous energy radiating from every pore.

"What the hell–"

"Grab your bag. We need to get out of here. Now. I'll explain later. Hurry, Matt. There's no time." She knelt by her suitcase, retrieved the spare Glock magazine, and exchanged it for her half-spent one, pocketing the other. Hannah was sitting up, her eyes wide with fear, and Jet walked over to her. "Honey, everything's okay. But it's time to go. Can you be super good and get moving?"

Tears streamed down Hannah's face as she nodded, frightened and confused by the shooting and now this.

"Be brave, sweetheart. I'll take care of you. Everything's going to be okay. I promise." Jet turned to Matt. "You got everything? I just need my hygiene kit and we're out of here." She moved to the bathroom and returned in seconds, packed her kit in her bag, and then shouldered it. "Hannah, you stay next to Matt, okay? Hold onto his shirt. It's dark out, and I don't want you to fall."

Hannah nodded again and moved to Matt, who offered her his infectious grin. "All right, princess. Follow Mommy." He looked Jet over. "How is Mommy, anyway?"

"I'll be better once we're on the road."

"Want to tell me what happened?"

"Bunch of bad guys. I thought they were after us." She shrugged.

"But they weren't?"

"Seems as though we aren't the only ones with problems."

Jet switched the lights off and cracked the door open. Seeing and hearing nothing, she swung it wide and stepped out. A young, scared couple was running for the stairs, no bags, and Jet let them get well ahead before she led Matt and Hannah to the pitch-black stairwell.

"Matt, give me your bag. Carry Hannah down the stairs. I don't want her tripping."

"I got it," he said and shouldered the bag before picking Hannah up. "Lead on."

They made it to the ground level, and Jet turned to Hannah. "I want you to close your eyes tight until I say it's okay to open them, okay? Promise me you'll do that, honey."

Hannah looked at her uncomprehendingly. "Otay."

"Ready? Now."

Hannah did as instructed, and Jet motioned for Matt to follow her. They skirted the dead gunmen, and Jet pointed to the lobby and then moved to the nearest body and scooped up his weapon. A Beretta with a suppressor. She felt in his pockets and found two spare magazines, which she slid into her side pockets before catching up to Matt and slipping the gun into his belt.

"Hey. Careful, huh?" he whispered.

"Let's hope you don't need it. A Beretta." Jet led them through the front entrance and was ten meters from the Explorer when she stopped dead. "Damn."

A Ford Excursion SUV was behind her vehicle, blocking it. She'd parked near the lobby to reduce the odds of a break-in, but hadn't factored the gunmen's truck into the equation. She stood staring at the big vehicle, debating whether to go back and search the corpses for keys, when a set of blue-white headlights lit the walkway and a silver Land Rover backed out of a nearby slot. Jet's gaze locked with the driver's – the man with the Desert Eagle. He said something to the passenger, and the Land Rover backed up until it was even with them. The tinted window slid down with a motorized whine. Two young men eyed Jet, and then Hannah.

"What's wrong?" the driver asked.

"We're blocked in. I think it's the gunmen's car."

He twisted around to look and saw three sets of headlights approaching on the road. He swallowed hard. "Good luck. I'll bet those are reinforcements."

Jet pulled her Glock out in a fluid motion and pointed it at the passenger's head. "Unlock the doors. You're giving us a ride."

"Screw her, Alejandro," the passenger hissed.

Alejandro looked at Hannah and then at Jet. "You're wearing out my gratitude," he said.

The headlights drew nearer – three black SUVs. Jet could make out an arm dangling out of the nearest with an assault rifle.

"Either you let us in, or we're going to get shot to pieces. And you'll be first," Jet said, her voice low as she shifted the gun to aim at Alejandro. He sighed, hit the power lock button, and the doors unlocked.

"You win. Make it fast. They're almost here," he said.

They piled into the back seat, and the Land Rover pulled away before Jet had gotten the door closed. The rifle opened up on full automatic and chunks of pavement flew into the air around them.

"Hold on," Alejandro yelled and floored it as he swerved and rounded the corner. Two of the SUVs followed while the third rolled to a stop at the motel entry.

The big Land Rover engine roared as Alejandro drove the vehicle to its limit and Jet strapped Hannah in. Matt and Jet twisted to watch the pursuing vehicles, which were already falling back on the long straightaway, their motors no match for the souped-up Land Rover's acceleration.

As they continued to pull away from the gunmen, Alejandro glanced in the rearview mirror at Jet, who was still clutching the Glock. "Easy. This is my brother, Rodrigo. I'm Alejandro. Put your gun away and buckle up, because judging by the welcoming committee back there, we're in for a rough ride."

CHAPTER 11

A lamp shone through the wooden blinds in the window of the third-floor condo in one of Medellín's best neighborhoods, an area that had been gentrified after the decline in cartel-related violence in the new millennium. Time had worked its magic on Colombia, and even though the country was still embroiled in a fifty-year-long civil war, with a good half of the nation under rebel control, life went on in the metropolitan areas, and the beleaguered city was enjoying a renaissance as a retirement destination for gringos.

The metropolis was nothing like it had been when Vince Drago had first taken up residence there seventeen years earlier, when it was still wide open. It had been a place where an enterprising young man with certain unorthodox skills could make serious money without fearing messy legal entanglements – and if that young man had a taste for nose candy, so much the better; cocaine was cheaper than flour in Medellín.

Drago rubbed his hand over his smooth chin – the goatee had been shaved off within hours of the bar fight – and eyed the screen of his computer monitor. He typed in a few commands and double-checked the blind email account again to ensure his eyes weren't playing tricks on him, and then sat back, a smile on his face. His agent had contacted him with a job, but one unlike anything he'd fielded in recent memory: high dollars to track and execute one target – and not even a guerilla or cartel kingpin surrounded by an entourage of killers.

It sounded like child's play. That immediately made him nervous; he was naturally distrustful of anything that seemed too easy. Harsh experience had taught him nothing in life was ever simple or facile. So when a client came along offering a dream contract with insane pay, his immediate instinct was to decline it.

He took a long hit of the joint he'd rolled and held the smoke deep in his lungs before exhaling a pungent cloud at the open window. There had to be a catch. Drago was a specialist, and a highly paid one to boot. Hiring him to do a routine hit was like using a sledgehammer to kill a fly.

He stood and went into his bedroom. After a few moments, he returned with a cell phone equipped with a signal scrambler. He powered it on and dialed his agent's number and waited as it rang.

"This better be good," the agent growled.

"It's Drago. We need to talk."

"Do you have any idea what time it is here?"

"Time to tell me about the contract."

The agent cleared his throat. "Fine. The fee is half a million, plus expenses. I'll send a dossier via encrypted email within…the hour."

"Who's the client?"

"No idea. I was contacted by an intermediary."

"Who?"

"You wouldn't know him."

"Try me."

The agent hesitated. "Simon Belem."

Neither man said anything for several seconds. Drago broke the silence. "You know who he fronts for."

"I asked. This isn't one of theirs."

"And they'd never lie about something like that."

"After your last dance with them, I think it's safe to say you're not on their Christmas list. This isn't company business."

"Then why that kind of money?"

"You have to find the target to collect. And…well, you'll see when I send the file over."

Drago's stomach did a small flip. "What?"

"The target has something you need to recover. For an additional bonus."

"Something," Drago echoed.

"Diamonds."

"How many diamonds are we talking about here? And what sort? In jewelry?"

The agent hesitated. "I don't see why you need to know that. What does it matter?"

Drago explained with an air of exaggerated patience. "It matters because how many he has and in what form will impact how he behaves. Will he be looking for a pawn shop? An international fence? Is he going to be unloading one or two, or trying to get rid of a handful? If they're worried that I'd try to take them myself, then they shouldn't hire me."

"Loose stones. Millions worth. How many they're unsure of. Perhaps tens of millions."

Drago flicked a match to life, lit the joint again, and took another hit. "The plot thickens."

"Is there anything else? If you take the deal, we get a quarter mil now and the balance upon completion. It's on the level. You should live so long that you get more like this."

"Don't lose that optimism."

"Good night. Call me in the morning and let me know how you want to proceed."

The phone went dead in his hand, and Drago switched it off. Forty-three minutes later, he received a 6MB file via an email server with military-grade encryption and a one-time-use password. Drago downloaded the file, printed it out, and then spent an hour reading it and crawling the web for news out of Buenos Aires and Mendoza. The only relevant thread was an aristocrat in Mendoza who'd apparently arranged for the plane that had been shot out of the sky – an incredibly sloppy bit of overkill even by Drago's elastic standards.

He called the agent again and ignored the grumbling way the man answered the phone.

"Bastard. I didn't even bother to go back to sleep."

"You know me well. Consider the contract accepted."

"I'll arrange a transfer, as well as a jet to Mendoza. Can you be ready in an hour?"

"You sound pretty sure of yourself. Tell me you didn't already have the plane on call."

"There are no secrets between us, are there?"

"One caveat. The file says I can expect intel support through you. Where are *you* getting it from?"

"Wherever I can."

Drago's inner alarm sounded again. "I don't need any surprises."

"That makes two of us. Relax. Everyone's after the same thing."

"I just want it on the record. This looks and feels like a black ops job. Not a hit. Don't get me into anything I can't get out of. And don't hold out on me."

"Never. The transfer will happen by the time you touch down in Mendoza. Call me on the way to the airport and I'll give you the plane info."

"Gear?"

"You won't be searched by Argentine customs. Bring the minimum you'll need. Anything specialized I can source locally."

"How?"

"I have friends in low places."

Drago packed a black nylon carry-on bag with three changes of clothes, a Heckler & Koch Mark 23 pistol with three spare magazines of hand-loaded ammunition, a laser aiming module and a screw-on suppressor, and a collapsible sniper rifle with two eight-round magazines and a long cylindrical suppressor, all concealed beneath the false bottom. It was heavy, the compartment lined with a layer of lead foil to confound any airport security X-ray gear, and it wouldn't withstand an in-depth search. Still, if his agent was on his game, there wouldn't be any reason for concern – on private charter flights there wouldn't be any security to clear, just a short walk across the tarmac to the waiting plane.

The jet was a Gulfstream III, older but easily capable of hitting Argentina from Colombia even if its range was considerably more limited than that of its more advanced siblings. Drago settled back into the luxurious seat, his bag strapped into the recliner across the aisle from him, and closed his eyes as the aircraft taxied to the main runway before accelerating and thrusting upward into the night sky, turbines pushing hard to get the plane over the mountain range in the thin atmosphere of Medellín's high altitude. He peered through the window at the tapestry of city lights disappearing beneath the wing and closed his eyes again, determined to get some rest on the five-hour flight south.

CHAPTER 12

San Felipe, Chile

Bastian stood by the reception counter, watching the hidden lobby security camera footage at hyperspeed as his men dragged the bodies of their comrades from the courtyard and loaded them into the back of the Ford Excursion like cords of firewood. The captain of the local police had called to alert him that he had ten minutes before the first car arrived – a courtesy that the Verdugos' generosity had bought that evening.

He'd begun his scan of the surveillance tape at the point Alejandro and Rodrigo had arrived. There was no way that six men had been taken out without serious reinforcements, and he wanted to see what he was up against. As he fast-forwarded through the hour and a half between when they arrived and when his shooters did, he couldn't believe that nobody else had come in. He'd have bet money that he would see at least a few of the Soto crew put in an appearance, but he would have lost his wager, because the lobby remained empty – and there was no other way in or out of the hotel.

His eyes narrowed as he watched his men enter the lobby at the start of the attack and then move into the courtyard after shooting the clerk. Followed by nothing in the lobby for four minutes, according to the counter, then the first of a number of couples and individuals running for the door. Bastian guessed the gun battle was already over by then – this appeared to be the guests clearing out after the shooting had stopped, which made sense.

Wait. There. He stopped the tape when he came to Alejandro, gun in hand, moving through the lobby, followed by his brother. Bastian pressed play and watched as nothing else happened, and finally a couple with a small child ran past the reception desk. Then nobody more.

Which was impossible.

Where were the shooters who'd helped the Sotos?

None of it made sense.

He rewound and stopped at the couple with the child. There was something…familiar there. What was it? The man was wearing a baseball cap, and from the elevated angle of the camera, Bastian couldn't make out much of his face. But the woman…

Bastian stared at the image and grunted, then paged through his iPhone messages until he came to one he'd received from Antonio earlier in the evening. He opened the attachment and stared at the photo, and then held the phone up next to the monitor as he muttered to himself.

"Well, I'll be damned…"

"What is it?" asked his second-in-command, Felipe, as he nervously checked the time.

"The woman. On the tape. If I'm not mistaken, it's the same one as in the photo Antonio sent us earlier. The one with the half-million-dollar price on her head."

"What? Let me see." Felipe rounded the counter and stared at the image for a few moments before nodding. "Could be. Hair's shorter. But the face…"

Bastian stood. "Time's up. The cops will be here in another couple of minutes."

"You're going to leave the tape?"

"I have to. That was part of the deal with the cops. Don't worry, though – all our men are dead, so they won't be talking. And if it gets the Sotos into even more hot water, hey, call that a win."

They jogged out to the SUV, and then Felipe veered left to where the gunmen's SUV was parked, keys in his hand. He slid behind the wheel and started the engine and was following Bastian's vehicle out of the lot when the first set of emergency lights appeared on the road from town.

Bastian placed a call on his cell phone as his driver put distance between them and the hotel. The cab stank of blood and human waste from the bodies in the cargo area, but he ignored it as he waited for an answer. When the call picked up, the voice on the other end of the line sounded excited, and there was considerable background noise.

"Where are you?" Bastian snapped.

"Behind the Sotos. But they're getting away. That damned truck of his is a rocket."

"Keep after them. Are you in the lead vehicle?"

"Yes."

"Did you see anything at the hotel?"

"We didn't stop. The Sotos were pulling away when we arrived."

"Damn."

"Why?"

"Looks like they had help. The woman Antonio broadcast a few hours ago."

"Woman!" A pause. "Now everything makes sense…"

"What are you talking about?"

"When the Sotos were in front of the hotel, they were talking to a family. Then everyone loaded into their car and they took off."

Bastian nodded. "When you catch up to them, kill the woman if you can't take her alive."

"Will do."

"And be careful. It looks like she's working with the Sotos. Which means the warning that accompanied the photo wasn't a mistake. She's dangerous as a snake. We've already lost six good men tonight to her. Don't make it seven."

"I understand."

"I'm heading back to the safe house. Call me with updates every ten minutes."

"Okay. It looks like they're heading north. Into the mountains."

Bastian frowned. "There's nothing there."

"Maybe that's the point. They've already gained maybe half a kilometer on us. They'll probably gain another before I call you again. They're going to try to outrun us."

"Keep after them. I'll make some calls and see if we have anyone up in Cabildo or La Ligua who can come the other way and cut them off."

"There are a lot of smaller roads once we're in the mountains."

"Don't lose them. Between the Sotos and the woman, this is the biggest payday we'll ever get."

Bastian's final call went out to Antonio, who was not only still awake but alert, in spite of the hour, which didn't surprise Bastian. This was arguably the most important night of his life: the culmination of months of planning and the effective change of power in the entire nation's underworld in a matter of hours. Bastian told him about the woman and the Sotos, and while Antonio tried to sound calm, Bastian could tell that he was annoyed that the attack hadn't gone as planned, as well as excited that they'd located the woman so quickly.

Leonid awoke from a sound sleep and gazed groggily around his hotel room before his eyes landed on his cell phone, which was glowing and vibrating on the night table. He reached over to it and sat up as he answered.

"Yes?"

"*Señor* Ross? This is Antonio. I'm sorry if I woke you."

"No problem. What can I do for you?"

"We've found your mystery woman."

Leonid switched on the bedside lamp and threw the sheets off, now fully awake. "Where?"

"She was involved in a gun battle at a hotel. We're in pursuit of her now. There's no way she can get away. She and her accomplices are on a mountain road with nowhere to go."

"Accomplices? What are you talking about?"

Antonio gave Leonid an abridged version of the events at the hotel. "I hope to have good news for you soon."

"Antonio, listen to me very carefully. This woman is not to be trifled with. She's more than a match for anything you can throw at her. No disrespect, but I thought my instructions were clear. I was to be notified—"

"Which you have been. Unfortunately, your agenda doesn't align with mine. The men in the car with her are of considerably more importance to me than she is, and watching them from a safe distance wasn't an option. As you say, no disrespect, but do not come to my country and lecture me on how to best proceed. I have my priorities clear. I'll call you when I have more information."

Leonid fumed at the crime lord's arrogant dismissal but bit his tongue. It would do no good to anger the man who had his quarry in sight.

"Very well. I'll wait for your call. I can't tell you how...disappointed I'll be if she gets away."

"Thank you for the reminder. I'll be in touch."

Leonid found himself staring at the cell phone, the line dead in his hand.

Idiots. They had no idea what they were dealing with. The woman had scaled a twenty-story building in Moscow, defeated advanced security systems, killed one of the most powerful oligarchs in Russia and escaped from an army of elite ex-commandos seemingly without breaking a sweat. Now it sounded like she'd painted a hotel with the blood of Antonio's top execution squad.

He took deep breaths to calm himself. Things were out of his hands. He could only pray that she made some critical mistake, because otherwise his money was on her escaping just as she had in Argentina.

Leonid hoped he was wrong but afraid that he was right.

He stood and paced as he called the other members of his team in Santiago and filled them in, and then contacted the remaining group in Mendoza. He wanted them in Chile at first light – they were to drive their rental cars over the pass and meet him in the morning. None of the men questioned the order, and he knew that they would be departing Mendoza minutes later.

Leonid sat back down, having done everything he could, and plugged his phone into the charger as he waited for news. The surge of adrenaline from closing in on his quarry made further sleep impossible. Ten million dollars had never been closer, and with any luck, within the next twenty-four hours he would be able to claim it and get back to Russia, finished with South American backwaters for good.

CHAPTER 13

San Felipe, Chile

The Land Rover streaked through the night, the powerful V-8 engine propelling it to ever higher speeds as it rocketed along the rural two-lane strip of country asphalt that paralleled the dry riverbank running north. Jet's knuckles were white as she gripped the door handle while holding Hannah's hand with her left. She sneaked a peek at the speedometer and saw the needle hovering at 160 kilometers per hour. Jet exchanged a glance with Matt and craned her neck to see the following headlights – now tiny in the receding distance.

"Where are we headed?" Rodrigo asked as Alejandro slowed for an intersection.

"Wherever we can lose these clowns."

"And then what?"

"And then we contact the men and go on the offensive against the Verdugos."

Rodrigo scowled. "But we don't know it was them."

"Gunmen shot up our nightclub and then our hotel, at the same time the cops took Dad out of commission. Who's second choice in your mind?" Alejandro asked derisively. "They want war, they'll get it. By tomorrow the streets will run red with their blood."

"What about this bunch?" Rodrigo demanded, gesturing with his thumb at the back seat.

Alejandro looked at Jet and Matt in the rearview mirror again. "Good question," he said thoughtfully.

"You can let us out wherever we can get a taxi. This isn't our fight," Matt said in Spanish.

Rodrigo glanced at the side mirror. "Easier said than done with them on our ass."

"Hang on," Alejandro warned as he abruptly braked and then swore under his breath as he accelerated again. "Too sharp a turn. We would have flipped at this speed."

"You know this area?" Rodrigo asked.

"I've camped in the mountains here when I was with Veronica," he said, referring to his ex-girlfriend. "She liked that kind of thing. I think there's a bridge up ahead that goes across the riverbed."

"Why don't we try to duck onto a side road?" Jet asked.

"I don't know where they lead, so if we dead end, we're screwed. I do know that this road continues north all the way to the coast, by Los Vilos. And every minute we're leaving them further behind. So I'm going to keep going. It's our best bet."

Alejandro goosed the throttle again, urging the vehicle faster, and Jet silently thanked Providence that there were no other cars on the road. At these speeds he wouldn't have time to react, and the gunmen behind them would be the least of their worries.

Several minutes later the road branched. He took the left fork and then slowed as they entered the small hamlet of Putaendo. He wended his way through the desolate streets, going as fast as he dared. Rodrigo turned to his brother.

"Why don't we cut down one of these streets and park? When they go by, we can backtrack, and they'll never know the difference."

"That assumes it's only those two cars. There was a third that stopped at the hotel. If we do that, we run a good chance of meeting them on the way back. I'd rather not risk it."

He accelerated again as they neared the bridge. He swung hard left, and they careened across the expanse, the gravel of the riverbed gray in the moonlight. Matt twisted around, keeping his eyes on the road behind them, and when they were across, he saw the headlights make the turn.

"They're still there. They must have seen our taillights." He glanced at Jet. "We should be running without headlights and using the emergency brake to slow. Then they'd have no idea where we went."

Rodrigo glanced back at him. "You two seem to know an awful lot about this."

Matt shrugged. "You pick things up over the years."

Alejandro wrenched the wheel, and they hurtled up an even smaller road, barely two lanes wide and pocked with potholes. The darkened form of small farmhouses, many little more than shacks, flew by as he continued to push the Land Rover past any sane limit.

"We'll be able to eat their lunch once we're on the mountain. It gets steep, and those tanks won't be able to keep up on the grade. Half an hour of that and we can loop back around on one of the winery valley roads. We'll have left them in the dust," he said.

Silence settled over the cabin as Alejandro concentrated on his driving. The large SUV's transmission pulled as the engine wound through the revs, and their speed passed through triple digits again on a long straightaway adjacent to the desiccated riverbank. The dark outline of the mountains stood in stark relief against the stars in the night sky as they roared past the last of the farmhouses. The slope changed, and they were climbing, the motor laboring as they ascended above the valley. Alejandro carved the corners as he floored the gas pedal, leaving the pursuing vehicles far behind.

A yellow lamp flickered to life on the dashboard. Jet leaned forward to see what it was as Alejandro cursed. He turned to his brother and snarled.

"How many liters of gas do we have left when the warning light goes on?"

"Damn. You're kidding me…"

"Look for yourself. It would have been nice to know we were running on empty about twenty kilometers ago."

"We must be burning a ton. Let's see…maybe eight, ten liters? Normally that would be about forty kilometers. But at this speed, maybe…twenty-five kilometers, at most?"

"That's a problem. There's nothing between here and Cabildo, and that's a postage stamp. Even if we made it – it would be ridiculously easy to find us there," Alejandro warned.

"I'll call someone. If we can lose them long enough for help to arrive, we should be okay," Rodrigo said and pulled his cell phone from his jacket. He stared at the screen and swore. "No signal."

"Of course not. We're in the mountains. The nearest tower's back in the valley."

"So what are we going to do?" Rodrigo demanded, his voice edged with panic.

"Keep going as far as we can. Now shut up and let me think," Alejandro snapped.

A green highway sign appeared out of the dark in front of them, signaling a split in the road, the left fork leading to La Ligua, the right to Alicahue. Rodrigo pointed at the sign. "Maybe we should try to make it to Alicahue?"

"No, we'll lose any advantage we have. That road turns to dirt in a bit, and it would cut our speed to nothing, not to mention leave a dust cloud to follow." Alejandro blew past the junction, the SUV rocking as it was buffeted by gusts of crosswind blowing down from the mountain. He picked up the speed for the last of the long, rolling hillside climb and then slowed somewhat as the road began twisting, the turns treacherous. Jet turned to watch the road behind them and estimated how far back the chase vehicles were – maybe a minute and a half or two, at most. More than adequate if they'd been smart about things back in the small towns and cut the lights, but out in the open like this...

They rolled around a particularly sharp curve, and the engine sputtered, hesitated, and then resumed pushing them along. Jet leaned forward. "We don't have much time. Pull over wherever you can and get out of the car. Matt, you take Hannah. I'll run it off the side of the cliff here. It's got to be, what, eight stories of drop?"

Rodrigo shook his head. "Are you insane? They'll be on top of us in no time."

"I'm anything but. If this works, they'll see the wreckage and think we misjudged a curve or had a blowout. With the gas tank empty, there's a better than fifty percent chance it explodes, which would be even better. Either way, I doubt anyone's going to scale the side of the mountain in darkness to confirm we're dead when they see the wreck. They'll just assume nobody could have lived," she explained, her voice even. "Don't hit the brakes. Use the emergency brake, and turn the lights out as we slow. They'll think we've gone around a curve. Then run for cover."

Alejandro nodded. "She's right."

Rodrigo shook his head. "And then what? We're out in the middle of nowhere, no cell coverage, nothing around. How do we get out of here?"

"We have to be alive to worry about it. If we wait till we run out of gas, we have zero chance," Jet said.

Alejandro peered into the darkness and took his foot off the gas. "Up there. See it? A flat area on the shoulder."

"No. Just stop in the middle of the road. Grab the biggest rock you can carry and bring it to me. I'll do the rest. Now shut off the lights and remember – only use the emergency brake."

Alejandro did as instructed, and they coasted to a stop.

"Everybody out. Run up the road around the corner, and then head into the mountains. If this works, we want to be well away by the time they arrive. Even if they smell a rat, this should buy us enough time to get away. Matt, grab my bag and Hannah and move." The money and passports were in Jet's bag. Matt's contained his clothes, which were replaceable, but without money and papers they'd be as dead in the water as if they'd gone over the cliff in the Land Rover.

The doors opened, and everyone climbed out of the car. The only sounds were the wind moaning through the ravine below them and the faint sound of truck engines in the distance, straining up the hill. Matt went to the rear hatch and opened it, shouldered Jet's bag, and went to Hannah as Alejandro searched along the roadside by the faint moonlight and returned lugging a large stone.

Jet turned to Matt. "Run. I'll catch up with you in a minute."

Matt loped off, the bag over one shoulder, Hannah hanging on to his neck as he supported her with his good arm. Jet eyed the rock. "Put it on the floor on the driver's side and get going. I'll maneuver it into position and do the rest."

Alejandro set the stone near the gas pedal and nodded to Jet, then grabbed Rodrigo's arm. "Come on. They're getting nearer."

Jet didn't wait for them to clear the area. She got behind the wheel and shifted the automatic transmission into low gear and pulled to the edge of the road. The drop was almost vertical to the rocky base of the chasm. She set the emergency brake, leaving the vehicle in gear, and jammed the rock against the gas pedal. The engine roared, and the SUV began to roll toward the edge, the smell of brake strong in the air. Jet trotted next to the vehicle and reached in as they neared the cliff and released the brake, then threw herself to the side as the truck shot forward. She hit the pavement hard and rolled with a grunt as she watched the silver form of the Land Rover plunge over the edge. She'd just gotten to her feet when it crashed into the bottom of the dry gorge, and she nodded to herself as a tongue of flame licked from under the hood.

Jet sprinted up the road after Alejandro and Rodrigo, wasting no time to watch the final seconds of the Land Rover's existence. She was rounding the turn when a fireball exploded behind her with a muffled *whump*. A trace of a smile tugged at her mouth as she poured on the speed, and then she saw the outline of the brothers ahead of her. When she reached them, she pointed to the hillside where she could see Matt already a dozen yards up the rise, and then followed in his footsteps as the sound of the pursuit SUVs approached from down the winding mountain road.

Alejandro and Rodrigo slipped and slid on the loose rocks as they tailed her, the slick soles of their expensive dress shoes all but useless for the task at hand. Matt continued ascending the side of the hill, his steps sure, dodging between cactus and scrub as he forged higher. Jet caught up to him and murmured in his ear. "Give me the bag. Hannah's heavier, but I can take one."

"I've got it."

"No point wearing yourself out. We're going to be walking a long time."

He shrugged the strap off, and she pulled the bag over her shoulder. "When we get a chance I'm going to dump this and move the important stuff into my pockets. The lighter we can travel, the better our chances," she said, and he nodded agreement. Hannah was watching her with wide eyes, and she smiled at her daughter. "This is fun, isn't it? An adventure. Camping, they call it."

Hannah looked unconvinced, sucking her thumb with an accusatory stare, obviously tired but overstimulated from the drive and the run up the mountain. They kept moving, the brothers fumbling behind them, and then they heard the sound of the pursuit vehicles rolling to a stop around the bend. Alejandro slowed, but Jet shook her head. "Keep going. We want to be out of sight if they wise up and start looking for any tracks. Right now our head start's our only advantage, so don't throw it away waiting to see what happens. They'll either come after us, or they won't. Either way, the more distance, the better."

Alejandro nodded, and she turned, Matt leading the way, a column of lost and weary travelers on a mountainside with only the wind and the glimmering heavens to guide them, leaving danger in their wake as they headed toward an uncertain future.

~ ~ ~

The driver of the lead vehicle flinched when the orange ball of flame blasted skyward from the ravine ahead.

"What was that?" the gunman in the passenger seat demanded, his Mac-10 machine pistol in his lap.

"Beats me. But we'll know soon enough."

By the time they pulled to a stop by the roadside, the Land Rover was a charred, twisted hulk far below them in the ravine. The driver got out of the car and moved to the edge of the drop, hands on his hips as he watched what remained of the SUV burn. The passenger and the three gunmen in the rear of the first vehicle joined him, and the second truck rolled to a halt next to them. The driver walked over to the new arrival and gestured at the wreck.

"He went off the side."

"Ha. I thought he'd lost us. At the rate he was going, he'd have been in Peru before we were out of the pass."

"Looks like maybe he should have slowed down, eh?"

"Well, that's one problem we can scratch off the list."

"Yeah, nobody's walking away from that. You see it blow?"

"From around the curve. I caught the last of it."

The driver sighed. "All right. Let's head back. I'll take a few photos with my phone, and when we get service, I'll send them to Bastian. He'll be happy."

"That's the understatement of the year."

The second SUV executed a three-point turn and trundled back down the hill as the driver walked back to the edge and memorialized the scene with his phone's camera. His men milled about, smoking and chatting as he took pictures from different angles. When he was done, he nodded.

"All right. Mount up. No point hanging around here."

The gunmen piled back into the vehicle, and the driver put the transmission into gear, glad the chase was finally over. Bastian had made it abundantly clear that failure wasn't an option, and he hadn't wanted to have to tell his superior that the Sotos had somehow evaded them yet again. That wasn't a recipe for a long life in his line of work, and he breathed easier on the trip back down the mountain, the driver now taking the curves at a moderate speed, happy to be headed back to their temporary headquarters for some deserved celebration after a job well done.

CHAPTER 14

Washington, D.C.

The older man pulled his long overcoat tight around him and clamped his hat in place as he walked into the evening wind on a crowded sidewalk in Georgetown, looking like any of tens of thousands of tired bureaucrats and lobbyists in a city overcrowded with anonymous gray men. He'd gotten the call only an hour before and had dressed and left his home in Virginia in a rush to make the rendezvous.

The coffee shop was a bohemian nod to 1950s beat culture, which the name made clear: Kerouac, the latest in a growing trend of pseudo-independent restaurants that were actually chains owned by multinational corporations. The older man pushed through the door and was greeted by a carefully engineered chaos, the overstuffed chairs with threadbare seats and peeling earth-tone walls as bogus as the framed black and white photographs of Ginsberg and Kerouac and the rest of the beat generation's icons, which he knew from a recent *Washington Post* article were identically hung in each of the chain's forty-four outlets, with another dozen planned inside the next ten months.

A bearded student wearing a beret and an Irish fisherman's sweater greeted him with a tired stare from behind a carefully worn counter, its edges scarred from eons of use that existed entirely in the minds of the carpenters who'd fabricated it to exacting corporate specifications.

"What's it gonna be, daddy-o?" the barista asked, his insouciant moue the only genuine expression in the place.

"Cup of coffee. Black."

"Javanese or Costa Rican?"

"Rican."

When the older man had paid and collected his oversized mug of coffee, he turned to scan the largely empty room – it was far too late in the evening for anyone but first dates looking to seem innocuous to each other, and his rendezvous, who was occupying one of two seats in the corner, studying a magazine as though it held the secret to eternal bliss.

He sat down across from the younger man and took an appreciative sip of the rich brew before setting it down on the table between them.

"You're sure it's her?"

"Absolutely. Took a while to filter through the system from Interpol, but it's a match. You can see from the side-by-sides." The younger man handed him a single sheet of photo stock with two images on it.

The older man's eyes pored over the images – one from the traffic camera near the residence of his son, Peter, taken moments after he'd been murdered in the dead of night, and the other a grainy shot apparently from a security camera, given the time and date stamp in the lower right-hand corner.

"Christ. This is already…too damned old. Where was it taken?"

"Mendoza, Argentina. A casino."

"Argentina! What the hell…" the older man spat.

"I know. Which explains why none of our efforts to track her have yielded anything. South America isn't known for its hypervigilant surveillance. Not much has changed since half the Third Reich disappeared there at the end of the war."

"Those that weren't welcomed into the DOD with open arms, you mean. Ancient history."

"Anyhow, this was circulated on Interpol for ID purposes, and it took some time for us to flag it."

"And?"

"And so far there's been no identification that I know of. But it puts her in Mendoza, which is a start."

"Not exactly a hub of our operational strength, though, is it?"

"We don't have anyone on that coast. Just a few low-level data collection operatives. Nobody field-trained."

"Lovely. Where does that leave us?"

"I asked the Buenos Aires head of station to nose around and see what he can come up with, but frankly, I think you'd be better served with a freelancer."

The older man looked around the area. "That bitch killed Peter," he hissed.

"Yes. But I'm not sure it would be in your best interests – in any of our best interests – for a death squad to be traced back to the agency. Especially since there's no official tie-in." The younger man paused, dreading the older man's reaction to the message he was delivering. "And a freelancer would have more latitude to, well, take certain liberties with the local laws that might not fly with an official team."

The older man's eyes gave nothing away, his stare as cold as the grave, his irises two drops of black oil in a dead sea. "I trust you have a short list of deniable contractors for me?"

"Of course." Another piece of paper changed hands, this one with three names on it. "I made a few calls. The top name is unavailable. So it's either number two or three."

The older man read the stats. "Impressive."

"None of these are amateurs."

"What kind of support can I expect?"

"You'll have the full unofficial cooperation of the Buenos Aires station."

The older man took another swallow of coffee and rolled it around in his mouth like he was sampling a fine wine. "Cost?"

"Won't be cheap. Figure a nickel."

The older man nodded. "Which of the two candidates would you recommend?"

"The husband and wife team."

"Why?"

77

"Because we're after a woman, the female's intuition could come in useful. Just an emotional preference from my end. Either would probably be equivalent."

The older man thought for several moments. "Can you deal with the contract if I decide to pull the trigger?"

"Of course."

"And you're sure we can't handle this through official channels?"

"My instinct says no. Even in our world, somebody's going to want to know the justification for devoting resources to this. But it will mostly come down to risk. There's no way it will make it through committee. Trust me on this."

"You know your shop better than I do."

"It's not like the good old days. There are no more cowboys. Everything's more regimented. Structured."

The older man shook his head and then finished his coffee. "How do you want to handle the funding?"

"I'll get you an account number. It would be best if the funds stayed offshore."

"I can arrange that." The older man stood and shifted his fedora further forward on his brow. "Sooner the better." He looked around the room. "I think we're done here. Anything else?"

"No."

The older man hesitated as he turned, as if a thought had just occurred to him. He fixed the younger man with an icy glare, his expression flat. "Don't screw this up. I want her."

"I know you do. I'll pull out all the stops."

The older man spoke softly. "Don't disappoint me on this."

"I won't."

CHAPTER 15

Jet glanced at Hannah, her little head bouncing against Matt's shoulder as he marched along behind Alejandro, who had taken the lead once they were well away from the road. She was asleep, which was a small miracle, but didn't surprise Jet. Hannah had proved not only resilient but also capable of drifting off under the most difficult of circumstances. For a moment, Jet envied her that ability, and she smiled wistfully.

The scrub was thinning out as they climbed. They'd found a trail that paralleled the road far below.

Alejandro pointed out droppings along the way. "Goats. They're all over this area. You can hear them at dusk and dawn. I still remember that from camping." He paused, looking around. "There are mines in this stretch. Silver and copper. I used to visit them with my girlfriend. Most are closed down, but they've recently reopened several."

"That's nice. But how will any of that little bit of trivia help us?" Rodrigo grumbled.

Alejandro shot him a black look. "If we can find one along this stretch that's still active, if we're really lucky, they'll have strung a phone line. If not, at least come morning we can expect workers to show up, at which point we can get a ride."

"Why would they give us a ride?" Jet asked.

Alejandro grinned at the stars. "I can be very persuasive."

Rodrigo nodded. "Our family runs this part of Chile."

Matt snorted. "Didn't look like it back at the hotel."

Rodrigo stopped, and Jet could see his jaw muscles tighten. "You have no idea what you're playing with here," he warned, his tone menacing.

"Rodrigo," Alejandro said, "they aren't the enemy. She took out most of those gunmen. Don't waste your energy. We're still a long way from the mine."

"I don't like his attitude," Rodrigo pressed.

"Save it for the Verdugos."

Rodrigo resumed trudging along the dusty track, and the tension of the moment diffused. An hour later they came over a rise and took a break on the summit. Rodrigo shook a cigarette out of a nearly flat packet and lit it. Alejandro peered into the distance. "You see that road? Dirt, off to the left, cutting across that slope? I believe that leads to one of the mines I'm thinking of. It's an old one that shut down operations, but a new company came in and began digging again. The price of silver has increased enough to make it viable."

"It's a long way off," Rodrigo complained, inspecting his ruined shoes with a frown.

"Not that far. We should be able to make it before morning," Alejandro said.

Jet stretched her arms over her head and shouldered her bag again. "I'm game. But I need to go freshen up. I'll be back in a minute."

When she returned, she was no longer carrying the bag. Her pockets were bulging, and she had an extra jacket for Hannah as well as one for herself, but nothing else. A duffel full of clothes would require far more energy to haul than it was worth, and she could always buy more clothes once they were off the mountain. "That's better. Lead the way, Alejandro. The sooner we get there, the sooner we'll know whether you can make a call and get help."

Alejandro checked his watch. "It won't be light for another five hours. We should be able to find one of the mines within two or three – this isn't that big an area, and they're all fairly close together. The only reason to cut a road into these hills is to access mines, so we get to that road and follow it, we're home free."

"What if it's not one of the operational ones?" Rodrigo asked.

"Then we keep going till we find one that is."

Rodrigo shook his head. "I was afraid you'd say that."

They made it to the road in a little under an hour and took another break. Jet strode along the edge and peered at the surface before returning. "Tire tracks. Fresh, given that it rains a fair amount here. That's positive. This is probably one of the working mines."

Matt nodded. "Let's hope so. Not that I don't enjoy a nice evening constitutional, but I'm about ready to call it a night."

"Shouldn't be that far now," Alejandro said. "Most of the mines are only a few kilometers off the main road."

"With our luck this will be the exception," Rodrigo said, probing his tender feet through his dress socks, his shoes by his side. "What a nightmare."

"No point in whining. This is the least of our worries. We still need to deal with…with other matters. Tomorrow's going to be another very long day," Alejandro cautioned. "Come on. Might as well hit it. We can rest once we're at the mine."

The trek lasted another hour and a half, mostly uphill, and by the time they reached the mine grounds, everyone was beat. Alejandro and Rodrigo went to reconnoiter around the few temporary buildings near the mine opening while Jet attended to Hannah, who had awakened and needed to relieve herself. Matt gathered wood and leaves and created a fire pit from stones to stave off the worst of the chill from the icy wind coming off the Andean slopes. Once her motherly duties were done, Jet returned with Hannah and sat next to Matt, who was waiting for the brothers to return so he could borrow their lighter.

"We're going to need some water soon. We've sweated a lot," he said.

"When they get back, that'll be our first order of business. One of the buildings is sure to have water if this is a working mine."

"What do you make of those two?"

"Alejandro seems to be the brains. I could do without his brother. He's dead weight," she said.

"Agreed. And they seem to be up shit creek. Let's not forget for all their assurances that they run this country that they got shot up pretty good at the hotel. If you hadn't been there, they'd be dead. We all know that."

"But I was. Makes me wish I'd just stayed in bed. The brother's right about one thing: this is a nightmare."

"Right, but it's not our problem. We just need to get out of here and get clear of this pair, and then we can go on with our lives."

"Good plan. Of course, when the Argentine fixer's guy shows up tomorrow, he's going to find a hotel full of police and no client. So back to the drawing board on getting out of Chile."

"True." Matt thought for a moment. "If their family really does run things here, maybe your boy Alejandro can help. I'd say he owes you big for saving his bacon, and then for coming up with a solution for the car."

"Good idea, but I wouldn't hold my breath. I get the feeling they've got bigger fish to fry."

"I'm just saying, you've got a marker with him. Or at least, you should."

Jet sighed. "I couldn't sleep back at the hotel, and now all I can think of is shutting my eyes. How upside-down is that?"

Matt looked at where Hannah was lying, her head in Jet's lap, slumbering as though in the womb. "Once we get some water, you can catch a little shut-eye. I'll keep watch."

"You're not just a pretty face, are you? Anyone ever tell you you're a nice guy?"

"Not recently. Something about being too busy running for our lives."

"Well, you are. And I'm lucky to have you. Even with a broken wing and the world's worst haircut."

Matt leaned into her and kissed her. "Likewise. Except for the wing and hair part."

A gust of cold wind blew across the dirt, carrying with it grit and dust and the smell of dry grass and stagnation. Gravel crunched underfoot as Alejandro returned, shaking his head. "No phone line. But it's definitely a working mine, or there wouldn't be any buildings here."

"Doesn't look like a very big operation," Matt observed.

"They're probably just doing some kind of an assessment. I don't see a lot of heavy processing equipment," Alejandro agreed.

"Could be they're trucking the ore to a larger mine?"

"Either way, I'd expect workers shortly after sunup."

Jet lifted Hannah's slack form and handed her to Matt before looking at Alejandro. "We need to get into the buildings and find some water. My little girl needs some and so do I."

"I'll show you the likeliest candidates. I don't suppose you know how to get past locked doors, do you?" Alejandro asked.

"You'd be surprised what a girl can do if she puts her mind to it." She hesitated. "Where's your brother?"

"Nature called."

"Ah. Well, lead the way."

They got lucky at the first trailer. Jet broke a window, and Alejandro boosted her through, and she opened the door from the inside. In the faint moonlight they made out a water cooler with a twenty-liter bottle atop, half full. Jet found a plastic pitcher on one of the desks, filled it to the brim and slaked her thirst, as did Alejandro. When they were sated, she refilled it and then took the pitcher back to Matt and Hannah. Rodrigo returned shortly thereafter, and Alejandro led him to the water cooler. When they reappeared five minutes later, Rodrigo looked considerably less annoyed – a first since she'd met him. Matt lit the fire, and they gathered around it, the warmth from the flames inviting in the cold darkness, the wood crackling and popping, the smoke cloying and thick.

"Let's try to get some sleep. It'll be light in an hour or two," Jet said.

"How can you sleep after all this?" Alejandro asked, frank curiosity in his voice.

Jet considered the last few days – gun battles, the kidnapping, the plane crash, the showdown with Tara, the full-scale war at Dante's factory – and smiled sweetly.

"It's been a long week."

CHAPTER 16

Santiago, Chile

Leonid ran from the bathroom to where his cell phone trilled and vibrated on the hotel room table. He snatched it up and held it to his ear.

"Yes?"

"Congratulations. Your problem is solved, which means you owe me half a million dollars."

Leonid absorbed Antonio's words. "Please explain."

"Your woman was in a car with two of my enemies. They were being chased on a mountain road and met with an accident in the form of a ten-story drop. They went over, and the truck blew up."

"Where?"

"About sixty kilometers north of us. A city called San Felipe. The crash took place in the mountains outside of town."

"I want to see for myself."

"I thought you might. I have arranged for one of my men to meet you up there and show you the wreck. Or if you want to forego the formality, I have photographs."

"All due respect, photos don't tell the whole story."

"Just so. When would you like to meet my man?"

Leonid checked his watch. "How long will it take to get there?"

"No more than an hour."

"Where do I meet him?"

"I'll send someone to pick you up. I presume you're staying at the hotel where we met, Mr. Ross?"

"That's correct, but unnecessary. I can make my own way."

"Ah, yes, but now I feel like I have five hundred thousand reasons to ensure that you don't encounter any difficulties getting there – or returning." Antonio's message was clear: he wasn't going to let Leonid out of his sight until the wire transfer was completed. It would be too easy for Leonid to verify the woman was dead, and then disappear, having acquired a half million dollars of value for nothing. "I will have a car there in twenty minutes, yes?"

"That's very gracious of you. However, I have several men who are part of my team who will want to come."

"The more the merrier. Just see that they're on their best behavior. We don't want any misunderstandings, do we?"

"Of course not. Twenty minutes."

"Look for a white Chevrolet Suburban. The driver's name is Carl."

The phone went dead. Leonid called his men and told them to be in the lobby in fifteen minutes and to come armed. He didn't trust the slick Chilean and wanted some insurance against a possible double cross. But based on the man's description of the crash, it would be the easiest ten million Leonid had ever made.

But Filipov, the attorney who had contracted the hit, would want definitive proof before he paid, which meant that Leonid had to get it, one way or another. The man wouldn't take a few snapshots and Leonid's word for it – he'd want her skull. Which was as it should be, Leonid thought. The customer was always right.

Leonid did a quick calculation of time zones and decided not to call Filipov until he had the evidence he needed in hand. It wouldn't do to get the attorney's hopes up only to dash them. No, better to appear on his doorstep with proof in hand and wait for payment in his office. Not that Leonid didn't trust him, but prudence dictated that he eliminate any temptation not to pay, and it would be impossible to argue with Leonid parked in the man's office with a body bag or a test tube containing the last of the woman's essence.

Carl was on time and showed no interest in talking, which was fine by Leonid. Half an hour outside town, they were blinded by police cruisers in the road. Spotlights roved over the Suburban as it drew to a stop. A uniformed officer took Carl's ID and radioed it in, and Leonid eyed his men in the back seat, who appeared relaxed, but who he knew all had their fingers on their pistol triggers out of habit. Hopefully the cops wouldn't search them or it would get ugly quickly – Leonid didn't know what the penalty might be for carrying unregistered, concealed weapons in Chile, but he suspected it was substantial.

The policeman returned with Carl's license and waved him through, averting one crisis. The big vehicle ate up the remaining stretch of road, and even with the unscheduled police stop, they made it to San Felipe on time.

Carl placed a call, murmured a few words, and then hung up, eyes never leaving the road. They drove down a quiet street and into a driveway that led to a farmhouse, ample acreage on either side ensuring privacy. The car stopped in front of the house, and Carl rolled down his window as a man emerged from inside – tall, a no-nonsense expression on his face, a pistol bulge obvious beneath his windbreaker. He exchanged a few words with Carl and then, after glancing at the men in the rear seat, turned his attention to Leonid.

"I'm Bastian, Mr. Ross. My boss says I'm to extend you every courtesy. Here are the shots I took of the accident," Bastian said in accented English and held out his cell phone.

Leonid took the phone and skimmed through the photographs. "Pretty dark, but it looks grim. Did you go through the wreckage?"

"No, it's too far down the gulch. Quite steep."

"Then let's go to the site. Oh, and see if you can find some rope. How many meters down do you think the wreck is?"

"Maybe…thirty meters? Nine or ten stories."

Leonid nodded. "Then forty meters should do the trick." Leonid's tone was friendly, but it was obvious that it wasn't a request. If Bastian was annoyed by the demand, he didn't show it, but merely nodded and returned to the house. Five minutes went by, and he emerged with a bundle of cord in one hand and strode to the black SUV. Carl waited until he'd turned it around, and then followed him down the drive.

Not surprisingly, the road to the mountain pass was deserted, and they made reasonable time. As Leonid had hoped, no emergency vehicles were at the scene. Leonid stepped from the Suburban and walked to the edge, and Bastian joined him, flashlight in hand. The fire had long since gone out, and Leonid could barely make out the charred remains. Bastian played the beam over the burnt form, and Leonid turned to him.

"One of my men will go down and have a look." He turned to the youngest of his team, a wiry man in his late twenties, and nodded. "Rudi, you know what to do," he said in Russian, and looked meaningfully at the cliff edge. Leonid glanced at Bastian. "Can I see that rope?"

Bastian brought over the line. Leonid cinched it to the Suburban's trailer hitch and gave it a good pull and then handed it to Rudi, who wrapped it around his waist and his forearm and moved to the drop-off. "Flashlight?" Leonid asked, and Bastian handed it to Rudi, who pocketed it before he lowered himself over the side.

"I hope he doesn't disturb any snakes. There are plenty of rattlers in these hills," Bastian said as they watched Rudi expertly rappel down the slope.

"That's good to know," Leonid said, terminating the discussion.

Three minutes went by, and Rudi called out from below. The terse words sent ice through Leonid's veins. He responded in Russian and turned to Bastian.

"There are no bodies in the wreck."

"What? I...maybe they were thrown clear? Or incinerated?" Bastian's cool veneer of confidence suddenly showed cracks.

"I told my man to look around, but my bet is he doesn't find anything. This was probably a ruse to get you to drop your pursuit. Bones don't incinerate in a car fire." Leonid spat to the side. "Which worked nicely, I'd say."

Bastian shook his head. "Why would they do such a thing? They were well ahead of my men. There was no reason. No, I think there's another explanation. They must have been thrown clear."

"I told your boss, Antonio, that the woman is a skilled professional. I warned him not to engage under any circumstances. This is why." Leonid paused. "You're lucky to be alive."

Bastian considered the scene at the hotel and said nothing as they waited for Rudi. Minutes stretched on, and then the rope went taut with a snap as he scaled the slope again. When he reached the road, he shook his head and gave a short report in Russian. "There's nothing. I did a grid search for twenty meters in all directions. No sign of anything other than the car, which is burned to a crisp."

Leonid relayed the information to Bastian, who glowered at the wreckage as his mind worked furiously before shaking his head again. "Impossible. There was an explosion. It must have vaporized them or blown them across the mountainside."

"No, I'm afraid not. There would have been something left. A bone or two. A skull. There's nothing, and my man walked the perimeter and searched among the pieces that blew off the car. So the target got away, while we're left standing in the dark with our dicks in our hands." Leonid was done with being polite. These incompetents had lost her, and God knew whether they'd ever pick up her trail again.

"Let's say you're right. Where would they have gone? The nearest town is over twenty kilometers away. No, it doesn't make any sense…"

"Perhaps they had another car waiting to rendezvous with them. I don't know. What I *do* know is that there are no bodies and no evidence of any kind that anyone got so much as a scratch in this crash, much less was killed. I'm afraid I'm right on this. You can verify it come morning, but I'd say she escaped."

"Which means…the men she was with also escaped," Bastian muttered, the gravity of the situation hitting home. The Sotos were still alive and out there somewhere. Antonio would go berserk, and when he was angry, he could be volatile. He fished his phone out and peered at it. No signal. He swore and eyed Leonid. "Come. We should return to the house. I need to make some calls."

Leonid retrieved the rope and tossed it to Bastian, who took the bundle and stowed it. The return drive was at considerably higher speed than the ascent, and Leonid could tell that Bastian was agitated by the way he pushed his SUV around the curves ahead of them. When they pulled into the farmhouse drive, he was already out of his vehicle and on his phone, pacing, in a heated discussion. Leonid and his men got out of the Suburban, and Bastian faced them, cell phone still glued to his ear.

"We know where they are. We're calling in reinforcements." He finished the call and pocketed the cell.

"How do you know their location?" Leonid asked.

"That's not important. But we will arrange for this to be the last hours of their life."

"I want to go with you."

Bastian nodded and looked Leonid and his men over. "Yes, I figured as much. And so you shall."

"It will be light soon. Time's wasting."

"You're correct, but I have my instructions. I have been told to wait until arrangements have been put into place to ensure that there can be no more mishaps. We will leave at dawn."

"I don't see why we're delaying," Leonid snapped.

"I understand your impatience, but there's nothing I can do about it. Best to relax. Come inside – we have everything you could want. We'll be on the road soon enough."

Leonid could see there was nothing to be gained by arguing, so he accepted Bastian's offer of hospitality and followed him into the house, keenly aware of precious minutes ticking by but unable to do anything about it.

~ ~ ~

Franco hung up on Bastian and called Colonel Campos, the number as familiar to him as his own. Campos answered on the fifth ring, his voice gravelly with sleep and a budding hangover. Franco apologized for rousing him and then got to business.

"I need your help, my friend."

"Of course, whatever you need," Campos said, his voice cautious.

"The Soto boys are at a mine north of San Felipe."

"Yes?"

"I need the army to stop the miners from going to work this morning and, if possible, to cordon off the area so nobody can enter or exit it."

"That could be problematic if the local police want to know why we're in the region. That's not our customary turf…"

"I understand. I'll deal with the police – they've had no problem taking my money so far. Look, I'll only need you there for a few hours. This will be over by breakfast. I'll send my men in, and they'll do the dirty work, so your hands will be clean. You just need to ensure they aren't disturbed."

"I'll need to think up a pretense. If my superiors ask why I shipped several truckloads of men there, I need an answer."

"Tell them you were following up on a tip about weapons smugglers. God knows the Sotos are guilty of that, and more. Whatever you need to do, do it, but I want that road closed down by dawn."

Campos drew a heavy breath and grunted. "I'll get dressed." He didn't need to say that Franco now owed him big. This went far beyond looking the other way when certain containers entered the port, or rousting unfriendly union workers who were agitating for higher wages from one of the Verdugos' shipping or loading companies. He was being asked to get his hands dirty, albeit from a distance, and Franco was under no illusions that the price wouldn't ultimately be high. Then again, so were the stakes. He needed the Sotos dead and would do whatever it took.

Franco returned to the bedroom, removed his black silk bathrobe and smoothed his pajamas. His wife hadn't awoken, and he looked at her sleeping form with a combination of loathing and resignation. She'd once been a great beauty, courted by rich men, and had chosen him for her husband, to her family's continued chagrin – beneath her station, as she'd taken to reminding him. But now…years and alcohol had taken their toll, and when he looked at her, it was like a cruel joke that all the mistresses and trysts could never right.

Franco sighed. He was an honorable man, and she'd borne him a son, which had been all he'd really wanted out of the union. It was for that son that he was risking it all to make the bold move against his hated rival – a move that could be either suicide or brilliance. Tomorrow would tell, and Franco, a man who knew no religion other than his own desires, uttered an unfamiliar prayer to a strange God, pleading with him to support his enterprise and bless it with success as he crawled back into bed, his head pounding from a tension headache that all the whiskey in the world couldn't wash away.

CHAPTER 17

Mendoza, Argentina

The first rays of dawn marbled the sky with tangerine and pink as the Gulfstream made its final approach over the vineyards surrounding El Plumerillo International Airport. The plane rocked, its tires smoked on the tarmac, and then it stabilized, the updrafts of buffeting wind diminishing at ground level. The sleek aircraft slowed as it neared the end of the runway and made the turn that led to the small terminal. Drago eyed the airport as they rolled to a stop and was relieved to see only one sleepy customs inspector standing near the building.

He checked his phone and saw a message from the agent, sent twenty minutes earlier. Drago read it with interest and then returned the phone to his jacket pocket as the pilot lowered the fuselage stairs, the din of the engines whining at idle an auditory assault from the rear of the plane.

When he stepped into the morning light, the air felt crisp and clean, as though the nearby Andean peaks had imbued it with an electric vitality. The customs inspector approached and stamped his passport perfunctorily, uninterested in his bag. Drago nodded his appreciation, glad that his agent had been true to his word in eliminating that hurdle.

He made his way to the parking lot, where the text message had promised a Chevrolet sedan would be waiting, the key under the driver's side floor mat and the door open. Drago found the car and, after orienting himself with the handheld GPS that had been left in the glove box per his request, he pulled out of the dirt lot, his first errand of the morning to check out the two addresses the agent had sourced for the aristocrat who'd arranged the jet that had been blown out of the sky. It was a starting point, even if it was unclear to Drago how it was connected to his concerns, other than a report that a woman had been working with the target in Mendoza and that she'd been on the plane.

A woman. He'd only had the contract for six hours, and there was already a new player in the mix – a mystery woman. Nobody knew anything about her, which caused butterflies to flutter in his stomach.

The connection wasn't much – wasn't anything, really, by his standards – but hopefully it would be enough. He'd need to sweat the aristocrat and see what he knew. Beyond that, the trail had gone cold in Buenos Aires three days earlier, which was a lifetime. The target could be in Malaysia by now, but a job was a job, and he hadn't expected it to be easy given the half-million fee. After all, no contract was ever easy if it required Drago's special skills.

According to the file, the target was a highly experienced covert operative who'd taken that which didn't belong to him – diamonds, exact quantity and value unknown. Part of what made the assignment troublesome was that he wasn't expected to just locate the man and put his lights out, but also to interrogate him and find any diamonds he still had left. Upon reflection, the contract price was fair – finding the target would take some doing, possibly weeks of his time, assuming he was successful at all.

Drago was under no illusions that he'd been brought into this for a simple button job. For all his agent's assurances, everything in the report had pointed to a black ops mission gone horribly wrong, which meant U.S. government involvement. Reading between the lines, the target had pissed off his employer, who'd ordered him taken out.

Only that apparently hadn't been as easy as hoped, which was where Drago came in.

The diamond angle had been explained as a simple theft by the target – the property of the contracting client. What a former covert operative had been doing with the property, or how it had come into his possession, was left out of the narrative. Again, this reeked of clandestine involvement: need to know was an obsession for some agencies, the CIA and DOD being two of the biggies.

It didn't really bother him that he might be doing their dirty work for them, but it did give him pause that they were in such dire straits they'd needed to hire him. His last job for the agency hadn't gone well. "Too much collateral damage" had been the assessment, meaning that butchering not only the target's staff of bodyguards but also his family in order to lure him into Drago's trap had been over the line – this, in a business where no lines existed until after the fact, when armchair quarterbacks bitched about what they would have done differently. It was one of the primary reasons he'd gone independent so many years ago: if a drug lord wanted one of his competitors taken out, there were never any regrets unless Drago failed, which had never happened. Nobody complained about the level of brutality required to accomplish the objective. They merely paid up and said thank you. As it should be.

But get a government involved and look out. Hand wringing, impossible caveats, threats to not pay once he'd performed, worries about some wiseass deciding that the best way for their dirty deeds to never see the light might be to eliminate him…all of these went with that territory, which is why he didn't like the work, preferring to stay in the private sector.

Having profited handsomely from his decision, he'd made the right choice.

Still, a half million dollars didn't fall into his lap every day, and it was easily five contracts' worth of profit when the expense provision was taken into account. Three years' pay at his going rate for one assignment. Whoever had picked the number had done so knowing there was no way he would turn it down. That made him feel like he was being played, but to what end, he wasn't sure. What he was sure about was that after this job, he'd be taking a nice year or two of vacation somewhere he couldn't be tracked – maybe somewhere like the beach towns of Venezuela. A man could do a lot of good living for that kind of money anywhere in that region.

He followed the frontage road to the highway that led south of town, keeping his speed at the limit. Twenty minutes later he spotted the exit that led to the first address. He took the turn, the gleaming contemporary white of a large winery, Bodega Norton, on the right, at the bottom of the small town of Luján de Cuyo. Crossing the overpass, he headed east through endless vineyards, civilization slipping away with each meter. An ancient tractor lumbered along in front of him, its exhaust pipe belching blue smoke, the old man driving it unbothered that he might be holding up traffic. Drago waited until the road widened enough to pass, and the man waved at him as he did so, his leathery face as lined as a Shar Pei's, his skin the color of burnished bronze.

A sign appeared on the right, and the GPS informed him that the turnoff leading to his first address was thirty more meters up, somewhere a half kilometer off the road, in the middle of the vineyards. Drago slowed as he neared what turned out to be a gravel track that stretched through the vines, and pointed the car down the gray strip, moving cautiously so as not to throw a dust cloud.

To his left rose a walled compound, the iron gates open, the large main house easily visible. Workers were already on scaffolds at the early hour, repairing what looked like bullet holes in the mortar – enough to suggest that a major battle had taken place. He sat watching the men and was startled by a polite honk from behind him; a glass truck was waiting for him to move so it could enter the grounds, presumably to replace the windows that yawned empty in the front façade.

Drago pulled forward and waved at the truck, his mind working furiously. There had been no mention online of an epic shootout in Mendoza, which was the only thing that could have caused the damage he'd seen. He'd done enough of it himself to recognize the signs, but it made no sense. And it gave him pause. How much clout did you have to have to keep something like that hushed up in a country with a supposedly free press?

Another truck approached from down the trail, and Drago rolled down his window and extended his hand, signaling for the driver to stop. The man obliged and leaned over to see what Drago wanted. Drago affected a bemused expression and grinned.

"Is the owner around, you think?" he asked.

"You one of the vendors?"

"That's right."

"Talk to Juan. He's handling all the buys. The owner's not here, which isn't surprising given all the damage."

"I'll say. I've never seen anything like it."

"I know. They say there were over three hundred bullet holes inside the house. It'll take weeks to fix everything. What a mess, eh?"

"Still, good for business."

"That's right." The driver waved and proceeded through the gate. Drago had seen enough and used the drive to turn around and make himself scarce before anyone got too curious. The owner wasn't there, which left one other possible address.

Drago passed the tractor again as he returned to the highway and offered a salute to the old farm hand, who'd no doubt been working the land his entire life as his father had worked it before him. There must be a certain peace in knowing your place in the universe, Drago mused, your lot in life clearly defined, with the only uncertainty how many summers you had before the ground reclaimed you. He shook off maudlin thoughts and tapped in the second address. The GPS blinked and displayed the new coordinates – also rural, and what looked like a good half hour from the shot-up compound.

His stomach growled, and he realized he hadn't eaten. He glanced at the screen again and pulled back onto the freeway, resolved to finding someplace for breakfast before paying his next visit, which would hopefully be more productive than his last. Aconcagua's snow-capped peak thrust into the cobalt sky to the west, reaching to the heavens for as far as he could see, and he mentally filed the area away as a possible destination once he was done with the contract.

He was humming as he drove back toward the city, its buildings gleaming in the sun, an interloper in God's country, man's puny outpost insignificant when framed against the majesty of the mountains and the endless azure sky. The beauty of the area notwithstanding, the contractor's comment about the number of bullet holes inside the house gave Drago serious pause, and he wondered, not for the first time, what he'd gotten into.

CHAPTER 18

When Hannah awoke the next morning, she had both her coats over her. Her little head peered out from the folds like a turtle. Jet stirred and cracked an eye open as Matt stood and brushed off his pants, gazing around at the mine buildings in the light of day.

Jet couldn't imagine the grounds looking any shabbier. Everything was coated with a layer of beige dust, and the ground was littered with discarded bolts and broken tools as well as the remnants of crates and pallets. An exhausted-looking forklift with oversized tires occupied a position on the periphery near two portable toilets she'd missed in the dark.

The buildings were little better, structural afterthoughts near the mine's entry, a dark aperture in the side of the mountain that looked like a worm had bored into the earth. Rodrigo and Alejandro were near the opening, Rodrigo limping slightly, smoking his first cigarette of the day. Jet roused herself and sat up, smiled at Hannah, and rooted in her jacket pockets for a breakfast bar – one of several items she'd scavenged from her bag. Hannah yawned and stretched, and Jet tore open one end of the package and handed her the bar.

"That's breakfast, honey. Don't do your usual act and refuse to eat. We don't have time for it, and if you don't eat, you'll go hungry," Jet warned, anticipating the battle she had to fight with the toddler almost every other morning. Fortunately Hannah seemed to appreciate the seriousness of her mother's tone and set to wolfing it down, traces of the strawberry jam filling coating her face as she ate. Jet smiled at the vision and shook her head and then tossed Matt one of the bars. "Here you go, big boy. Man needs to keep his energy up."

He caught it and inspected it. "Mmm. Prune. Once a fella gets to a certain age, it's the little things that impress…"

"I grabbed everything I could fit. If you don't want it, I'll trade you. I got grape."

"I like to think of prunes as really wrinkled grapes. Makes them go down better. I'm good."

Alejandro walked over to them, leaving his brother by the shaft. "Good morning. I just realized I never caught your name."

"Sorry. It's Naomi," Jet said, keeping with her current passport's moniker. "This is Doug and Hannah." Matt's passport identified him as Douglas Hess, his former Argentine identity now discarded along with Jet's Rebecca ID.

"Pleased to officially meet you. I wanted to thank you again for the help. The car was a good idea."

"No problem," Jet said. "All in a day's work, along with gunfights in the middle of nowhere."

"Which was impressive as hell, by the way. I think I already mentioned that, but it bears repeating."

"You know, I was thinking about one thing, though. You mentioned last night that you were attacked at a nightclub?"

"That's right. We barely escaped with our lives."

"And then again at the hotel."

"Correct."

"How do you think they found you?"

"I…I don't know. I mean, it's common knowledge that we're partners in the club, but the hotel…I figured someone must have talked."

"That's a possibility. But there's another you might want to consider."

"What?"

"They could have put a tracking device on the car."

"I actually thought of that. Moot point now, but it's a good one, nonetheless."

"True, but along those lines, they could also be triangulating your cell phones."

"I lost mine at the club."

"But your brother has his."

Alejandro's face changed. "Damn. I'm such an idiot. Of course." He turned to Rodrigo and waved him over.

Rodrigo reluctantly hobbled toward them. "What is it?" he demanded.

"Your phone," Alejandro said.

Rodrigo went white. "What about it?"

Alejandro held out his hand. "Let me have it. That might be how they've been tracking us."

Jet nodded. "It's a definite possibility. You need to pull the battery."

Rodrigo rolled his eyes as he withdrew his phone from his pocket, flipped off the back, and removed the battery. "There. Satisfied?" he asked Alejandro.

"Don't get all defensive. It's a good point. If they have the right contacts through the phone company, they could track us to within a few meters," Alejandro explained.

"Whatever." Rodrigo walked back to the mine, obviously annoyed at having been ordered around by his brother in front of strangers.

Alejandro shook his head. "I have to apologize for Rodrigo. He gets defensive. And I imagine it's been hard on him, watching his car destroyed, being chased all over hell and back…"

"You're both alive, and you also were in a gun battle. I don't see why he's being temperamental. You're the one who got shot at," Matt said. "Maybe he just doesn't like us."

"No, it's just been a long night, and he's in pain. He doesn't mean anything by it," Alejandro insisted.

Jet shrugged. "I overheard you talking on the trail. Your father was arrested yesterday?"

Alejandro's face hardened. "That's none of your concern."

"No offense, but doesn't it seem like a lot of things went wrong in a short period of time? As you say, it's none of my business, but it sounds coordinated. If it was, then being tracked on your phones is the least of your problems."

Alejandro stared off into the distance before giving a grudging nod. "You have a point. It occurred to me that we might have a leak in our organization."

"If you do, then you can't be certain that you aren't telegraphing your moves the second anyone else knows about them. Seems like pure luck that you got out of yesterday alive. You may not be so lucky today," Jet said.

Alejandro's eyes narrowed as he studied her. "What's it to you, anyway? Why the interest in my well-being?"

"We have a problem. You might be able to help us. Like I've helped you so far."

"A problem," Alejandro repeated.

"Yes. We need to get out of Chile. Without attracting any attention from immigration. We're thinking a boat fits the bill."

Alejandro considered it. "I see. And what is it that has caused you to have this need?"

"Let's just say that we ran afoul of the wrong person. Leave it at that."

"Someone in Chile? I know everybody. It's not that big a country, population-wise. I could have a word with them – that's usually sufficient."

"No, not here. Let's just say that borders might pose a problem."

Alejandro switched into business mode. "Do you need papers as well as your transportation facilitated?"

"If they're high quality, sure. Never hurts to have more papers. Does that sound like something you could handle?"

Alejandro smiled. "There's almost nothing I can't handle, Naomi." He kicked a rock. "Once I get off this mountain, we can talk. I have some obvious housekeeping matters to attend to, but after that, yes, I can help you with this. Do you have money?"

"Some. Enough."

"Even better. Nobody works for free. It will be expensive to find a discreet captain and an immigration official who will look the other way."

"I'd hope you could do a good deal, considering what we've been through together."

"Any deal I do will be a good one for you," Alejandro said. "Don't worry about any of this. It's not difficult. In Chile, anything is possible."

"That's good to hear," Matt said.

Jet smiled. "Anything else I can do to help, just ask. I have some skills."

Alejandro nodded. "Yes, I've noticed. But I think we're close to being done with the dangerous phase of our adventure."

"What will you do?"

"Convince the miners to give us a ride to the nearest phone, get my people coordinated and arrange for a pickup, and deal with business. Once things have settled, we can discuss your predicament further."

"What time do you think they'll be here?" Jet asked, glancing at her watch. "It's coming up on seven."

"I'd imagine any time. I'm surprised nobody's arrived yet."

Jet watched Hannah get to her wobbly feet and look around. Now that she'd eaten her bar, it was potty time. "I hope you're right."

Alejandro rolled his head, trying to loosen up his stiff neck muscles, and adjusted his shoulder holster. "So do I."

CHAPTER 19

Mendoza, Argentina

Towering trees shimmered in the wind on the periphery of the home at the second address, a country villa the size of a small hotel, also ringed by vineyards, the nearest neighbors so far away Drago could barely make out their house. He'd arrived a half hour earlier, left his car near the main road, and walked the rest of the way, his bag over his shoulder and his pistol in his pocket, the suppressor alongside it where he could fit it in a matter of moments.

The villa would pose a challenge – he'd spotted four competent-looking security men patrolling the exterior, all of whom appeared to know their business. That didn't cause Drago to hesitate, but merely to formulate a more involved plan. They'd have to be neutralized in a manner that would prevent the occupants from noticing, which would be no mean feat in broad daylight. Then again, there was a reason he was considered to be the best. Now it was time to earn his money.

The security men stayed outside while he watched, but he couldn't depend on that. He could just go by what he'd observed through the small binoculars he'd brought. Through the high-magnification lenses, the men's faces looked like they'd been carved from mahogany, although he thought he detected an air of boredom in their eyes – a positive for him, because complacency could buy him the time he'd need to dispatch them.

He decided his best odds would come from using his sniper rifle, which would be reasonably accurate at up to five hundred meters, even with the wind. Drago practiced with it regularly in the Colombian countryside, so he had full faith in his abilities, and he

103

was no more than two hundred meters away, making for easy shooting. He spent another hour timing the security retinue's routine and noted that the leader, an imposing man with a head of thick black hair and mirrored aviator sunglasses, tended to stay on the front porch, out of the sun, while his subordinates did rotations around the grounds.

Drago assembled his rifle, affixed the scope, and was watching the lead guard through the telescopic sight, the crosshairs on his temple as a matter of habit, when a stir among the men caught his attention. A handsome woman in her sixties emerged from the front door, followed by a younger one – obviously her daughter, based on the resemblance – holding the hand of a little girl. The older woman knelt down and kissed the little girl on the cheek, and then a dignified elderly man strode onto the porch. Drago didn't need to guess that this was the patriarch – his aristocratic bearing, shoulders as square as a doorway, his posture ramrod straight, announced him as such even from that distance.

The head bodyguard hurried to one of two white Toyota Land Cruisers parked near the front entrance and opened the passenger door. The older woman moved to climb in as the little girl waved to her, the morning sun shining on her bronze skin, and then the silver-haired man marched to the driver's side as the daughter and her child returned to the house. The guard tapped two of his men, who rushed to the rear doors and got into the SUV, leaving two to guard the villa in their absence.

Drago weighed his options. He could wait until his target had left, kill the remaining guards, hold the daughter and her child hostage and wait for the aristocrat to return – assuming he would, which was a safe bet since he wasn't carrying luggage – or he could waylay the vehicle and take on the two guards in the rear seat on the fly.

He made his decision as the SUV backed away from the house and swung around to pull down the long drive. He'd try for the vehicle.

Drago got to his feet, shouldered his bag and the rifle, and moved from his position in a crouch, jogging along the road, putting more ground between himself and the house. For what he had in mind, the quieter subsonic pistol rounds would do: with any luck at all, nobody would hear the shots in the house, and assuming he could take out both guards before they could fire at him, nobody would be the wiser. Divide and conquer, he thought and squatted out of sight of the road among the vines as he screwed on the Heckler & Koch pistol's suppressor.

He heard the crunch of gravel before he saw the SUV go by in a blur, and then he was moving to the edge of the vines. He fired twice at the rear tire and heard it pop. Brake lights went on, and the vehicle slowed before coasting to a stop. He edged closer as the back doors opened and the security men got out, followed by the old man. All three stood by the tire, inspecting its shredded bulk, and then one of the men swung the rear cargo door open to get the jack and spare tire.

Drago's rounds punched into the man's torso – three shots grouped within five inches of each other, he noted automatically with approval even as he swung the barrel at the second guard, who'd barely registered his partner crumpling next to the cargo hold when Drago blew his throat out with two well-placed slugs. Blood splattered the elderly man's face and jacket as the guard collapsed, and then Drago ran toward him. He closed the twenty-five yards in seconds even as he trained the weapon on the man, who looked like he was debating going for the guard's holstered pistol as Drago approached.

"Don't even think about it," Drago warned in Spanish. "Hands up. Do it or I'll put a bullet in you. That's your only warning."

The man raised his hands. "You picked the wrong man," he said quietly, his tone confident, his gaze unwavering. Drago had to admit he was an imposing figure even at the wrong end of a gun barrel.

"Maybe so. Get back in the car. Slowly. We're going for a ride."

"And if I refuse?"

"Then your lovely wife gets it in the back of the head to show I'm serious. It's all the same to me," Drago said, and he could tell by the look on the man's face that he believed him.

"What do you want?"

"To talk. Nothing more."

"Who are you?"

Drago motioned with his weapon for him to get back behind the wheel. "The angel of death. Now do as I say or I start shooting again, and once I do, I can be hard to stop."

The man looked him up and down, and then complied. Drago kicked the cargo door closed and stepped over the dead bodyguard and then slipped into the rear seat, ignoring the look of raw terror on the woman's face. He kept his gun pointed at the man, never taking his eyes off him even when he addressed her.

"Don't scream or try anything, or you're dead. Do you understand?"

She nodded. Drago could smell fear beneath the cloying expensive perfume she was wearing.

"Good," he said and pulled the door closed behind him.

"Where to?" Sofia's father asked.

"Back to the house. I need privacy, and it looks nice."

"Absolutely not. Might as well shoot me right now. There's no way I'll endanger my daughter."

Drago shrugged and thumbed back the hammer on his pistol and shifted it to the back of the woman's head. He paused, considering, and then whispered to her, "If I kill you, my hunch is he'll become even less cooperative, so instead I'm going to shoot you in the kidney. The agony will be excruciating, but it will take a while for you to die, and if your husband tells me what I need to know, you'll have time to get to a hospital so he can save your life. Sorry about that," Drago said and fired through the back of the seat.

The woman's scream was tortured, but Drago didn't flinch.

"You bastard," Sofia's father hissed through clenched teeth, trying to twist to get at him.

Drago held the pistol steady. "All right. The clock is ticking on your wife's life. You want me to do a repeat performance on you so you can't drive her to the hospital? Keep talking."

"What do you want?"

"I need to know the whereabouts of the woman you arranged the jet for. The one that exploded."

"What? How would I know that?" he demanded, but Drago could sense something in his tone. The man was good, he'd give him that, and most might have believed him. But not Drago.

"Where is she? If you don't tell me, I'll put a bullet in your wife's other kidney. You can live with only one kidney. But with both ruined? It's no kind of life at all."

The woman's face was white from shock. "Tell...him..."

Drago nodded. "Yes. Your wife is sensible. Tell me where she is and you'll live."

"I...I don't know. I swear it. She disappeared two nights ago."

"Where was she going?"

"I don't know."

"Did she have anyone with her?"

"Her husband and her daughter."

"Her husband. What does he look like?"

"Tall. Handsome. Maybe...mid-forties. Caucasian. I think he's American or Canadian."

"Sounds about right. Where did they go?"

"I told you. I don't know."

Drago shook his head. "Your poor wife." He turned to her. "Forgive him. He's willing to allow you to suffer the tortures of the damned to protect them," Drago said and moved behind her as he pressed the suppressor against the rear of the seat.

Sofia's father froze. "No. Please. There's something else. I...I really don't know where she was going. But...I gave her the number of a friend who could arrange things. She might have contacted him. He might know."

"A friend. I see. And who is this friend?" Drago asked, his voice reasonable.

"Alfredo Sintas."

"A good name. Where can I find him?"

"He lives in San Rafael." He gave Drago the address.

"Alone? Wife? Kids?"

"No. He's a widower. His children are grown."

"You have a cell phone?"

"Of course."

"Call him. Tell him you're going to be in town and you want to meet him at his house. In an hour."

Sofia's father dialed Alfredo's number. When he answered, he kept the discussion short, the suppressor cold against the back of his head. Alfredo agreed he'd be home and waiting for his arrival. He hung up, and Drago nudged his skull with the suppressor. "Toss the phone back here."

He did as instructed. "Now what?"

The soft point .45 slug blew a spray of the older man's brains onto the windshield and starred it where it punched through the glass. Drago turned and put a bullet into the woman's temple, ending her suffering, and then scooped up the telephone and got out of the SUV.

It would be midafternoon by the time anyone found the bodies, drawn by the buzzards circling the bloating corpses overhead. Drago slipped the phone into his pocket and ran down the drive, his stride easy, a rhythmic predator's lope. The bag and rifle bounced against his back as he raced to his car to have a chat with Alfredo – hopefully soon enough to be able to catch a light lunch afterward.

CHAPTER 20

Jet was fussing with Hannah's hair when she heard the motors from the dirt road, big vehicles climbing the steep hill. She shielded her eyes from the sun with her hand and squinted into the distance as Matt returned to her side with Alejandro and Rodrigo in tow. When she turned to face him, her face was tense.

"What do you think miners would be driving?" she asked Alejandro.

"A work truck, or maybe a couple of vans."

"Not newish SUVs, though…"

Alejandro peered into the distance. "No. Is that what's approaching?"

"Yes. Four of them." She stood and looked hard into Matt's eyes. "Something tells me those aren't miners."

Alejandro watched as the vehicles approached. "But…that's impossible."

"Seems like there's been a lot of that going on over the last twelve hours, hasn't there?" She paused. "Come on. Let's get out of here."

"They'll be on top of us before we can get over the hill," Matt said. "We've got to go into the mine. Anywhere else and we'll be sitting ducks."

"You want to go in there?" Rodrigo asked. "No. Not me."

"Then you can roll out the welcome mat," Jet said. "He's right. They'll be here in under a minute. Come on, honey, let's go," she said to Hannah as she picked her up. "Time to explore the magic cave." She glanced at Alejandro. "Good luck. I don't like your odds."

Alejandro eyed the dust cloud from the road, and then his brother. "Rodrigo. There's no way we can outrun them."

He shook his head. "I'm not going in there."

Jet tried one more time. "In the mine we have an advantage – they can only send in so many men, and you can choose where you make your stand. They obviously know you're here. Out here the advantage is theirs. The mine's the smart choice."

Alejandro nodded agreement. "I say we go in. Now."

Matt was already moving toward the dark opening, and Jet was backing away from the brothers with Hannah – she'd spoken her mind, and now it was time to move.

Rodrigo glared at his brother. "Alejandro, I can't tell you how sick I am of you making decisions and telling me what to do. You want to go into the mine, you go. I'd rather take my chances out here. I think you and the girl are wrong." He pronounced *the girl* like an insult.

The engines grew louder, and Jet spun with Hannah and ran for the mine. The trucks would be there within thirty seconds, tops. If the brothers wanted to bicker and stay outside, waiting to get killed, it wasn't her problem. Hers was getting out of this alive and keeping her daughter and Matt safe.

The entry was larger than she'd thought from afar, at least five meters high and seven wide, but she could see that it narrowed as the daylight died in its bowels. Matt motioned to her to hurry, and she met him inside. The air smelled stagnant, like moist rock and dust.

"Come on. We need to get well out of range. If they send men in, we don't want to be where they can see us," he said. His voice echoed off the tunnel walls.

She heard a noise behind her. Alejandro was at the mine entry.

"He's an idiot. He's making a run for it up the mountain. I couldn't stop him."

"It's too late to do anything now – he made his choice. You need to get deeper before they arrive. Once they do…" She didn't have to finish the thought.

Alejandro studied her determined expression and looked at Hannah. "If they send men in, you'll be in danger, too. All of you."

"This isn't my fight."

"I know that. But they won't make that distinction. You're here with me…I wouldn't rely on the Verdugos for mercy."

She closed her eyes for a moment and then nodded and put Hannah down. "Doug, take Hannah. He's right. Get going. I don't want you getting hit by any ricochets."

Matt stepped forward. "Are you serious?"

"There's no other way. They'll hunt us like rats unless we can hold them off."

"There are usually other ways out besides the main entrance," Alejandro said. "I know a little about mines from friends in the business. There will be ventilation shafts. We might be able to get out through one."

"Might," Matt echoed.

Alejandro faced him. "Do you have a better option?"

The roar of the first SUV arriving quieted them. Jet whispered to Matt, "Please. Do as I ask. Keep her safe. I'll come find you. But hurry up and move. It's going to get ugly here any minute."

"I hope you know what you're doing," Matt growled through clenched teeth and scooped Hannah up with his good hand. "Come on, darling. We're going cave exploring."

Hannah looked at Jet with frightened eyes, and Jet touched her cheek. "Don't worry. Everything will be fine."

Hannah spoke in a tiny voice. "Prometh?"

Jet nodded solemnly. "Of course I do. I love you, honey."

"Me too," Hannah said, breaking Jet's heart. And then Matt moved deeper into the mine, his shoes crunching on the ore underfoot, following the rusting remains of a rail system into the mountain.

Jet freed her Glock and slid away from Alejandro.

"When they come, you take the ones on the left, I'll take the ones on the right. But make every shot count. Use the rocks as cover." She pointed at a pile of stones next to a metal cart that looked like it predated the automobile. "I'll be over there." She edged to an indentation in the mine wall where several iron boxes were corroding, still filled with ore from the mine's depths.

"Won't the shooting trigger a cave-in?" Alejandro whispered.

"No plan's perfect. What's the alternative?"

He glared at the mine opening and nodded. "If I make it out of this alive, you can consider the boat trip on me."

"That's a generous offer. Let's keep you breathing, then, shall we?"

The headlights from the lead SUV shone into the mine, but didn't reach their position due to a slight bend in the tunnel. Alejandro had his Desert Eagle out, and Jet noted that his hand was steady. Good. They heard the SUV's doors slamming, and then a second and third set as the other vehicles arrived.

Three flashlight beams played along the walls as men entered the mine. Jet stabbed her finger toward the lights, and Alejandro nodded, understanding. They needed to take out the men with the lights. Without the flashlights the attackers would be blind, backlit by the sun streaming through the opening, making the mine threshold a killing field for anyone trying to cross it.

They didn't have long to wait. The bouncing beams approached with the thud of boots on rock, and Jet saw the first intruder: a man carrying an assault rifle, the flashlight secured below the barrel, a worst-case scenario for them because the weapon's greater range would overpower Jet and Alejandro in a shooting battle. That underscored all the more why they'd need to optimize their element of surprise. They wouldn't get more than one chance.

Jet shook her head when Alejandro glanced at her, and she motioned with her hand to not shoot yet. Her message was clear: let them get close enough so they could take out all the flashlight-toting gunmen with their first salvo.

Another man appeared, also with his flashlight affixed to his rifle, the third right behind him. Fools, Jet thought, allowing them to get closer...closer...closer.

Her Glock's bark sounded like artillery fire in the tunnel. Two of the men dropped, and Alejandro's Desert Eagle roared three times, cutting the third down. None of the riflemen had been able to fire a shot, but that quickly changed as their colleagues opened up, firing blindly into the mine. Jet flattened herself against the ground and tried to create as small a target as possible as slugs winged and whistled off the rock walls. Another gunman edged toward her, this one without the benefit of a light, and she took his head off with a single shot.

More random fire, a flurry of rounds, but because of the bend, none hit them. They waited for the inevitable, and another unlucky man crept forward. One explosive cough of the Desert Eagle and he went down. His companion, following him in, emptied his entire rifle magazine into the darkness and was feeling for a spare when Jet's Glock took him out.

The tunnel went quiet as the attackers debated the wisdom of walking into a killing machine. Jet knew she'd been lucky that the men were inexperienced at this sort of an assault. If they had any brains, they'd fall back, maybe try to burn their quarry out using smoke. She offered a prayer to the universe to keep them from thinking of that. So far they'd shown themselves rank amateurs, and it had cost them six of their own in barely a minute.

But she couldn't rely on them not coming up the learning curve quickly. Her ears were ringing from gunfire, the high-pitched ever-present keening of tinnitus more than familiar. She didn't see any shadows that announced more shooters entering the mine, so she inched over to Alejandro's position and murmured in his ear.

"Cover me. I'm going to get us some rifles. If I'm right, two of the lead gunmen are out of sight of the mine opening. Follow me up, and if anything shows its head, shoot it."

Alejandro nodded and rose from his position behind the rocks. The dead attackers were no more than ten meters away. Jet and Alejandro edged forward together, weapons clutched in two-handed combat grips. Alejandro hung back after the first five meters and took up position, his weapon at the ready, as Jet continued on. She couldn't detect any sign of life from where she was, but she also understood that she was nearly deaf, and that if one of the cowboys at the mouth of the mine decided to squeeze off another thirty rounds, one could easily hit her while she was recovering weapons.

Jet found four spares in the first shooter's vest. She gritted her teeth as she pulled his rifle from the man's dead hands, noting that it was the familiar standby of guerillas and criminals everywhere, the trusty old AK-47 – this one probably Chinese-manufactured, judging by the newness of the finish. She switched the flashlight off and pocketed the magazines, and then, after waiting a few beats so she could detect any movement from the mouth of the mine, repeated the process at the next corpse. She was just finishing when gunfire exploded from the opening, and she hugged the ground as lead flew past her position and several rounds thudded into the dead man immediately in front of her.

When a lull in the random shooting came, Jet fired off half the rifle's thirty-round magazine on full automatic. That would give their assailants something to think about. Now they'd be walking into full-bore machine-gun fire. Jet was betting there wouldn't be many eager volunteers for that duty. She snatched up the second rifle and sprinted back down the tunnel, trusting Alejandro to pick off any pursuers. She wasn't surprised when there weren't any.

Round one had gone to the good guys, but she knew it was just a matter of time until their luck ran out. They needed an escape route, or eventually they'd run out of ammo – or worse, someone would show up with a grenade or a stick of dynamite, and the game would be over.

Chapter 21

Bastian ignored the blood streaming down his arm from where a stray ricochet had grazed his bicep. What should have been a straightforward search-and-destroy foray had unexpectedly turned into full-scale war, and he'd lost half his most experienced shooters in the blink of an eye. He peered into the mine as though he might see a way out of the situation in its inky depths, which was how Leonid found him moments later.

"This won't work," Leonid said. "I told you she was smart. You're sitting ducks walking into the mine, and by now it sounds like she's got some of your Kalashnikovs."

"You keep saying it's her. How do you know? Alejandro's a tough customer."

"I have no interest in this Alejandro. What I know is that she's your worst nightmare. A seasoned executioner. She doesn't scare, she doesn't panic, and I'd be willing to bet she's clocked more hours of this kind of combat than all of you combined." Leonid tried to keep the derision out of his voice, but it was difficult.

"You want to try?" Bastian snapped. "I don't appreciate your insults."

"What, walk into sure death? No, thanks. I told you I thought it was a bad idea to do this as a frontal assault, but you ignored me. Now you understand why it was."

Bastian had to concede the Russian's point. "So what do you suggest?"

"Can you get the soldiers up here? See if they have any flash bangs or flame throwers. But remember that I need a body or you won't get paid, so they can't just blast the mine to dust."

"Right now I could give a shit about getting paid. I need to take the Sotos down," Bastian snapped.

"Well, you're doing a crap job of it. Get on the radio, call in the troops, or you'll be standing here at nightfall with a freight car full of bodies, all of them yours," Leonid said disgustedly and then left the gangster to his ruminations while Leonid explained the situation to his men. He had enough experience with these sorts of setups to know a loser when he saw one, and the mine was the worst kind of trap for anyone going in. He wanted no part of it, and the only way he saw them prevailing was to throw soldiers and high explosives into the mix – preferably stun grenades that would blind and deafen the defenders. The Verdugos didn't have that sort of ordnance, so it would be up to the military. A simple equation to an ex-special forces commando like himself, but obviously not for a street fighter like Bastian.

Bastian spoke into the radio and explained the situation to Colonel Campos, who was personally overseeing the exercise and was down at the base of the mountain, where he'd erected a roadblock and checkpoint. Campos clearly wasn't happy that he was being called upon to escalate his role in the proceedings and told Bastian to stand by while he contacted Franco to discuss it.

Five minutes later the radio crackled to life. Campos snapped a terse warning that he was sending up a contingent of soldiers to deal with the standoff, and that Bastian should get his men out of there – this would now be a military exercise, and as such it would be too big to sanitize after the fact. Campos didn't want to explain to his superiors why he was now an errand boy playing cleanup for some of Chile's most notorious gangsters, taking sides in a territorial battle. They'd cook up some kind of explanation for the casualties in the mine, but he couldn't afford his men to see carloads of armed hoodlums standing around watching his troops risk their lives so they didn't have to.

~ ~ ~

Jet joined Alejandro deeper in the mine, where he was using his new rifle's flashlight to illuminate the tunnel. He supported her as she climbed up a decrepit wooden ladder and used his pocket knife to cut the wires of the overhead lighting, ensuring that the gunmen wouldn't be able to start up the generator and eliminate the darkness – darkness that was their closest ally at this point, equalizing the attackers' superior numbers and rendering their firepower moot.

"What do you think they're planning?" Alejandro whispered.

"I already told you. They're going to try to burn us out or bury us alive – their only options. Which means we need to get as far away from the entrance as possible and start searching for an alternate way out. Or it's just a matter of time."

Alejandro spat dust and nodded. "I agree."

Jet followed the rails farther into the mountain, and then her flashlight reflected off Matt and Hannah's eyes. She ran to them and hugged Hannah, who was sobbing softly, obviously terrified by the darkness and the shooting. Jet looked up at Matt, whose face was streaked with dirt.

"We caught a break– but they'll be coming back, and this time, probably with the right gear. Alejandro says these mines will have ventilation shafts and possibly other entrances, although I wouldn't bet that if there is another access point it won't have a few gunmen watching it."

"Then what do we do?"

"First, move as far into the mine as possible so you and Hannah are safe, and Alejandro and I will scout for ventilation passages. I don't see any other way." She handed Matt the rifle and spare magazines. "Think you can manage that one-handed?"

"They say motivation's everything."

Jet smoothed Hannah's hair. "Shhh, my love. You've got a light now, so there's no need to be frightened. We're going to find someplace nice and safe for you and Matt to hide while I find a way out of here. You've been very brave, but I need you to be even braver now, okay?"

Hannah looked unconvinced. She nodded, but the tears didn't stop, and Jet felt a pang of anguish at the anxiety her daughter was suffering. Jet kissed her and pulled her close again, her shudders like knife stabs to Jet's heart, and then Hannah spoke, very softly.

"I want stay. With you."

Jet glanced at Alejandro to ensure he was out of earshot, and whispered to Hannah, "I know, honey, I know. And you will. But you need to go with Matt, just for a little while, so I can find an exit, okay? Then I'll be back, and we'll get out of here, and you'll never have to come back, ever again. I promise." Her words sounded hollow to her, but she pushed aside the creeping despair that was washing over her and stood, her shoulders square. "Come on. We may already be out of time."

Matt led the way with his rifle flashlight. Jet carried Hannah, her pistol wedged in her belt, and Alejandro brought up the rear, his flashlight off, to better see any light advancing toward them from the tunnel mouth. They passed an ore cart that had run off the rails, and then an entire section of track disappeared before restarting further along the horizontal shaft. She estimated they'd come at least two hundred meters when the tracks stopped. Six more ore carts rested on the last section of rail, blanketed in dust, obviously unused for eons.

They paused and heard the unmistakable sound of boots from far behind them. She leaned into Matt and murmured to him.

"Run. They're making their push."

Matt complied, and she followed his beam bouncing on the walls. Alejandro did his best to keep up, and after a few minutes they couldn't hear the footsteps any longer. Jet spotted several side passages with piles of old picks and pry bars strewn along the floor, and then pointed. Matt disappeared inside the closest, but returned a few moments later.

"It's another vein that must have petered out. Goes back a little, and then dead-ends into rock."

They heard more scrapes and shuffles from the direction of the mine opening. Jet looked around and made a tough decision. "Is there anything to hide behind, or in?"

"There's some barrels and a moldy tarp. Why?"

"I don't want you or Hannah in the line of fire."

"I seriously doubt that anyone's not going to look down these passages."

"It's your only chance, and it's better than catching a bullet out in the open."

"You're stretching. Think about it for a second."

More noise from the tunnel convinced her. Their pursuers would be on top of them any second. "Fine. Move. Get as far from here as you can with Hannah. We'll hold them off."

"That's not much of a plan."

"They'll catch us eventually. We might as well be able to pick the place for the next skirmish. With the passages at least we've got some cover. Don't argue. Get going."

Jet handed Hannah to Matt, and he shifted her over, the rifle unwieldy but manageable. "See you in a few."

"Count on it."

He turned and sped away, his light fading and then disappearing around another bend in the tunnel. Jet turned her attention to Alejandro beside her in the darkness.

"You ever fired an AK?"

"Sure. It's practically second nature."

"Good. We'll fire, fall back, fire, fall back. Make them fight for every meter of progress and pay for it in blood, and don't let them get close enough to blind you with their lights. If you get hit, call out."

"All right."

They both heard boot soles on shale and stiffened. Jet darted to the passage across from the one Alejandro was taking cover in. Nothing happened, the dank cool air quiet and calm, and then more rustling greeted them from down the tunnel. A soft glow illuminated the brown walls from around the bend as the gunmen neared, and then Alejandro squeezed off bursts at the first shooter that appeared in his sights.

His volley knocked the man off his feet, his flashlight shattered, and then a barrage of automatic weapons fire lit the passage. Chunks of stone flew from the walls as rounds blew fragments everywhere, and Jet wedged herself further in the small opening she'd chosen. She was just preparing to fire back when she saw the telltale shape of a grenade land four meters away, and then she instinctively stuck her fingers in her ears and closed her eyes as she pulled back into the safety of the side passage.

The concussion from the blast was palpable, like a blow to the chest, and then she was falling as the ground collapsed beneath her. The last thing she saw was Alejandro across from her, an expression of shock on his face as the floor disappeared and he vanished in a cloud of dust, as though the earth had swallowed him whole.

CHAPTER 22

When Jet regained consciousness, she was lying on her back in cold water amidst the rubble from the mine floor cave-in. She opened her eyes and flexed her fingers and then her feet, reassured that she was still intact, if shaken, her gun still gripped in her hand. She looked over toward Alejandro, who was sprawled on a mound of mud, groaning. She forced herself up and crawled toward him, but was caught by surprise when she slid downward and landed in deeper water, which was washing away much of the dirt beneath them.

Alejandro shook his head as she reached him, and she saw the barrel of his rifle, with the flashlight still attached, poking from the mound. Jet wrenched it free and froze at the sound of voices from above – the attackers were cautiously making their way toward the hole in the tunnel floor left by the collapse.

"Can you move?" Jet hissed in his ear.

He tried to sit up. On the second try he managed to with a muffled groan.

She pointed at the opening above them. "If you can, follow me. They'll be here in a few seconds."

She moved off to her left, feeling along the wall, and quickly found herself submerged up to her chest in cold water – water that was moving, implying a source, and more importantly, an outlet somewhere. A splash sounded behind her. She stopped as Alejandro joined her, AK held over his head.

They let the current push them along, moving them faster than they would have dared in a dry passage, and Jet realized that they must be in another part of the mine – a lower section that had flooded and been abandoned. She heard excited chatter from the cave-in area behind her, which inspired her to keep moving in the stygian blackness, trusting the current to guide her forward.

A light flickered to life behind them, and she could see from the reflected glow of flashlights shining into the passage that they were around a gradual turn in the submerged tunnel. She stopped moving, not daring to breathe, and listened for sounds of pursuit – assuming anyone was foolhardy enough to go into a mine shaft that had just collapsed, courting a burial for eternity beneath tons of rock. More voices echoed off the walls as Alejandro drew next to her, and they both gazed back at where the floor had collapsed, waiting for some sign of what to expect.

The voices grew louder as the number of men around the edge of the cave-in area increased, but thankfully, nobody was following them.

Yet.

She jerked her head at Alejandro and held a finger to her lips and then pointed into the blackness ahead. He nodded, understanding, and they set off, their passage silent as the water moved them along. The invisible floor below them was smooth, polished by centuries of the underground stream washing away at it.

The light from their pursuers faded, and they were once again blind, using their hands to guide them along the wall as they progressed deeper into the earth. Jet checked her watch and, when ten minutes had gone by, paused again.

"It's safe to use the light. They probably think we were buried in the rubble. An easy mistake to make," she murmured.

"Let's hope so. Where do you think we are?"

"Another section of the mine, or a much older mine beneath the one we were in. I'd guess older, perhaps even dating back to the Spanish – I haven't felt any rails, and the width is only half of the one above."

"That makes sense. But how do we get out of here? I have no idea whether an older mine like this would have any vent shafts. Probably not..."

"The current's strong, so that means it's letting out somewhere. I say we follow it and find out where."

"What if it's into an underground river? They have those, you know."

"That wouldn't be so good. Let's hope for something outside."

"Do you...do you think they'll give up?"

"No way of knowing. Maybe, maybe not. But if we keep moving, I can't see them catching up to us."

"So we could wind up drowned somewhere under the mountain instead of shot," Alejandro said bitterly.

Jet shrugged. "We don't have a lot of options."

Alejandro removed the flashlight from the rifle and switched it on. The small lamp seemed blinding after the prolonged darkness. He traced the beam along the tunnel and nodded. "I think you're right. This looks old. The walls are uneven, nothing like the other mine. It was probably dug in the nineteenth century and then abandoned when the ore began to run lean. Maybe earlier. Hard to say."

"You know more about silver mining than I would have expected for a...a businessman."

"I'm not uneducated. For a long while I fantasized about owning a ranch out here, raising horses, maybe growing grapes. I devoured everything I could on a wide variety of related subjects and spent most of my university years in these mountains. Nearly every weekend."

"We have to keep going. We know there's nothing back there for us except death."

Alejandro took the lead, and they glided along seemingly forever. They passed a fork where the main tunnel split off and decided to go with the passage that had the strongest current. After another long slog, she checked the time again and saw that twenty-five minutes had elapsed. The frigid water was beginning to take its toll on them both, and she wondered how long they could keep going before it stopped them. Even though it wasn't freezing, it was cold enough to leach their body temperature, and Jet knew well that the first signs of hypothermia would be sluggish thinking and loss of motor skills.

They rounded another twist in the tunnel and found themselves facing a dead end – one minute they had been in a narrowing passageway, the next, confronted by a wall. Jet exchanged a glance with Alejandro and took a deep breath, then went under as he directed the flashlight beam into the water by the base of the wall. When she came up for air, gasping, she shook her head.

"The water's rushing through a small opening. Maybe large enough for us to get through, maybe not. But there's no telling where it goes, or if there's any air – it could be wormholes that shoot through the rocks, carrying water and nothing else. If that's the case, going in would mean drowning."

"I'm not sure I feel that lucky."

"What about the other passage?"

"I guess we don't have any alternative, do we?"

"Let's work our way back. It's worth a shot. This looks like certain death."

It seemed to take twice as long to backtrack, and when they reached the other passageway, they hesitated in front of it. "If this goes nowhere, then what?" Alejandro asked.

"Then we need to come up with a better plan," Jet said, trying not to think about Matt and Hannah and what might be happening to them. It was possible the gunmen would call it quits after the cave-in, not wanting to tempt fate by pushing still deeper into the mine, but Jet couldn't bet on it, in which case their survival would depend on Matt's ability to evade them. Matt was good, but not superhuman, and Jet's mind conjured up a host of nightmare scenarios, each worse than the last.

Alejandro moved into the new passage, his teeth chattering, and Jet knew they were in trouble – she wasn't sure how much longer they could hold out. But the thought of her daughter hiding in the mine above kept her going, and she refused to give in to the mental drift from the drop in her body temperature.

The tunnel narrowed further, and Alejandro looked back at her, his gaze grim. She slowed and then cocked her head and listened.

"There. Do you hear that?" she asked.

"Hear what? My ears are shot from the gunfire."

"Splashing. I hear splashing. Keep going."

Alejandro continued plodding forward, carried by desperation as much as current. They rounded another curve, and he disappeared from view. She gasped as his head sank beneath the surface, and then she too was pulled down as if by a subaqueous invisible hand.

Jet struggled to hold her breath as she was pushed along, her velocity increasing, and just as she thought she was blacking out, the proverbial light at the end of the tunnel manifesting in her mind's eye, she realized that it wasn't in her mind at all – there was a glimmer above her. She kicked upward with all her might, and her head broke the surface. She sucked in air reflexively, and Alejandro sputtered nearby as he treaded water and coughed.

Jet looked around as sweet, cool air flooded her lungs. They were in a cavern, and at the far end was an opening through which sunlight was flooding. She swam for the gap, and Alejandro joined her, their wet clothes slowing their progress. When they made it, they found themselves at the top of a small waterfall where the subterranean reservoir spilled down the mountainside, forming a brook that trailed off into the brush.

"I don't know about you, but I've had all the swimming I can stomach," Alejandro said, eyeing the green grass that grew along the banks of the creek.

"I'm with you." Jet crawled onto the rocks at the side of the opening and studied the slope, and then, after a moment's hesitation, lowered herself down. Alejandro watched her progress, and when she was standing on terra firma, followed in her tracks. They stood, dripping in the sun, and Jet raised an eyebrow. "Where's your rifle?"

"I dropped it when I went under. And I lost my pistol as well. Fell out of the holster."

She pulled the Glock from her waistband and dumped water out of the barrel. "At least I still have this. But I'll need to dry it out. Give me a few minutes."

Alejandro nodded, and she set about fieldstripping it, inspecting each piece before reassembling the gun. "It should still fire. I just want to make sure there's no grit in the workings. It wouldn't do to have it jam." Jet fitted the last part in place and stood. "So now what?"

"Now we have to find a way off this mountain so I can get my people involved," Alejandro said, his tone dark.

"I suppose circling back around and taking on several dozen men is out of the question?"

"With one waterlogged pistol? I think not."

Jet tilted her head back, luxuriating in the sun's warmth after too long in the cold water. "Well, you're the Chilean wilderness expert. I want my daughter back, and standing around here isn't going to do it." She opened her eyes and leveled a cool emerald stare at Alejandro. "Lead the way."

CHAPTER 23

Colonel Campos swiveled as one of his subordinates by the mine entry called his name. He'd been alerted about the cave-in and casualties by radio and had issued instructions to inspect the length of the mine, leaving no inch unsearched. His instructions had been carried out to the letter, as he'd expected. What he hadn't expected was to capture not only Rodrigo, who had surrendered shortly after the army had arrived, but also a man and his daughter – the man unarmed, although an AK-47 and a silenced pistol had been found on the floor of the tunnel before he'd been discovered hiding in a dead-end passage near the heart of the mine.

Campos approached the man, who had been dragged to the entry by two soldiers. His daughter, no older than three, stood next to him, holding his pants leg and bawling quietly. Campos took in the man's features, noting the leanness of his jawline and the unflinching intensity of his stare, and glanced at the filthy cast on his arm.

"It's not your lucky day, is it?" Campos said.

The man didn't respond.

"Is this your daughter?"

A curt nod, nothing more.

"What were you doing inside the mine?"

Nothing. No response, not even a flicker.

"Perhaps you don't understand the seriousness of your situation. You were involved in a gunfight in which a number of my men were injured. That makes you enemy combatants. Both of you. Which means you have no rights. I can do anything I like to you. And I intend to. If you don't cooperate, you'll never see the little girl again. Do I have your full attention now?"

Another nod.

"What were you doing in the mine?"

"Trying to escape gunmen."

"Gunmen. I see. And why were they after you?"

"I don't know."

Campos snorted. "You don't know."

"That's correct. All I know is they were shooting at us, so we ran into the mine."

"We. Who's we?"

"My daughter and I."

"Who else?"

"That's all I remember."

Campos eyed him doubtfully. "So you have convenient amnesia?"

"I've been hiding in a mine for hours with a child. People have been shooting and blowing things up. Maybe it's shock. I don't know."

"Shock. I see. Not bad, but it won't hold up under scrutiny, especially with a witness."

Matt didn't blink.

Campos grinned. "That's right. We caught another of your group. A young man with more brains than you, obviously. He's singing like a bird. And his story is nothing like yours."

Hannah looked up at Matt. "Want…my…mama!" she wailed, her voice torn with grief.

Campos stepped back. "Silence!" he roared.

The little girl continued crying. "Mama!"

Campos flinched at the shriek and glowered at Matt. "Control your brat, or I'll have my men do it for you," he ordered.

Matt shook his head. "Because she's also a dangerous enemy combatant, right? A two-and-a-half-year-old terrorist?"

Campos sneered at him. "You have quite a mouth on you. But I think you'll change your tune shortly." He nodded to the approaching lieutenant. "Take them to the outpost for interrogation. I don't want anyone talking to them until I get there." Campos had commandeered a deserted army encampment in the hills south of the mine and was using the buildings as his field headquarters. It was under the radar because it was officially closed down, and had the added benefit of being on government property, so he could fortify it as he liked without attracting any scrutiny from the local population.

The lieutenant saluted. "Yes, sir."

One of the soldiers led Matt to a troop transport, and the other picked up a kicking and screaming Hannah and carried her to the vehicle. The colonel's soldiers watched in silence, and a flutter of trepidation twisted in his stomach – there were limits to what he could do without stepping over a line from which he could never return, and he'd need to keep his nose clean or one nervous infantryman could cause him a world of grief. He was already on tenuous ground, but if he brutalized an infant and a foreign national... Even his command over his men had its limits – limits a smart man wouldn't hurry to test.

~ ~ ~

Alejandro moved like a ghost through the tall grass, surprisingly graceful for a city boy, Jet noted, as he neared the barbed-wire fence that enclosed the pasture they'd spotted. A dozen horses stood on the other side of the wire – three geldings and the rest mares, healthy, their coats shining in the sunlight. Jet could see that the adult horses had marks from bridles and saddles, so they were accustomed to being ridden – an inelegant but convenient mode of transportation in a rugged area with no roads in sight, much less any cars. She spotted a small farmhouse in the distance, so far away that it looked like a toy casually discarded at the other end of the valley. A shabby barn sat closer to the horses, on the other side of the pasture, unpainted and barely standing, sunlight shining clear through its walls.

Alejandro made a snicking sound with his mouth, and one of the mares regarded him with soft brown eyes. He slowly approached the fence and held his hand out, making a fist, as though he was holding something – perhaps a treat or a lump of sugar. The horse shuffled over, and he reached up and petted her, scratching around her ears, and then smoothing her mane as he purred endearments. A second smaller mare came over, followed by two of the ponies, and it quickly became obvious that all were not only tame but starved for affection. Jet joined Alejandro in rubbing their faces, and after several minutes he nudged her.

"Think you can keep these ladies company while I uproot that fence post?"

"I'll give it my best shot. But make it fast, would you?"

"That's my intention."

He walked to the post and began working at it, shifting it back and forth until it fell, taking the fencing with it. He inspected his work and then moved to the next post and repeated the process. The horses seemed not to notice or care, and Jet had her hands full petting all of them, their big heads pressing her for favored position.

Alejandro stepped back once he had the second post felled. "I'm going to get a couple of saddles. Stay here."

"It might be easier if I just walked over to the barn, don't you think? The horses seem more interested in following me than in making a break for it. Poor things are probably bored out of their minds and would do anything for a run." After a final pat on the head of the nearest mare, she marched across the pasture, followed by all but one pony and a shy mare that had hung back. Alejandro shook his head and hurried around the fencing to the barn, where a gate was held closed by a rusting length of wire twisted around one of the posts.

He emerged from the bleak structure a few moments later with a blanket, saddle, and bridle. "Do you know how to secure this?" he asked.

"No. Do you?"

"Fortunately I spent summers as a boy at my father's estancia, and we had horses. Which one do you want?"

Jet turned and found herself facing the mare that had been trying to edge the rest away, vying for more stroking. "I think this one wants me."

Alejandro swung the gate open and moved to the horse, which stood calmly while he placed the blanket on her back, strapped the saddle in place, and fixed the bit between her teeth. He handed the reins to Jet and returned to the barn. Jet whispered to the mare, "You're a good girl, aren't you? I knew it the moment I laid eyes on you."

Alejandro was back within a half minute with another saddle. He made the snicking sound with his mouth again, and the mare that had originally greeted him ambled over to his side. He had the saddle on in seconds, and after fitting the reins, he mounted her in one smooth move.

Jet was less graceful getting onto her horse, but managed. She'd only ridden a few times before, on her forbidden rendezvous with David so many years before. A wave of melancholy washed over her at the memory, but she banished it – she didn't have the luxury of sentimentality.

"Where to?" she asked.

"To find a phone. We need reinforcements. My organization will be bouncing off the walls with my father in custody and my brother and me out of touch. Once I'm in contact, we'll have options."

"Well, then, lead on."

Alejandro gazed at the sky to get his bearings and then set off in what seemed like a southern direction. The horses seemed happy to run. The day was beautiful: flowers in bloom, a susurrant wind rustling the treetops, nature beckoning. Soon they were out of sight of the barn, following a trail, and for a moment to Jet it could have been five hundred years earlier and they Spanish plunderers, so quiet were the surroundings, not a trace of modern civilization anywhere, only the steady clumping of the horses' hooves.

Jet cleared her throat and spoke quietly, her mind having been working over their situation.

"There's another possibility, you know."

"Possibility of what?"

"How your enemies know where to find you every time."

"Really? What?"

"Your brother."

Alejandro pulled on his reins and the horse stopped. "What are you saying?"

"He was with you at the nightclub. You said the gunmen entered while he was in the bathroom, but when you made it out of the club, he was sitting in his vehicle outside."

"That's nonsense. He's my brother."

"And then at the hotel. Nobody knew you were there. And yet they found you."

"As you said, could have been a tracking device on the car or tracing the phone."

"Right. But explain the mine. No car tracking device. And the battery out of the phone."

"And no signal," Alejandro reminded her.

"No, that was earlier. We don't know if there's a signal at the mine. It's higher, so it might have enough line of sight to hit one of the towers in the valley. The only thing we have to go on is your brother's say-so."

"Which is sufficient for me."

"He got very uncomfortable when you asked for his phone, do you remember? Like someone had punched him. As you might expect if he'd made calls on it to your enemies."

Alejandro grew quiet, thinking.

"And then he inexplicably refused to go into the mine with us. To not go would be certain death – there was nowhere to run to. And yet he was adamant. Which would make sense if he knew there was nothing to fear."

"Why are you doing this?" Alejandro asked, his voice tight.

"Your father was arrested. So the head of your organization is out of commission. Then you're attacked, and your brother is conveniently absent."

Alejandro's expression darkened, but she pressed on.

"At the mine, he seemed really resentful that you were telling him what to do at a crisis moment. That seemed completely out of character when it was happening. You were trying to save his life, and he was getting angry. Who responds that way?"

"He was probably afraid. Maybe he's got a thing about the dark. Or claustrophobia. I don't know."

"Right. Or maybe he wanted to stay outside to avoid being killed when the gunmen went in to wipe us out." Jet paused. "Correct me if I'm wrong, but I got the impression that with your father out of the loop, you're next in line. Is that not right?"

"No, you're right."

"So if he resents you anything like what I saw, it would be awfully convenient if you were taken off the game board. Then he would be running things. Which, if he'd already negotiated a deal with your rivals, might leave him in the strongest position he'd be likely to see in his life."

"I don't want to hear any more."

"No problem. I just wanted to put that out there. Do you have an alternative explanation of how they found us at the mine?"

Alejandro gave his horse rein, and it began moving again. Jet allowed him space – she'd made her point, and now he had something to think about on the long ride to wherever. He pulled away from her and cantered to the top of a rise where a copse of trees had managed a foothold on the inhospitable stone and stopped, his hand raised. Jet slowed as she neared, and then spotted what he'd seen.

Down at the base of the other side of the hill ran a narrow road framed by heavy brush, an oak tree rising from one side of it – and a green army jeep parked in the shade with a soldier lounging against it, smoking, while his companion relieved himself behind the tree. Jet and Alejandro exchanged a glance, and she spurred her mare forward. The smoking soldier looked up but didn't register alarm at the sight of a woman astride a horse. This was the country, after all, so it wasn't unexpected or unusual. He waved at her as she approached, and she waved back, the Glock's bulk at the base of her spine reassuring.

Jet's hair gleamed black as a raven's wing as she closed the distance, and when she was less than ten meters away, she dismounted. Alejandro had hung back and was allowing his horse to

133

meander on the hill's crest, so the soldier's attention was entirely focused on the beautiful young woman who had materialized on horseback during his dull duty.

"Hi, there. You wouldn't happen to have an extra cigarette, would you?" Jet asked, throwing the soldier a brilliant smile.

"Sure," he said and fumbled in his uniform pocket. He found his pack and looked up to find himself staring down the Glock's ugly barrel.

"Remove your sidearm using only your index finger and your thumb. Don't make a sound or you're dead," she whispered.

The blood drained from his face, and he complied, moving slowly.

"Good. Drop it on the ground and step away from the gun, over by the tree."

The soldier tossed the pistol into the grass and took three steps toward the tree.

"Okay. Stop," Jet called out in a louder voice. "Hey, I think your buddy here has a problem," she said.

The second soldier moved from the other side of the thick trunk, fiddling with his belt, and froze when he saw Jet holding the gun on him.

"What is this?"

"Play along and you won't get hurt. I want you to reach for your weapon using your left hand and toss it on the ground. One false move and I shoot you."

The soldier glanced at his companion and then returned his gaze to Jet.

She gestured with the gun. "Slowly. Do it now. I don't have time for this."

He reached across and drew his weapon and then dropped it like it was a live snake. "Now what?"

"Now go stand by your friend."

The soldier complied, and Jet signaled to Alejandro. He rode up and smiled at the vehicle.

"I think our problems are solved," she announced.

"We could use the break," he agreed, dismounting.

She returned her attention to the soldiers. "Get your shoes off."

"What?" the first man asked, incredulous.

"You heard me. And keep your hands away from your knives, or it'll be the last mistake you make."

When they'd removed their boots, Jet nodded approval. "Now drop your pants. And take off your shirts."

The men unclasped their web belts and did as instructed. Once their uniforms were bunched together on the ground, Jet leaned into Alejandro and murmured.

"Would you get their clothes? And if they have handcuffs, secure them together, hands behind their backs, facing away from each other."

Alejandro moved to the men and barked instructions. He quickly located a pair of handcuffs in a case on the first soldier's belt and tossed them to him, snarling a terse order. The man sat down and shackled his hands behind his back. Alejandro had the second soldier do the same, with the exception that he had him pass the manacles through the first man's cuffs before snapping the left one shut, effectively securing them in a position where they wouldn't be able to move far. Jet inspected his work and nodded.

"Behave yourselves, and we'll alert someone that you're here." Jet studied them, little more than boys, and her voice softened. "I wouldn't try to stray from this tree – we'll clock the distance on the odometer, but if you make it very far there's no guarantee that anyone will find you before nightfall, and at that point you could die of exposure before you're located. So sit tight." She glanced at Alejandro. "I think the one on your left's more my size."

They had the uniforms on minutes later, and Alejandro inspected Jet. "Very nice. It might just work." He turned to the soldiers. "Now, gentlemen, before we get going, you're going to tell us everything you know about your operation. Where any roadblocks or patrols are, where your headquarters are, the works. Please don't think you're being smart by lying, because if we find out something's different than you said, we'll be back, and at that point, well…we'll view you as the enemy rather than a couple of honest guys who were in the wrong place at the wrong time."

Alejandro grilled them, emphasizing that he had the ability to reach anywhere in Chile to exact his revenge, and when he stood, he seemed satisfied with their responses.

"You heard them. The main roadblock's by the mine entrance. A couple of checkpoints on the road. An abandoned outpost for their field headquarters. Sounds about right."

"Think they left anything out?"

"Maybe, but I don't get that feeling. They know my family's reputation – that was obvious – and they understand that I'll take it personally if they tried to get us into hot water. These guys are grunions, doing their time. I doubt either one of them wants to get dumped into the ocean wearing concrete shoes."

Jet nodded. "You want to drive, or shall I?"

He looked down at his sleeve. "I'm the corporal, so I will. But you better hope we don't get stopped – from a distance this could work, but not up close."

"Why not?"

"There are no females in the armed forces in Chile. And no offense, but even in that getup, it's hard to miss that you're…well, not a man."

"Ah." She moved to the jeep and lifted out a FAMAE SAF submachine gun. "This is nice."

Alejandro retrieved the discarded pistols and handed her one. "FN-750 9mm pistol. Locally made, as is the submachine gun. Both use 9mm parabellum bullets. Quite good, and reliable."

She holstered the pistol after looking it over, and sat in the passenger seat, her helmet strapped on tight. Alejandro collected their clothes, folded them, and stowed them in the back of the Jeep before he took the wheel. Soon they were bouncing down the little road, the only vehicle in sight.

"We can't forget to notify someone about them. They're little more than teenagers," Jet said, and Alejandro nodded.

"I'll let the local police know once we're safe. They'll be able to find them by nightfall."

"Where are we headed?"

"We have a house in San Felipe that only a few of the ranking members of the family know exist. Small – where we keep weapons, contraband, and not much else. It's really just a living room, kitchen, and bedroom. But it has a phone."

"What about a car?"

"That, unfortunately, we're going to have to be creative about."

"So we steal one?"

"That's one way to do it. Do you have any experience hotwiring?"

Jet smiled as they hit a particularly nasty rut. "You could say that. But my daughter and Matt are back in the mine. I can't just leave them there."

"I know. But if the army's involved they were likely captured, which means they're probably alive. Unlike the Verdugos, the army won't just kill everything that moves. So the chances are good that they're in custody. The best way to help them is for me to get back to civilization and organize my forces. I'm not without my own contacts in the army, but they aren't going to do me much good riding around in a Jeep. I need to rally my troops and use the phone, not a gun. That's the best way."

"Have you thought about your brother at all?"

He sighed. "I can't come up with any explanation for the attack at the mine that doesn't involve him tipping them off. It sickens me, but I can't. I'll have to handle it later. Right now I need to get back to my home turf and organize a counterattack before anyone expects it. Once I've done that, I can deal with your daughter. Make sense?"

She studied his profile. "How much pull do you really have, Alejandro?"

"My father effectively runs this place. That should tell you how risky this little adventure was for the Verdugos. They had to believe there would be no effective retaliation or they'd never have chanced it – which further supports your theory about my brother."

Jet didn't like the idea of leaving the area without Matt and Hannah, but she couldn't think of a reasonable argument. Alejandro was right, and as much as she hated to, she had to trust him. He'd have a better chance of locating and freeing them once he was at the helm of his troops than she would playing commando.

When they reached the main road, Alejandro turned left, toward San Felipe – leaving the army, and her daughter, behind. Jet's gut twisted as if she'd been hit in the stomach with a board, but she forced herself to think objectively. There was no outward sign of her inner battle, her face placid as the wind buffeted her, and to any observer she would have looked as calm as Buddha. They passed several troop transports heading up the mountain, and Alejandro waved. Jet realized he was thinking more logically than she was. There was only so much she could do on her own, and right now their greatest advantage was that the world thought they were dead, buried in the bowels of a mine forgotten by time.

She looked off at the distant Andes, the peaks sharply traced against the taut turquoise sky, and bit back the frustration that threatened to overwhelm her.

She would get Hannah back. No matter what.

CHAPTER 24

San Rafael, Argentina

Drago's first impression of San Rafael was overwhelmingly green. Everywhere he looked seemed to be an eruption of trees – olive groves, poplar, pine, oak, and larch, the land a verdant contrast to the arid valley he'd driven through to get there. As he neared town, he trailed a thirties-era flatbed truck laden with bales of hay. Three young men who could have stepped out of the last century rode on the bed with the load. As far as he could see, farmland, vineyards, and unimaginable agricultural abundance thrived in the majestic shadows of the towering mountains.

Alfredo Sintas lived in the wealthiest neighborhood in San Rafael, each home its own small winery. Carefully pruned vineyards served as his backyard and lawn. After doing a slow reconnaissance of the area, Drago parked a block away on a quiet side street and studied the secluded oasis of privilege filled with expansive villas and luxury automobiles. He didn't bother with his bag, preferring to leave it locked in the car, and took his time walking to Sintas' house, a dark brown baseball cap pulled low over his brow and a pair of cheap sunglasses shielding his eyes.

He walked up the drive, checking his watch as his gaze roved over his surroundings to confirm nobody was watching. He had little worry, but it was a habit born of long experience, and his glance took in everything while seeming to wander aimlessly.

A newish BMW sedan was parked in the driveway in front of the garage, and Drago felt the hood with his hand as he brushed by it – cool to the touch, so not a recent arrival. He'd debated more circuitous approaches but had decided on the direct route: a knock at the door, a case of mistaken address. He was nearing the front porch when he spied a man in his sixties at the side of the house, wearing a red sweater and slate-blue corduroy trousers, chopping at the dark brown soil of a vegetable garden with a hoe. A man in touch with nature, Drago thought approvingly, as he moved to the side gate.

"*Señor* Sintas?" Drago called, his tone harmlessly friendly and slightly puzzled.

"Yes, that's right," Sintas said, looking up from his work, equally perplexed.

"Ah, good. I'm afraid your friend isn't going to make his appointment," Drago said, opening the gate.

"My friend? What are you talking about?"

"I'm sorry. I can't remember his name. Older fellow, lives in a magnificent villa on the outskirts of Mendoza? Drives a Toyota Land Cruiser?"

"Hector Garibaldi?" Sintas said as Drago stopped inside the gate, ten meters away. "Why, he just called. What happened?"

"Was that his name? Sorry. I'm terrible with that sort of thing." Drago pulled his pistol from where he'd had it at the small of his back. "What happened was that he had an accident. He sent me here in his stead. He promised you'd be able to answer my questions for me, and assured me you'd be cooperative."

Sintas eyed the weapon, confusion playing across his face. "Who are you? What do you want?"

"Ah, as to who I am, that's not important. As to what I want, that's easy. Let's go inside, and we can discuss it." Drago motioned with the gun, a small smile on his face, looking almost embarrassed that he'd had to disrupt the man's idyllic morning.

Sintas hefted the hoe, and Drago could read his intent. "*Señor* Sintas, I really don't want to hurt you, but if you follow through on your ill-advised idea about making a try for me with the hoe, I'll be forced to shoot you in the stomach, which I can assure you is incredibly painful. What will then happen is your bowels will leak into your abdominal cavity, slowly poisoning your blood, which can take many hours and is an agonizing death under the best of circumstances." Drago sighed. "Now, I don't think either of us wants that. I'd prefer to be invited in, to sit and talk, perhaps like new acquaintances if not old friends, learn what I need, and then leave you in peace, aware that you've sat with death and walked away unharmed. There aren't many men who can make that claim, but I'm feeling generous today, and it's too beautiful out for more killing."

"You're insane."

"Ah, well, perhaps. But that doesn't change anything, does it? Put the hoe down, keep your hands where I can see them, and let's go inside. I trust there's nobody else in there? No housekeeper or mistress?"

Drago could see the internal struggle as Sintas calculated whether he could reach Drago with the hoe before he could fire. He arrived at the sensible conclusion – which was no – and did as instructed, his eyes narrowing as he slowly lowered the hoe handle and laid it on the ground.

"What are those? Tomatoes? And is that basil?" Drago asked.

Sintas ignored the questions. "What do you wish to know?"

"It's a small thing. Probably not worth either of our time. Let's go inside and discuss it. The alternative is not a pretty one, as I mentioned. We can be civilized about this, yes? We aren't animals, after all."

Sintas moved to his side door with the deliberate care of a much older man. Drago closed the distance to him lest he get any ideas about inadvisable heroics and followed him into the house. The decoration was dated and more feminine than Drago had expected – no doubt the deceased wife's touch. The hardwood floors showed signs of recent work, the varnish fresh and shiny and the joinery meticulous.

"Please, sit. Over here," Drago said, leading him to a couch in the living room. Sintas complied, and when he was seated, Drago sat across from him in an easy chair.

"What do you want to know?" Sintas said, his eyes boring into Drago as though he could kill him with the intensity of his stare.

"Your friend Garibaldi gave your contact information to a troubled young woman, with the encouragement that you could arrange for anything she might need. She's helping a very dangerous fellow. You don't want any part of this, I assure you. Has she contacted you?"

Sintas didn't blink. "No. I have no idea who you're talking about."

Drago exhaled, clearly disappointed. "You know, it's an interesting thing. A practiced liar will tell a lie and never blink while he's doing so. The tendency is for an honest man to look away for an instant, or for his eyelids to flutter. But a skilled liar will hold absolutely still, having mastered the giveaways that people automatically and correctly associate with prevarication." Drago paused as Sintas glared hate at him. "You didn't blink. If I wasn't as practiced a liar myself, I'd have believed you. Unfortunately, I am, and I can tell you're lying."

"I'm not."

"Yes, you are. You just did it again, when you insisted you weren't. So that's two lies." Drago sighed resignedly. "I'm afraid I wasn't clear. I require this information, and you will tell me. You will do it either willingly, in which case we shall part as friends, or unwillingly, in which case you've seen your last sunset, tasted your last dinner, drunk your last glass of fine wine. The choice is entirely yours. Believe me when I say that I hope you choose wisely."

Sintas glowered at him defiantly. "I told you the truth."

Drago adjusted the position of the pistol ever so slightly and squeezed off a shot. The round blew the older man's kneecap off.

Sintas' scream of agony shattered the stillness of the house. Drago didn't move, his smile fixed in place. After several moments of watching Sintas writhe in pain, Drago stood and walked to the kitchen, taking his time, and removed an ice tray from the freezer. Another howl of anguish echoed through the house, and he dropped four into a plastic bag, reconsidered and added two more, and then moved back into the living room. He stood in front of Sintas and inspected the bloody wound, then set the bag down on the coffee table and returned to his seat.

"Hold the ice on it. It will begin to numb in a few minutes. Not enough so it stops hurting, but enough so you can speak coherently."

Sintas' mouth gawped, but nothing came out but a wheeze.

Drago nodded. "I hope I've made myself clear. Because of your reluctance to be honest with me, you'll be walking around on one stick for the rest of your life. But you'll be alive. Piss me off any further and it'll be two sticks. I can see you're paying attention, so I'm going to share something with you." Drago sat back. "The American Indians used to have a remarkable way of torturing their prisoners. I mean, they had many; it was considered great sport. But the one I'm thinking of in particular shows how inventive they were. They'd broil the victim's appendages, slowly, over many hours, and when the nerves went dead, they'd cut their hands and feet off, and then repeat the process on the stumps. They could make the process take days." Sintas seemed to be following what Drago was saying, so he continued. "You need to ask yourself whether you want to continue to try to lie to someone who carries that sort of information around in his head, hoping for a chance to use it."

Twenty minutes later Drago left the house, walking unhurriedly. Of course he'd lied about allowing Sintas to live – which Sintas, being a liar, had also intuited – so he'd had to alter his approach and make him beg for a quick death instead.

In the end, he got the information he wanted. His quarry was in Chile, a town called San Felipe. Or had been until recently. The woman was looking for a way out of the country – something unofficial. She'd missed her appointment with Sintas' man that morning and hadn't called yet to reschedule, but Drago was optimistic. He had Sintas' cell phone, so when she did, he'd know. And when he found her, he'd find his target.

From there, it was simply a matter of choosing the correct persuasion.

CHAPTER 25

San Felipe, Chile

The winding road down the mountain seemed to take forever to navigate in the Jeep. Jet kept the SAF submachine gun in her lap the entire time, wary of their escape having been too easy. She busied herself by listening to the chatter on the handheld radio clamped to the dash in a metal holder, and almost jumped out of her seat when a deep voice came on the air and reported that the captives were on their way to the provisional headquarters.

Jet turned to Alejandro. "You heard that. Captives. That has to be Matt and Hannah."

"Probably, and there's a slim possibility that it also means Rodrigo, but there's not much we can do right now. I have contacts in the military I can talk to once we're safe, but we're not there yet."

"That's bullshit. Of course there's something we can do. We just escaped from a mine that should have been a death trap. Don't talk to me about not being able to do anything."

"Look, even a temporary army headquarters is going to be swarming with soldiers. We're talking serious fortification. There's no way we'd be able to get them out in broad daylight. You'd be dead before you got out of the car."

"I have to try," she countered. "That's my daughter we're talking about."

"I know. But you have to do more than try. You have to succeed. Which means you'll need more than a gun and guts. You will need a plan and probably a lot of help. So calm down, let's deal with our present circumstance, and then we'll see what can be done. Nobody's going to be helped by you going off half-cocked."

Jet fumed in silence, but grudgingly conceded to herself that Alejandro made sense. While her instinct was to go in with guns blazing, it would do Hannah no good to have her mommy killed while trying to rescue her.

Once they rolled into town, Alejandro's posture changed and he visibly relaxed, but he was still detached and quiet, no doubt thinking through his next moves and the likelihood that his brother had turned traitor. Part of her sympathized with his predicament, but a larger part refused to get more involved than she already was.

"Where's this safe house?" she asked.

"On the west side of town. In a quiet residential neighborhood."

"How do you intend to get in?"

"I know the combination. We have a realtor's lock on the back door with a key inside."

"Do you control San Felipe, or do the Verdugos?"

"We do. Or rather, I would have said that we did until yesterday. After the hotel shootout, I'm not taking anything for granted."

"Can't you just make a call and get a dozen armed men to appear by magic?"

"Under normal circumstances I'd say sure, but…" He sighed. "I don't want to jump to any conclusions, but Rodrigo was in charge of this area, along with Los Andes, while I spent much of my time in Santiago. If you're right – and I'm not saying you are – and he participated in these attacks, then it's also possible that some or all of his men might not be loyal." He hesitated. "I'd just as soon leave them out of it for now."

Alejandro stiffened when a police cruiser swung out of a side street and took up position behind the Jeep. Jet flipped the safety of the FAMAE SAF off and did her best to avoid staring at the squad car in the rearview mirror. She clutched the weapon with a death grip as they went one block, and then another, and then the police car turned into the parking lot of a small restaurant. Jet returned the safety to the locked position and began breathing again.

The safe house was located in a working-class neighborhood, the homes jammed in close to one another, iron bars across the doors and windows, the vehicles older and the houses in disrepair. It was obvious to Jet that the population of San Felipe wasn't prosperous, which could work in their favor: older cars were less likely to have state-of-the art alarm systems.

Alejandro made a right onto a tree-lined lane and glanced at her. "The house is halfway down this block on the left-hand side." The Jeep crept along at a moderate pace as it approached the dwelling, and then Jet grabbed his arm.

"Keep driving. There's a man in that green sedan twenty meters up, my side. See his head?"

"Now I do. You're good."

"There are a bunch of cigarette butts on the street beneath his window. He's been there for a while."

"Shit." The single syllable held not only anger, but sadness. There weren't a lot of possible explanations for a watcher being outside of a safe house that only the top members of Alejandro's organization knew about.

"Just keep driving, maintain your speed, and laugh as you pass him like I'm telling you the funniest joke you've ever heard. Most soldiers are young and just putting in their time trying to make the best of things, and we'll appear a lot less suspicious if you're laughing than if you've got that grim look," she warned. "The mind tends to automatically discount smiling or laughing people when searching for threats."

He followed her lead and was cackling as they drove by the man in the Chevrolet sedan, who gave them a hard look and then returned to his cigarette. When they rounded the corner and were out of sight, Alejandro's expression settled back to his typically serious one.

"So much for that idea," he said.

"What about buying a cell phone? Or are there pay phones here?"

"Buying one isn't a bad idea. But what we really need first is an anonymous vehicle and to get out of these uniforms now that they've served their purpose. Maybe we should go back, sneak up on our watcher, and take his car?"

She shook her head. "Unnecessary risk, and it might alert your enemies that something's wrong if he's supposed to check in. There's nothing to be gained by doing it."

"So we steal a car?"

"What do you think of that one?" she asked, considering an older tan Toyota van parked in front of a small apartment building.

"Looks good. What do you want me to do?"

"Is there a hardware or stationery store around here?"

Alejandro considered the question. "I think we passed a little office supply place on the main street. Why?"

"Find a grove of trees or some bushes so I can change into my own clothes, and then we're going shopping."

Fifteen minutes later they were back on the same side street, this time with Jet wearing her shirt and pants, a metal ruler in one hand she'd notched using Alejandro's pocket knife. He dropped her at the corner, and she sauntered unhurriedly down the block, watching for any inquisitive neighbors. When she was alongside the van, she took a last look around and then slid the ruler down the passenger window. Five seconds later the lock popped open, and she slipped inside.

She reached beneath the steering column and felt for the ignition wires. When she'd located them, she sliced them free using the knife, stripped the ends, and crossed them. The starter cranked over, but no ignition. She tried again, and on the third attempt the little motor revved to life.

Jet pulled from the curb and drove to the end of the block, where Alejandro was waiting in the Jeep. They rounded the corner, and he ditched it in front of a vacant lot, and then quickly moved to the van's passenger door, submachine guns and the handheld radio clutched to his chest. Jet was already rolling away when he slammed the door shut and set the guns to the side.

"Get into the back and change," she said. "We'll stop at a phone store on the way out of town."

"Better yet, drive to Los Andes. There's less chance of seeing anyone who might recognize me. I'm hardly ever there."

She did as instructed, and by the time they stopped in front of an electronics store, he was out of the uniform, his shirt wrinkled and his trousers a shadow of their former immaculate glory.

He looked down at them and grimaced. "I look like a hobo."

"That's okay. I'm not choosy about the company I keep."

"How do you manage to still look good?"

"Cheap synthetics. Wait here. I'll get the phone." She felt in her pocket and withdrew the ziplock bag with the passports in it. Alejandro's eyebrows rose as she sorted through three and selected an Argentine one. Jet shrugged and slid the rest back into the bag.

"You need money?" he asked.

"I don't have any Chilean, so yes."

He handed her a wad of bills. "Good luck."

"Easiest thing I've done today. It's just a phone."

When she returned after a long wait, she tossed him his change and a little Nokia with a mobile charger. "All right. You're in business. Where to next?"

He checked the time. "Up at the next street, make a right. That will take you to the highway south. Santiago's about an hour drive."

Jet nodded and eyed the gas gauge, which thankfully indicated over a third of a tank of gas – more than enough to get them to the capital. She slid the transmission into gear and eased into traffic, keenly aware that every kilometer took her further from Matt and Hannah.

Alejandro was on the phone almost the entire trip, coordinating with his father's subordinates and giving them sanitized updates on what had transpired. He warned them that Rodrigo had been captured by the Verdugos, so any calls or instructions from him were to be treated as though they were made under duress and reported to Alejandro immediately.

The news on Gaspar Soto wasn't good. The attorneys had been stonewalled when they'd demanded to see him that morning; now it appeared that he wasn't being held at the downtown headquarters jail, and no new information was available. They were escalating their protests to the highest levels, but so far there was no information about Soto senior and no specific time when any would be forthcoming – a testament to the amount of money the Verdugos must have spread around, besides being patently illegal. But apparently in Chile the law was a fickle mistress and could be flouted or ignored by those in power with relative impunity. The head of the legal team vowed to get to the bottom of the matter before the day was over, but Alejandro appeared unconvinced as he hung up and sat silently brooding for the final kilometers into the city.

Santiago was a hectic clog of cars, all honking and near misses and daredevil abandon that reminded her of nothing so much as Buenos Aires – the world capital of insane motorists, rivaled only by the Italians for sheer suicidal bravado. Alejandro directed her through the afternoon traffic to a privileged area of classic French-influenced buildings. After circling the nearby streets and seeing nothing suspicious, he told her to park down the block while he scouted out his girlfriend's apartment.

"What does she do?" Jet asked as he slipped one of the soldiers' pistols into his empty shoulder holster.

"Her family's in banking and real estate. She helps manage their portfolio."

Jet eyed the imposing building. "Is she likely to be there during the day?"

"She works from home."

"And she won't mind you showing up? With another woman?"

"She's not like that – our relationship's more informal than you're imagining, and she doesn't get involved in my affairs." Alejandro swung the passenger door wide, stepped onto the sidewalk, and leaned into the open window. "I'll be back. She has several rental properties that are vacant at the moment. I'll borrow one until this gets sorted out."

"Watch your back."

"You too."

Alejandro walked away, looking like he'd lost a bear-wrestling contest in his torn dinner jacket and ruined pants, and Jet wondered for the hundredth time whether she was doing the right thing in trusting him. Her self-reliant side hated depending on a man whom she barely knew for anything, much less Matt's and Hannah's lives, but she stifled her doubts as she watched him cross the street and approach the building. There were no other options she could see, so like it or not, Alejandro was her only chance at seeing her daughter and mate alive ever again.

CHAPTER 26

The van was running on fumes by the time Alejandro returned. Jet took in his crisp pastel blue shirt, leather jacket, and jeans, and nodded as he opened the passenger door.

"I see you found a set of clothes," she said.

"Yes. I keep a spare bag at her place."

"Were you able to find anything more out?"

He nodded. "I'm expecting a call."

"We're just about out of gas," she said, eyeing the gauge.

"Doesn't matter." He held up a set of car keys with a BMW logo on it. "My car's in the underground parking."

"Is it wise to drive around in a vehicle that's associated with you?"

"Ah, I should have said *one* of my cars. Normally I have an armored SUV and a driver for security reasons. This is one of my toys."

"I see."

"I'll pull around. We can load up the guns and radio and be on our way."

"And the van?"

"I'll arrange for someone to get rid of it. Be right back."

Jet killed the engine and studied her reflection in the rearview mirror. She looked tired and in need of a shower. She rubbed a smudge of dirt from her cheek and was running her fingers through her stiff hair when she was assaulted by a wave of light-headedness, accompanied by a vision of Hannah cowering in the mine, crying. Sour bile rose in her gorge, and her mouth flooded with saliva. She swallowed hard just as the muted roar of a large motor vibrated her window.

Alejandro peered over a pair of sunglasses at her from behind the wheel of a black BMW X6. Jet eyed the aftermarket oversized tires and wheels and the gleaming onyx paint without comment and reached behind her for the submachine guns. She opened the door, transferred the weapons to the rear of the BMW, and then hopped into the passenger side.

The little Nokia trilled as Alejandro pulled away. He punched the call button and listened intently, muttered a few words, listened again, and then hung up with an oath.

"Bastards. They have my father at San Miguel prison. It's one of the worst hellholes in a system that's as miserable as you can imagine. Why they put him in there…" Alejandro trailed off, the venom in his voice threatening to choke him. "He should have been in the central jail. I mean, they can't even tell the attorneys what he's being charged with, and he's been transferred to one of the most violent facilities in the country?" Alejandro's eyes blazed. "We have to get him out of there. You have no idea how dangerous that place is."

"How? I mean, if you can't get anyone in authority to answer the phone?"

Alejandro slammed his hand against the steering wheel in frustration as his temper flared. "It's…I don't know who in the organization I can trust besides a core of my father's friends. There had to be inside information leaked for them to know he'd be at the restaurant at that particular time. I know you think it's Rodrigo, but even if you're right, there might be others."

Alejandro gunned the engine and sliced between two cars and then swerved into a left-turn lane and hung a U-turn, tires screeching.

"Where are we going?" Jet asked.

"I want to drive by the prison."

"What will that accomplish?"

"I need to think."

Jet opted not to argue the wisdom of going by the jail, and let him stew in silence. She, more than anyone, understood the anguish he was feeling at having a loved one held prisoner, in constant danger.

The prison turned out to be a series of multistoried concrete buildings behind a tall wall in the center of the city with guard turrets every seventy meters or so. They circled it three times as Alejandro grew increasingly agitated. When he coasted to a stop at a traffic light, he turned to her.

"I have to get him out. Now."

"Do you have any pull inside the prison?"

"Of course. We have pull everywhere."

"With the guards or the prisoners?"

"Before this I would have said both. Now I'm not sure. But certainly among the prisoners. A fair number of them are our men."

"And the Verdugos?"

"The cops have learned the hard way not to put the Verdugos into any prison in Santiago. Their crew goes to jail in Valparaíso."

"How about breakouts?"

"There have been a number. But they aren't reported."

"Can you organize a breakout?"

Alejandro considered the idea. "The system here is like most of South America. The jails are basically run by the inmates. They have everything you can think of – weapons, drugs, alcohol, cell phones – everything but a means to easily escape. The guards have the attitude that they're only there to keep the inmates in, not to control them. They're afraid to go into the buildings, as they should be. But one thing they take seriously is keeping the animals, as they refer to the prisoners, in their cages. Anyone trying to make a break for the walls is shot. Even so, some manage to sneak out, but a man like my father…he's not young."

"It sounds like you should call whoever runs things inside and let them know he's there. They may not even know he's there if they have him in solitary. You need more information than just that he's been imprisoned. Like where precisely he is in the complex, whether he's hurt, whether he can move around freely."

Alejandro nodded. "Yes. Excellent. I will relay the message. Hector is one of the trusted inner circle. You'll meet him shortly. He can put that in motion."

Alejandro made a call and spoke in rapid-fire Spanish, his tone as ominous as any she'd heard. When he hung up, he glanced at her.

"It is done. I should know something by the time we reach the rental."

"Where are your men gathered? Are they staying out of sight, or do you have a headquarters of some sort?"

"Hector is at my father's estancia. It's south of the city. Of course, we have the offices for our shipping company. But I think it would be a bad idea to go there – it's an obvious place they'll have watched. The same for my father's place. I don't want to risk it, especially if there are doubts about my brother."

"What about my daughter? Were you able to learn anything?"

"I've set wheels in motion. My contacts in the army are investigating. I expect to have news at any moment."

Jet studied Alejandro's profile, wondering if he was lying. She didn't think so. But that didn't mean anything. David had apparently spent most of the time he'd been with her lying, and she'd never suspected – a mistake that had almost cost her everything.

Ten minutes later, Alejandro parked in a multistory condo development's underground garage and killed the engine. He circled around, opened the rear cargo door of the X6, and then retrieved a golf bag. Jet handed him the submachine guns, which he concealed in the bag before shouldering it. "This way," he said, heading toward the stainless steel doors of an elevator.

The condo was a two-bedroom unit on the sixth floor, modern and sparsely furnished. He gave her a quick tour, and when she saw the washer and dryer, she nodded. "Does your girlfriend have any clothes here?"

"I don't know. I've only been in this place once before." They moved to the closet, where there was nothing but a cheap white cotton robe on a hanger that looked like it might have been left by the prior tenant. Jet examined it and carried it to the laundry nook. She eyed the soap and turned to Alejandro.

"I didn't have the luxury of having a new set of clothes, so I'm going to wash what I have and take a shower. Do you mind?" she asked.

"No. Of course not. I'm sorry. I didn't even think about it…"

"That's understandable. You've got other things on your mind. But while we're discussing necessities, I'm starved. Is there any way to get some food delivered?"

Alejandro stared at her like she'd announced she could levitate, and then smacked his forehead. "Damn. I completely forgot. Yes, of course, but it's likely to be pizza or something equally appetizing."

"Pizza sounds wonderful. Just cheese for me."

She went into the bathroom and stripped off, emptied the pockets of her cargo pants and emerged with her clothes. Alejandro was on the phone, pacing in front of the window. She poured in some powder and started the washer, and then retreated to the bathroom, where she luxuriated in a long, hot shower, even though there was no soap. When she was done, she stood, dripping, and wiped as much of the moisture off her body as she could with her hands. She then donned the robe and inspected herself in the mirror. A few scratches on one cheek, the scab beginning to lift on the other. Traces of discoloration beneath her eyes from lack of sleep. And the moist robe clung to her more closely than she would have liked. But all in all, she'd been worse. Much worse.

When she returned to the living area, Alejandro was still engrossed in a discussion and barely noticed her. She occupied herself by breaking down her pistol and assuring herself that it was still clean, and then went back into the bathroom and collected her money, papers, and the small satchel with her diamonds. A knock at the door startled her. She chambered a round in the FN-750 and emerged from the doorway, weapon at the ready. Alejandro saw her, and his eyes widened, and then he nodded and barked something into the phone before hanging up. He moved to the door, looked through the peephole, and then opened it.

The delivery boy received a memorable tip and departed with a grin. "It's safe to come out. No ninjas attacking, just food,"

Alejandro said, and Jet walked over to him, pistol by her side. He appraised her wordlessly and opened the box, and they stood at the breakfast bar and devoured the pizza, Alejandro fielding calls as he munched.

Once satiated, she threw her clothes into the dryer and waited for him to get off the phone. When he eventually did, he had a worried look on his face. "I've got news about your daughter and your husband. They're being held at the field headquarters, from what we can deduce. In the mountains, six miles from the mine. But according to my source, there are at least thirty soldiers there. So I'm not sure what can be done until they try to move them."

"What if they don't? Or if they do before we can get to them? I need to be up there, not here. This was a mistake," she said.

"And do what?" He eyed her in her damp robe and shook his head. "Even if you have remarkable abilities, which you clearly do, that would be suicide, and we both know it."

"Maybe. But it's my loved ones, not yours, so you can afford to be cavalier about it."

"Look, I made you a promise, and I'll keep it. I'm a man of my word, even if I have my faults. But I need to get my father out of jail first – that's my top priority." His gaze locked on hers.

She held his stare without blinking. "What can you tell me about the army headquarters?"

"I'm waiting for a diagram. It should be emailed to me within the hour. I haven't forgotten about your daughter. I've just got my hands full with trying to figure out how to get my dad free. The sooner that happens, the sooner I'll be able to put all my resources into helping you. I mean it."

Jet studied his face for any sign of duplicity. She believed him. "Do you know much about the prison? Do you have any sort of layout for it?"

He nodded. "Yes."

"Let me see it. If breaking him out of jail is the only holdup to going back to San Felipe, maybe I can help."

An amused smile played at the edges of his mouth. "You have a lot of experience with this sort of thing?"

She looked off into the distance, seeming to mentally drift away for a moment before returning her attention to Alejandro. "You could say that."

CHAPTER 27

Alejandro left the condo to meet one of his men and get the details on San Miguel prison. He returned ten minutes later accompanied by a short, swarthy man in his fifties with a weasel face and eyes that seemed to look through her. Alejandro introduced him as Hector, his father's most trusted lieutenant.

"How do you know you weren't followed?" she asked as she shook his hand.

"Sweetheart, I've been doing this forever. I wasn't followed," he said, his words clipped, his tone insulting.

Jet glanced at Alejandro. "You better hope not."

Alejandro spread a freshly printed set of documents on the breakfast bar. Satellite photos from Google Earth, a diagram of the prison grounds, photographs of the exterior, a neatly printed column of numbers.

Hector tapped the latter with a stubby finger. "These are the guard shifts. They do three changes per day. One at six a.m., another at two p.m., another at ten. We got it from a contact inside."

Jet could smell nicotine and sweat radiating off the man's rumpled suit. "How many guards?"

"Too many. Up to a hundred on any given shift. All armed."

"What do they do in the event of a disturbance? If there's a fight or a fire…or a riot?"

"Generally they stay on the wall or in a safe area and let it play out," Hector said. "In the case of a fire, we know too well how they respond. Eighty-three prisoners died in a fire a few years back. It was a national tragedy. There was an investigation and accusations that the guards were slow to allow the firefighters in, but as with most things here, nothing ever came of it."

Alejandro cleared his throat. "They rarely get involved in fights. Better to let the inmates kill each other, and then mop up after it's over."

"What about rioting?"

"Same sort of ambivalence. The fire that killed the inmates happened during a riot," Hector rasped, his voice seasoned by decades of tobacco and hard liquor. "Like I said, they tend to leave the prisoners to themselves. Which for Gaspar Soto is a double-edged sword. The good news is that he's surrounded by loyal men. The bad news is that it only takes one determined assassin to defeat everyone's efforts to keep someone safe if they're willing to give their life trying. And there are dozens of men in that prison who would kill anyone if it meant their family would be taken care of. Men with no chance of ever getting out, who live like rats."

Jet's eyes widened. "Then he's in with the general population?"

"Yes, he was just released into it a few hours ago, and our men are trying to keep it quiet. But it's hard. Gossip sweeps like brushfire in a prison. It's only a matter of time until someone tries for him," Alejandro said.

"But he's free to move around and isn't hurt?" Jet asked.

"He suffered a minor concussion and had some bouts of double vision, but our men say he's getting better as the day wears on," Hector said. "I spoke with him not an hour ago. Sounded fine to me, if a little weak."

Jet was studying the diagram Hector had brought. "These walls are a meter thick and reinforced concrete, correct?"

"Right. You can forget ramming a truck through it. Or even a tank. Hell, you could crash a plane into those walls and it wouldn't do much," Alejandro said.

Jet's eyes lifted from the page, and she looked at Alejandro. "What did you just say?"

Alejandro frowned. "That ramming through the walls is a no-go. I already thought about it."

She nodded slowly. "Let's talk about the electricity for the prison."

Hector tapped the diagram. "City power. Backup generators here and here," he said, indicating a small building. "When there's a blackout, the generators kick on within ten seconds, supplying power to the doors and spotlights. So that's not an option. And our source tells us that the main exit doors automatically lock in the event of an outage."

"These are the exercise yards?" Jet asked about the three open areas at the far side of the rows of buildings.

"Correct."

She beetled her brow as she studied the photographs and stepped back with a sigh.

"What is it?" Alejandro asked.

Jet moved to the window, where the afternoon sun was streaming through. She paced silently before it, lost in thought as the sunlight warmed her, and then returned to where the gangsters were waiting for her to speak.

"I know how we can get him out. Tonight, if you can work fast," she said softly.

"What? Just like that?" Hector said, his tone derisive. He rolled his eyes, obviously angry at having his time wasted.

Jet cleared her throat and offered a condescending smile. "Well, it wasn't that hard. It's really just a process of elimination. Pay attention and maybe you'll learn something," she said.

Hector bristled and his lip curled into a sneer. Alejandro shook his head almost imperceptibly in warning. The older man appeared to think twice and choked back his retort like he was swallowing a fistful of live ants.

"How would you do it?" Alejandro asked her.

"You'll need to talk to someone the power company and identify the location of the transformers that supply the prison. I presume you have access to satchel charges that might have walked away from a military base? You'll need several of them. And timers. Or foolproof remote detonators," Jet said.

Hector snorted in contempt. "You don't listen very well, do you? I just explained that the backup generators—"

"Go on automatically," she interrupted. "Which brings me to my next question. How difficult would it be for someone in the prison to either cut the belts on the generators or pour sand into the fuel system? We'll want them disabled, so when the power turns off, they fail and there's no electricity."

Alejandro considered the question. "We have a number of the prison staff on our payroll. It would be expensive, I'd guess. The person doing it would be taking a huge risk." He tilted his head and eyed her. "Why? What would you accomplish by sabotaging them? All it would do is black out the prison. That wouldn't get my father out, so what's the point?"

"True. But let's back up and talk about the transformers. Do you have any demolitions experts? Ex-military?"

Hector grunted. "Of course. Many of our men were in the service."

"Good. Then I won't have to do that part myself. For a while there I was afraid you might not have anyone competent." Hector's color rose, and Jet could see his neck redden. She turned to Alejandro. "Now, how about at the airport? Anyone you're paying off in the tower? Air traffic control?"

Alejandro looked at her as though she'd asked whether he could play the cello. "Why would we have someone like that on our payroll?"

She ignored his question. "Or maybe someone who owes you money or buys drugs from you?"

Hector's eyes narrowed. "I could ask. Why? What are you getting at?"

"If you can get your demolitions people on the transformers so that the power gets cut at ten o'clock when the guard shifts are changing, that would guarantee maximum confusion, wouldn't it? And if the backup generators failed, the entire area would be plunged into darkness, right? Probably for blocks around it, too."

Alejandro nodded. "Yes…"

Jet glanced out the window again. "It looks like it's getting cloudy. That could work well. Last night in San Felipe it was getting foggy as we headed into the mountains. Does it also get foggy in Santiago?"

Hector was completely lost. "Sure. Sometimes the airport shuts down for hours. Depends on how hot it was during the day and how cool the night is. Why?"

"Think it will be foggy tonight?"

Alejandro thought for a moment. "It could be."

Hector cut in. "I still don't understand what the hell you're getting at."

"No, I bet you really don't." She shrugged and returned her attention to Alejandro and described what she had in mind. Both men listened with growing expressions of incredulity on their faces. When she finished, Alejandro began making phone calls, and Hector studied Jet like she was insane, or a genius. He tapped a cigarette out of a flattened pack and stuck it in his mouth and then pulled a steel Zippo lighter from his pocket and lit it, his gaze never straying from hers.

"That's got to be the most ridiculous, implausible scheme I've heard in my entire life. And I thought I'd heard them all."

Jet didn't say a word. Alejandro had an impassive look on his face as he waited for someone on the telephone to give him an answer. When they did, he gave an order and hung up. "We got it. And we're lining up the painter as we speak."

She glanced at her watch. "You have about six hours to put it all together. Not a lot of time, but doable."

Hector took a long drag on his cigarette and inhaled deeply and then blew a long blue trail of smoke at the window.

"I'll ride shotgun."

CHAPTER 28

The ride to Gaspar Soto's estate took forty minutes, the last ten of which were spent in the back of a white panel delivery van with Hector at the wheel and Jet and Alejandro in the back, out of sight. Two cars filled with Soto enforcers had joined them, creating a caravan as they approached the twenty-acre compound. At the iron gates, four seasoned men with assault rifles blocked their way and only opened them once Hector had barked rapid instructions at them. Inside the high walls, mature trees lined the perimeter as far as she could see – large oaks, their tops rippling in the wind. Off to the right in the near distance, horses pranced in a corral as several hands worked with them; to her left, acres of vineyards stretched for ages.

The house was modest compared to the rest of the bucolic estate, two stories with several outbuildings. The van rolled to a stop in front of a circular stone fountain with an antique figure of Neptune gripping his trident as its centerpiece, and Hector turned to them as he shut off the engine.

"They're working on it in the back."

The rear doors opened, and several of the gunmen moved to either side of the vehicle, their expressions tense, as though they were expecting an attack at any moment, which was more than partially true. Alejandro had been coordinating the defense of the compound and now had fifty of the Sotos' most trusted soldiers on the grounds. Everyone knew that it was just a matter of time until full-scale war broke out in a battle to the death. There was too much at stake for the Verdugos to leave anything to chance, and there had already been reports of some of the Soto strongholds in the city being hit, although without much success; the Sotos employed the cream of the underworld and their numbers included a large retinue of ex-commandos and mercenaries – more than a match for the Verdugos' street toughs.

Alejandro led the way through the house, which was furnished in priceless antiques. Oil paintings from a bygone era adorned the walls. They reached a set of French doors at the rear of the salon, and Alejandro pushed them open. On the lawn, two men were rolling metallic green paint onto the back of a Bell 206-B3 helicopter, having completed the front of the cabin in white. Hector walked over to the aircraft and inspected the job and, after a brief discussion, returned to where Jet and Alejandro were standing.

"They'll be done in fifteen minutes and, allowing for some drying time, will apply the *Caribineros de Chile* lettering on the tail. By the time we're done, it will be indistinguishable from a police helicopter," he reported.

Alejandro edged to the side and had a subdued discussion with one of Hector's associates. When he returned, his face was glum.

"We have a problem. The pilot won't do it. We offered a king's ransom, but he refused. He's a straight shooter, old school, and has been with my father for twenty years. But he pointed out that if anything went wrong, flying the helicopter would be either life in prison or suicide."

"Can't say as I blame him," Hector said. "Did you try a more persuasive approach? Maybe his family?"

Alejandro shook his head. "I can't do that. My father would disown me. That's not how you reward trusted friends."

Hector spit on the lawn and lit another of his unending stream of cigarettes. "So now what do we do?"

Jet looked up at the sky. "It'll be dark soon. Has anyone gotten word on the air traffic situation? Do you have someone at the airport you can get to?"

Alejandro placed a quick phone call and then shook his head. "Unfortunately that came up dry, too."

Jet nodded. "Well, it just means that the bird will need to stay low and go in fast. It's still possible to pull it off, but it will require more scrambling. You'll need to have a car waiting and get your father clear, because without someone at the airports to run interference for you it will be just a matter of minutes before the landing area is swarming with police."

Alejandro glanced at Hector and moved next to him. Jet walked over to the helicopter as they chatted, and noted that it was in good condition – it looked like a nineties variant, in nearly new shape, evidently no expense spared on maintenance. Crime clearly paid well indeed. When she returned, Alejandro was back on the phone and Hector had an ugly smile on his face.

"What?" Jet asked.

"You're not the only one capable of innovative ideas, young lady. We might have a way to deal with the radar systems." He told her what he had in mind.

"You think you can do that?"

Hector shrugged. "For enough money, you can accomplish almost anything."

Alejandro hung up and nodded. "Another problem solved. It's taken care of. But there's still the issue of who's going to fly the chopper. If we can't resolve that, the rest of this is for nothing."

Jet sighed. "Didn't I mention that I'm certified to fly both fixed wing and helicopters?"

Alejandro shook his head. "No, it never came up."

"It's been years, but they say it's like riding a bicycle. I'll need an hour or two in the cockpit to familiarize myself with the layout."

Hector dropped his cigarette butt on the grass and ground it out with his shoe, ignoring Alejandro's frown of disapproval. "You're going to fly that thing?"

Jet shrugged. "It's not going to fly itself, is it?" She regarded Alejandro. "But it makes dealing with the airports all the more important, because I won't be going as fast as someone who knows the area well."

"I'm going with you," Alejandro announced.

Jet shook her head. "No, you need to stay and coordinate everything. And…if things don't go smoothly, you need to honor your commitment and get my daughter and husband back. Whatever it takes."

Alejandro shook his head. "I'm going."

Hector exhaled loudly. "Alejandro, much as I hate to admit it, she's right. You can't run interference *and* deal with any surprises in the air. And if this doesn't work, you'll need to take the helm of the organization in your father's absence. That won't be possible if you're captured or worse. This is how your father would want it. If you don't believe me, call him and talk to him yourself."

Alejandro stalked off, phone pressed to his ear. Hector watched him leave and turned to Jet. "I, on the other hand, will be right next to you the entire time."

She shrugged. "Suit yourself. Hope you can shoot better than you dress, because it may come down to that."

"I can more than carry my end of the log."

"Good. Bring a lot of ammo. And something with more punch than those 9mms. An AK if you can, with a boxcar of extra magazines."

"You read my mind."

"Can you get your hands on some night vision gear?"

"Should be able to."

Jet glanced at the helicopter and then back at Hector, whose eyes were as flat and dead as a pool of oil. For all his annoying qualities, she had no doubt that he could more than handle a gun.

"Then we may just have a chance after all."

~ ~ ~

The mountains northwest of San Felipe, Chile

Sweat ran down Matt's face in spite of the chill in the concrete bunker where they were being held next to the main building of the abandoned military outpost. Hannah sat in the corner of the improvised cell – a cinderblock storage room with a guard standing watch outside. Matt was working on the handcuff that secured his good hand to a metal pipe, his skin torn raw from his efforts, but no closer to success than when they'd been dumped in the room two hours earlier. Hannah had stopped crying and had retreated into herself. A soldier stopped by once to give them water, but besides that, they'd been ignored. The little girl had been quiet, not even complaining about having to use the bathroom as Matt twisted his wrist in frustration inside the metal cuff.

The door opened and two soldiers stepped in. The taller of the pair moved to Matt and pulled him to his feet while the other watched, his hand on his sidearm. Matt considered crushing the closest man's nose with his head and charging the other, but with his hand cuffed to the pipe, his odds of success were slim, and he didn't want to invite reprisals that might involve Hannah.

He'd overheard the reports to the colonel running the operation when they'd been transported to the outpost: Jet had vanished in the cave-in – dead, with a crew digging in the rubble for her and Alejandro's bodies. So now he was the little girl's only hope in the world, and he couldn't risk her safety with a foolish attempt destined for failure.

The soldiers unshackled him and led him to the main building, the shorter of the pair staying several prudent steps behind him should Matt try anything. Matt counted a dozen men near the vehicles and suspected that there were more on the periphery, which would make any attempt at a breakout suicide, even if by some miracle he could overcome his two escorts – not likely with a broken hand and no weapon.

The lead soldier opened the door to the main building and pushed him through. Matt found himself facing the colonel, Rodrigo, and a dark Chilean in jeans and a windbreaker. Next to him was a lean, tan man with a military haircut and a no-nonsense bearing – by far the most dangerous person in the room, Matt could instantly tell. The soldiers led Matt to a wooden chair and sat him down and then cuffed him to the arm.

"Well, well. I see you aren't only a coward, but also a turncoat. Nice," Matt said to Rodrigo. "Let me guess. You found an area with cell service up by the mine?"

"You're a bright one, aren't you? We'll see how insulting you feel after we're done with you," Rodrigo sneered.

The colonel stepped forward and slapped Matt with a backhand. Matt licked blood off his lip and said nothing. He was in the enviable position of not knowing anything, so there was nothing he could tell his tormentors that would be useful to them.

The man with the buzz cut approached him and studied his face before sitting down across from him.

"What is the expression? It's a fine kettle of fish you've gotten yourself into?" the man said in Russian-accented English.

Matt remained silent. What a Russian was doing in the Chilean mountains at a military outpost with a couple of gangsters and a high-ranking army officer was a mystery, but Matt's instinct was to say as little as possible.

The Russian turned to the Chilean. "Bastian, do you have any questions for our friend before I get started?"

Bastian nodded. "Where were you and the woman supposed to meet if you got out of the mine alive?"

Matt blinked. Meet? What was that all about? Unless…

"I have no idea what you're talking about," Matt said.

"Come, come. We know the woman escaped. Neither her nor Alejandro's bodies were found," the colonel said. "And one of our patrols came across two soldiers who were assaulted by them in the next valley. So we know they stole a Jeep and their uniforms. Let's not make this difficult. Where were you to meet if you were separated?"

Matt eyed the colonel. "We had no plan. How would I know that she would be trapped in a cave-in and escape? Although I have to say that's wonderful news."

"Yes, I understand the cave-in wasn't predictable, but let's try this another way. Where would you go if we let you free?"

That was an easy one, and Matt didn't have to invent an answer. "I…I have absolutely no idea. Probably back to the hotel."

Bastian cursed under his breath. "This is a waste of time. The hotel's crawling with police. He's not going to tell us anything. Or there's nothing to tell."

The Russian nodded. "Perhaps. But he knows a few things I'm interested in."

Matt stared him down, but felt a quiver of unease.

When the Russian spoke again, his voice was a purr. "Who is your young lady friend? What's her name and her background?"

"Her name? That's what you want to know? Naomi. Naomi Dove. As to her background, how the hell would I know? I just hooked up with her a couple of weeks ago. She's tripping around South America with her kid. She was lonely and I got lucky." Matt looked around, hoping they were buying it. "Or unlucky, it looks like now. What's all this about?"

Matt's only hope was to deny everything and play dumb. His story was non-disprovable, and Hannah was too young to be of any use. He'd assume the role of a single man on the prowl who'd met a woman in need and decided that he'd get more out of the deal than he invested. Completely believable and logical.

The Russian wasn't buying it. Not a word, Matt could see.

"She was involved in the gunfight at the hotel."

"If you say so. I don't know anything about that. I was in the room with the kid. She went out for a soda. Next thing I knew it was the Wild West, and then we were running for our lives."

Rodrigo shook his head. "They were acting like husband and wife on the trail. He's lying."

"Look, she's gorgeous and fun to hang out with. What do you want from me? I didn't ask to get shot at in some mine in the middle of frigging nowhere, and I sure as hell have no idea why you're so interested in some spacey chick I met in a bar."

Half an hour later, the soldiers dragged Matt back to the storage room, blood soaking the front of his shirt, his face bruised and cut from blows. Leonid watched him go and walked to one of the windows. Bastian stood and moved next to him.

"What do you think?" Bastian asked.

"Not a single thing he said was true. Not one."

"That was my impression. But how do we proceed, knowing that?"

Leonid glanced up at the sky, the afternoon's bright light fading as high overcast drifted from the west and dusk approached. A woodpecker flitted from tree to tree, bursts of color marking its flight as its bright plumage flashed in the dying sun. He turned to Bastian.

"We know she's alive and that we have her daughter. So we need her to know it, too. Think about it – what woman wouldn't do anything to save her child? If we make this the worst-kept secret in the world, she'll eventually hear about it, and then, trust me, she'll come to us. The trick will be being ready when she does. As you've seen by now, she's not an ordinary adversary." He paused, as if considering a riddle, his expression pensive. "But with enough firepower, even the most lethal predator can be stopped. We just need to get her in our sights, and I'll do the rest."

~ ~ ~

Igor and Fernanda sat at a sidewalk café on the downtown pedestrian boulevard in Mendoza, sipping espresso and nibbling croissants as Fernanda spoke on her cell phone with their agent.

"We're at a dead end," she said. "We've questioned everyone at the casino and spoken with the gentleman in the police department you suggested, but there's nothing on our target – she's vanished as though she never existed. I'd suggest that you circulate her photograph to anyone you can think of in this region. Maybe we'll get a hit. But right now there are no leads."

"That's disappointing. I'd hoped with you on the ground there…"

"We're all disappointed, but that's not going to get us any closer to finding her. Turn over some rocks. Put her face in front of every pimp, drug dealer, mugger and lowlife in South America. It's all we can do, unless you've got a rabbit you can pull out of your magic hat."

"Very well. Stay in Argentina until you hear from me. At worst you'll have a day or two of fine wine and gourmet food."

"While I appreciate the vacation tip, that's not going to get us paid, now, is it?"

"Leave your phone on. I'll call when I have something."

Fernanda hung up, placed the phone on the table, and watched as a group of high school students walked by, talking overly loudly, a few of the boys smoking, the girls with forbidden piercings adorning their young faces. A kit of pigeons paraded in lockstep across the cobblestones to where a pair of old women were throwing them chunks of stale bread while a lone saxophonist blew a haunting riff from a doorway, his case empty except for a few tarnished coins. She regarded Igor and sighed.

"I love Rio, but I could get used to this."

"You'd be bored inside of a week, my love."

"We could always fly back and whack someone for old time's sake whenever we got the urge."

He slid his hand across the table and took hers. "Always the romantic, aren't you?"

"That's why you married me."

"That and the sex."

She glanced at her watch. "Speaking of which, we have some time to kill. Race you back to the room?"

"That's my girl."

CHAPTER 29

San Felipe, Chile

The flight to Santiago from Mendoza had taken an hour to clear for the flight plan and another half hour for the actual flight. Unfortunately, Drago didn't have anyone available in Chilean immigration to walk him through, so he'd been forced to leave his weapons in a locker in Mendoza for later retrieval. Renting a car had been a pain, everything taking twice as long as it should have, and by the time he made it to San Felipe, twilight was bruising the sky with magenta and purple.

Drago drove to the hotel, but was taken aback when he saw what must have been the town's entire police force in front of it. He parked in the lot and made his way to the office, where a heavy-set woman stared at him from behind the reception desk like a vulture. A worker was replacing the glass in one of the windows, and Drago's practiced eye took in the bullet holes on the far side of the courtyard, each marked with a piece of blue painter's tape, presumably for ballistics.

"What happened here?" he asked, his tone friendly.

"Hotel's closed until day after tomorrow," the woman snapped, her patience obviously frayed.

"Oh. That's a shame. I need a room."

"Not here, you don't. There are technicians and police everywhere. Sorry."

Drago nodded sympathetically. "How about the restaurant? I could use a cup of coffee."

"I've got one girl working. She can do coffee, but no food."

"Sounds like a deal. Are those bullet holes?" Drago said, peering through the window at where the police were largely standing around, talking and smoking.

"Like I said, the hotel's closed. Yes, there was a shooting here. First and only time in thirty-seven years we've had any problems at all. A gang from out of town, they're saying. Bastards. I'll be lucky if I see any customers this season now, even though none of it has anything to do with the hotel."

"I'm sorry to hear it. If it's any consolation, I'll be back. But in the meantime, where would you recommend staying?"

She reluctantly gave him the name of another hotel. "They're okay. Not as nice as my place, but still, not terrible."

"Thanks. I appreciate it."

Drago entered the restaurant and sat by the window. A couple of pensioners were nursing their coffees at the next window, clearly entertained by the comings and goings of the police. Drago ordered a cup of coffee from the bored waitress and leaned over with a wave at the old men.

"Hell of a thing, isn't it?"

Both shook their heads and frowned. "It's a different world these days," the one facing Drago said. "No place is safe anymore."

"A crime. What happened?"

"Gangs. What else? Shot the place up. I heard there were a dozen of 'em killed. Slaughtered 'em like hogs."

"Really? Any idea what it was about?"

"Who knows? Drugs, money, power. Animals, all of them."

"Good Lord. Were there any survivors?"

"Not that I know of. Although I'm suspicious of all the army in the area today."

"Oh?"

"Haven't you noticed? There's some big deal happening in the hills. I keep my nose clean, you know, but you see things when you've got time on your hands. Hear things."

The other pensioner nodded at his friend's sage observations. "There was another shootout up there somewhere around a mine.

My nephew runs a market at the edge of town. He overheard the soldiers talking."

"I didn't realize San Felipe was so dangerous."

That got both old men started on the general moral decline of Chile in particular and young people in general. Drago listened politely, milking what more he could from them, and then excused himself from the discussion to place a call on his cell. When his agent answered he sounded out of breath.

"Yes?"

"I'm in Chile in a shit hole called San Felipe. Seems like something went down at the hotel the Argentine told me about. But that's ancient history. Do you have any contacts that could monitor the Chilean military and get me info on a shootout at a mine outside of town? I just heard about it, and I'm going to ask around, but I'm leery of attracting too much attention."

"You think that has anything to do with your man?"

"San Felipe is the kind of place where the locals sit around outside watching the snow melt for excitement. There was a gun battle at the hotel where his girlfriend was supposed to meet the Argentine's contact, and now another one at a mine close to town. What do you think?"

"I'll get right on it."

"Do that. You know my number."

Drago disconnected and engaged with the old men again, but that well had run dry. He chatted up the waitress but learned little new, other than that there had been about ten guests staying at the hotel when the gunfight had taken place the prior night, and all had cleared out before the police arrived.

"Can you imagine what that must have been like? Were any of the guests hurt?" Drago asked, pretending to be charmed by the young woman's rustic beauty.

"Not that I heard. And one of the policemen said that it was super weird because there were no bodies when they got here. Blood everywhere and the walls looking like a shooting gallery, but not one body. Creepy."

Drago didn't think so. The gangs had wanted to remove as much evidence as possible before the cops arrived. That they'd been able to told him the locals had been in on it. "Yeah. I can't believe you're even working today."

"Tell me about it. But what's funny is that with all the police, I've had a pretty good day so far. They tip okay."

Eventually Drago decided to drive up into the foothills and see if he could spot any of the rumored military presence. There was no telling when the agent would get back to him, and he was going stir-crazy, having gotten so close so quickly only to hit a wall. He stopped at the only market on the way out of town and chatted up the man behind the counter, but learned nothing he didn't already know, except that the clerk had heard the shootout had happened at least twenty-five kilometers up the main road.

Drago exited the little market and pointed the car north, hoping to at least get a glimpse of the army deployment before the agent called. It was either that or listen to another hour of oldsters lamenting the collapse of civilization, and he didn't think he could manage that without a few stiff drinks under his belt. He was just entering the curvy part of the mountain road when two army Jeeps passed him going in the opposite direction, three soldiers in each.

An auspicious sign, he thought to himself and slowed by another ten kilometers per hour. After thirty more minutes he reduced his speed to a crawl as he joined a column of cars in the near complete darkness that inched by a dirt road with an armored troop transport blocking it, a contingent of rifle-toting soldiers surrounding the vehicle. A faded sign announced the road as private property and that trespassers would be reported to the authorities by Epsilon Mines.

Drago passed a number of other tracks leading into the hills, but none with any armed presence. Near the top of the pass he spotted a compound far up the side of the mountain, its lights blazing, and when he rolled down his window, he could hear the steady far-off drone of a diesel generator. He recorded his position as a waypoint on his handheld GPS and turned around at the next road. When he checked his cell, he saw he had no signal and picked up his pace to get back to town.

As he neared San Felipe, his cell phone chirped at him, and he saw that he'd missed three calls, all from his agent. He hit redial, and the familiar voice answered on the second ring.

"I've been trying to reach you for an hour."

"I was indisposed."

"I got a report of some chatter on the military frequencies in the hills around San Felipe. A mention was made of two prisoners being held."

"Where did you get the report from?"

"A trusted source."

Drago smelled the CIA or NSA all over that, but didn't comment. There were few groups that could precisely target radio communications anywhere in the world, and he didn't want to question the man too closely.

The agent continued. "I have coordinates for the location of the only base in the area. Recent intel shows that it's now occupied after having been abandoned for years. I've forwarded you all the information I have."

"Good."

"Is there anything else?"

Drago thought for a moment. "Yes." He told his agent what he needed, and after a long pause the man responded with his usual deadpan tone.

"It could take a while."

"Be better if it didn't."

CHAPTER 30

Santiago, Chile

The guard's uniform seemed too large for his thin frame. His web belt with its baton, radio, and handcuffs hung loose as he circled the area that housed the prison's backup generators. He had a face like a hatchet, a sparse mustache, and looked younger than his thirty-seven years, though his shoulders were perennially hunched as if the burden of his age had broken him prematurely.

A corrugated metal roof extended over the generators, a large stainless steel diesel fuel tank positioned well away from the oversized motors. He'd been told exactly what to do, and it had sounded simple enough on the telephone, but now, with his fellow guards only meters above him in the watchtower, nothing seemed more difficult.

Fortunately, as he knew from his own experience on the wall, the guards would be looking inward, not out into the perimeter area where the equipment was housed. There was always the chance that one of them might see him, but he already had a story outlined that, if not ironclad, was plausible enough to buy him the time to get clear of the cursed prison, never to return.

Voices echoed from the nearby tower, and he froze. Laughter, an overly loud insult, more laughter. He flipped open the lock-blade knife he'd retrieved from his boot and approached the first generator. Even in the dim light he could make out the belt he was to cut.

It was harder than he'd thought it would be, tough, and he'd broken a sweat by the time he finished sawing the second one apart and moved to the third. Only that one final deed and his job would be done, his debt to the Sotos paid, with a substantial bonus to sweeten the deal. His downfall had been gambling, not drugs or women, but it had almost been his undoing and had resulted in his being a virtual indentured servant to the family, chartered with smuggling in contraband and weapons and phones. Now, with a few swipes of his knife, he was done with all that – or at least, would begin to get paid for his efforts rather than working off an ever-burgeoning debt, presuming he went unobserved and could return to his shift unsuspected.

The final belt fell from the pulleys. He stepped back, slipped the folding knife back into his boot, and returned to the main building. He'd excused himself from his duty on the tower earlier to use the bathroom, letting his companions have a good laugh over his discomfited expression and complaints over the quality of food served from the backs of pickups at the curb outside the prison gates.

~ ~ ~

A utility truck parked in front of the concrete-and-steel enclosure a block from San Miguel prison. A man in gray coveralls and an orange hard hat got out of the passenger side and carried an oversized tool kit to the structure's door. Two minutes after arriving, he'd jimmied the padlock and entered the dark space, a small work lamp on his hat lighting the way. The eight transformers were half the size of an economy car, and a hum vibrated the air as he placed the satchel charges beneath the connection points. After checking his watch, he switched on the detonators' digital timers and set them all for exactly fifty-seven minutes later – ten o'clock p.m. on the nose.

He patted each charge like a beloved pet. After looking around to ensure he hadn't missed anything, he returned to the door, which he bolted shut and padlocked again.

Nobody noticed the truck pull away on the darkened street, nor would they have been interested in a power company vehicle on its appointed rounds. The driver gave the passenger a high five as they rolled through the intersection, the lights of the prison receding behind them, and the passenger spoke into a two-way radio.

"We're locked and loaded. Repeat. Locked and loaded."

~ ~ ~

Lorenzo peered down the corridor to ensure he was unobserved, and then took the stairs to the roof two at a time. He opened the steel door, moved out onto the flat tarpaper surface, and hurried to the steel rungs leading to the tower. A breeze was blowing from the west, and he paused to watch a plane stop at the end of the runway before lurching forward, jet engines roaring as it reached takeoff speed and lifted into the night. Patches of white fog drifted over the surrounding fields, thickening into a white wall at the edge of the runway lights – not yet dense enough to interfere with the airport's operations, but an ominous portent.

Once the plane's blinking lights were out of view, he ascended a metal ladder to the platform above the radar arrays and shrugged off his backpack. He withdrew two compact charges and placed them on top of the junction boxes containing the heavy cables that led to the spinning arrays, and felt around in his bag again.

The radio-controlled detonators were tuned with a special handshake signal to prevent an errant frequency from setting them off. He finished arming the charges in less than a minute, and he smiled as he climbed down the ladder, his backpack now empty except for a sandwich and a newspaper – and the transmitters.

He'd just made ten thousand American dollars, which he was already mentally spending on a motorcycle he'd had his eye on and a proper set of kitchen appliances to keep his wife happy. All he had to do now was press two buttons at ten p.m. and the money was his, no strings attached.

It didn't trouble him in the least that his act would shut down Chile's international airport for at least a full day, stranding thousands and costing the airlines and government hundreds of thousands of dollars. The motorcycle was metallic red with an oversized rear tire and a powerful engine, and his domestic situation would improve for months because of his unexpectedly thoughtful household gifts.

The government and the airlines weren't looking out for his best interests, so he felt no reason to return the favor. He'd press the buttons at the appropriate time, dispose of the transmitters as instructed, and collect his pay with a clear conscience and an untroubled heart.

~ ~ ~

Alejandro stood by the helicopter as Jet did her final preflight checks, the big overhead rotors spinning slowly, the turbine roaring. Hector sat in one of the rear passenger seats with the window open, an AK-47 with a night vision scope next to him and a metal ammo container with ten thirty-round magazines at his feet. Jet adjusted the night vision goggles strapped to her head, verified the coordinates on the dash-mounted GPS, and gave Alejandro a thumbs-up.

"It'll take approximately ten minutes to get there. I'm going to be flying low and maintaining radio silence. Hector will call you on the cell when we're going in," she said.

"We'll be standing by." Alejandro glanced into the darkness at the edge of the clearing where a semi-rig was parked awaiting the helicopter's return, a group of men playing cards by the rear of the cargo bed. They would disassemble the rotor blades within minutes of the aircraft landing, and it would disappear into the truck, to be transported to a safe location where its original paint job could be returned to its factory luster.

She increased the revs. Alejandro waved and trotted away with his head down. Jet gave the powerful turbine more throttle and shifted the pedals as the rotors increased their speed. The surrounding grass blew horizontal from the downdraft, and then the helicopter was airborne, lifting into the night sky until the compound was just a postage stamp as she set a course for Santiago, its lights twinkling through the haze of fog that had materialized once darkness had fallen.

Hector checked and rechecked his rifle, cradling it like a newborn, and then hefted it and peered through the night scope at the landscape rushing beneath his feet. He'd jungle-taped the magazines end to end so he'd be able to change them faster, flipping spent ones over and seating new ones without having to reach for more in the heat of battle. Jet glanced back at him approvingly – he definitely knew his way around a gun. He adjusted his bulletproof vest and gave her a look that betrayed less confidence in her piloting abilities than she had in his firearm skills.

A portable police scanner sat in the copilot's seat, the volume up loud so she could hear it over the din of the engine and beating of the blades. She increased the helicopter's speed to a hundred twenty knots and checked her watch. A quick mental calculation told her that she'd be within range in seven minutes.

~ ~ ~

The riot began on the top floor of the southernmost tower as flames flickered out of the barred windows. Unlike the conflagration that had killed so many inmates in 2010, this one was purely for show, and all flammables had been removed from the area where the mattress burned.

Screams of alarm went up immediately, choreographed by the Soto lieutenants that operated the family's thriving prison drug distribution network. Anything could be had behind San Miguel's walls for a price, from a girl sneaked in by understanding gendarmes to a pistol to an inmate's favorite brand of alcohol. The Sotos had the most evolved infrastructure and the largest reach in the prison, and there were hundreds of inmates affiliated with the group, all of whom had been alerted that there would be a major disturbance starting at 9:55 p.m.

A few random gunshots echoed through the cavernous overcrowded cell blocks, mostly for effect, but a few in genuine retaliation for ill-considered insults or settlement of old scores. Prisoners pounded on the doors that sequestered them in the buildings, and after enough screams of "fire," the guards manning the building where Gaspar Soto was housed opened the gates so there wouldn't be a repeat of the prior blaze's devastating human toll.

Gaspar strode through the throng of prisoners surrounded by an entourage of his family's most dangerous enforcers, still wearing his tuxedo shirt and trousers from the prior night, dried blood staining the front. The crowd of inmates parted like a human sea before a tanker's bow, and Gaspar made his way to the edge of the building where he would be least visible from the guard towers, just in case a trigger-happy shooter on the last minutes of his shift decided to bag a trophy.

One of the henchmen, his shaved head revealing a web of scars from countless street fights, checked his watch and leaned in to Gaspar. "One minute."

Gaspar nodded and studied the chaotic scene before him – prisoners milling around, a few fake fights on the periphery to attract the guards' attention, a dead body of a hated rival passed overhead like a slam dancer at a rock concert. Inside the cell block, the windows of the top floor glowed as flame licked from the apertures. Unbeknownst to the guards, several Soto loyalists were waiting near the burning mattresses with water to douse them when the lights went out.

A cell phone warbled, and the shaven-headed bodyguard handed Gaspar the phone. Hector's voice had never sounded better.

"Get ready. It should happen any second. Stay on the phone."

"Okay." Gaspar could hear the thumping of helicopter blades on the line – the most welcome sound he could have imagined.

A series of muffled explosions greeted his ears, and the prison lights dimmed before flickering and going black. One of the bodyguards barked into his cell phone, and the fires on the upper floor darkened amidst clouds of smoke.

"It's done," Gaspar told Hector.

"We should be there in about two minutes or so. Get into position."

~ ~ ~

The air traffic controllers stared at their screens in horror. The worst nightmare of any airport was losing its radar. The monitors blinked at them, but the four aircraft that were on approach had disappeared.

"Shit. What happened?" the supervisor demanded, punching buttons and raising a radio to his lips.

A young man with longish hair looked up at him with a drawn expression. "All the feeds are dead."

"Do we still have the planes on the comm line?"

Another controller did a series of checks, his voice even, betraying no alarm, and then nodded. "Yes. We're still live with all four. One has fuel issues and needs to touch down within thirty minutes at the outside."

The supervisor wiped a limp hand across his face. "Find out what the hell happened. I want this fixed immediately. In the meantime, advise the inbound to assume a holding pattern with at least a thousand meters between them. If we aren't back online in ten minutes, divert all flights and bring in the one in fuel trouble using his radar. Obviously, all departing flights are canceled until we have our eyes back."

"Yes, sir."

~ ~ ~

Jet saw the entire area around the prison go dark when the helicopter was a minute out; she'd already slowed her speed in anticipation of the blackout. Hector was talking to Soto, and once the lights went off, she shut down her running lamps and brought the aircraft directly over the exercise yards. She flipped the night vision goggles down over her eyes, switched them on, and was relieved to see the yard light up in the screen's green glow.

"We'll be on the ground in twenty seconds. I'm going in hard, so hang on. Could be a nasty bump. It's been a while since I've flown one of these things."

"Now she tells me," Hector grumbled, his gun barrel hanging out the window.

Jet wasted no time in losing altitude. They dropped quickly and landed in the exercise yard with a bone-rattling jolt. Hector threw the door wide, gun at the ready, and Jet could make out the crowd of unruly prisoners – and a man she presumed to be Gaspar Soto rushing to the helicopter, his men shielding him from the towers.

Beams of light cut through the night from the guard posts, and in spite of the distance, the fuselage of the helicopter reflected their glow. Flashlights had always been a risk, which was one of the reasons they'd gone to the trouble of painting the bird to look like a police aircraft – a few seconds of hesitation as the guards tried to figure out whether the police had arrived to help with the riot could mean the difference between a safe escape and being shot out of the sky.

Hector reached out a hand to Gaspar and pulled him into the cabin. He slammed the door shut behind Soto, and Jet lifted off just as rifle shots thumped into the cabin housing. Hector opened fire at the tower where the muzzle blasts had lit up the night with their orange blossoms, and emptied half his magazine in a fully automatic burst. More shooting echoed from the tower. A few rounds struck the side of the helo, and then Jet was clawing out of range and banking away.

Hector turned to Gaspar, whose face was white with shock. He put the assault rifle aside and leaned forward.

"Where are you hit?" Hector yelled over the engine's roar.

"Bastards. We nearly got away clean," Gaspar snarled and moved a bloody hand from the side of his abdomen, just below his rib cage. A slug had punched through the cabin and caught him. Hector took a long look at the wound before sliding a nylon bag from beneath the seat. He peered into the sack and pulled out a field dressing.

"Lift your shirt," he said.

"Damn. Hurts like a bitch," Gaspar said, but complied.

Hector wiped away the worst of the blood and taped the dressing in place and then fished his phone from his pocket and placed a call. Alejandro answered on the first ring.

"Your dad's been shot. We'll need a doctor and probably an operating suite. Call Salazar and have him ready," Hector said.

"How bad is it?"

"Bad enough." Hector held the phone away and leaned toward Jet. "How long until we're back at the house?"

"Maybe eight minutes."

"Gaspar's hit. Abdomen. Make it five if possible."

Jet twisted in her seat and eyed the gangster, taking in his pallor and his blood-soaked shirt, and then returned her attention to piloting. She increased the speed to a hundred thirty knots and then pulled the night vision goggles off her head, dropped them next to the police scanner, and called over her shoulder, "I'll do my best."

Gaspar seemed to register her for the first time. "Who's she? Where's Adrian?" he demanded, asking about his pilot.

"Adrian wasn't available. This is Naomi. A friend of Alejandro's," Hector said and gave him an abridged version of the day's events.

"Why didn't you tell me any of this on the phone?"

"You know cells can be monitored. It wasn't worth the risk, and we didn't want to hand the bastards any evidence they could use against you."

Gaspar grunted and closed his eyes.

Hector's cell rang, and he answered it and then shouted to Jet, "Change of plans. Alejandro just got tipped that a police convoy's on its way to the estate. He says he'll meet you at the soccer field a kilometer and a half west of it. Can you divert and find it?"

"Ask him if he can bring three cars. Have them leave their headlights and emergency blinkers on so I can spot them," she answered.

Another hurried discussion and Hector was back.

"He's on his way. It'll be close. The prison breakout was the excuse they needed to raid the estate, and they're wasting no time."

"As long as everyone's gone by the time the cops show, it doesn't matter. Is there anything incriminating there?" Jet asked, more out of curiosity than anything.

"Of course not. I keep everything in my head. They'll get nothing," Gaspar rasped before sitting back with a wince.

"Relax. The hard part's over. We'll be on the ground in no time," Hector said.

"Maybe sooner than we'd hoped," Jet called from the pilot seat, her voice tight.

"What's that? What are you talking about?" Hector snapped.

"We're losing oil pressure. One of the bullets must have hit something."

"How bad is it?"

She squinted at the gauges and noted that the engine temperature was climbing.

"Just a matter of time until we're going down."

CHAPTER 31

Jet reduced the helicopter's speed in a bid to avoid having the turbine seize, and paged through the GPS settings until she found the overlay for the area around the estate. She zoomed out and scanned the vicinity and, after a few stressful moments, spotted the soccer field. She punched in a waypoint and returned to piloting, the police scanner suddenly bursting with transmissions.

One in particular caught her attention, and the blood drained from her face. She turned her head and called to Hector.

"They've mobilized a helo. It's in the air."

"It doesn't matter. Their radar's down."

She shook her head. "Maybe the airports are dead, but the helicopter might have an array. It won't be as powerful, but if they have a good suspicion of where to look, it could pick us up."

"That didn't come up in your planning, did it?"

"It was always a possibility. But there was no way to disable it, so I didn't see it as worth mentioning. We've got some time, but probably not much. I'm going to drop down so we're just above the buildings. Are there any high-rises I should know about within five kilometers of the estate?"

Hector thought about it. "I don't think so. But I wouldn't drop too low, just in case I'm wrong."

Jet focused on piloting the aircraft, one eye on the temperature gauge and the other on the city lights below. She tilted forward and slowly lost altitude until she was only sixty feet above the ground. Another glance at the GPS told her that the field would be somewhere on the right within another kilometer or two, and she watched the surroundings through the windshield, looking for the headlights.

Another burst of static from the scanner and a terse missive issued forth from a strained male voice. Jet listened, and her pulse began pounding in her ears. The police helo was headed toward the estate. It would be no more than five minutes behind them, maybe less, depending on how fast it was going.

She saw headlights and winking emergency blinkers in the center of a dark patch up ahead. That had to be it. She plotted a course for the field, noting that the fog was getting denser now that they were out of the city limits.

"Hang on. We're almost there," Jet said. The temperature gauge continued to climb as the oil pressure dropped, but she ignored it and concentrated on landing. She slowed to a crawl and then dropped gradually, watching the altimeter until the helicopter set down with a thump on the grass. Hector threw the door open as she reduced the revs to idle. She yelled at him over the din. "Get him out of here. The police bird's going to be on top of us any second."

Alejandro appeared at the door. He helped his father out of the aircraft and hugged him, ignoring the blood that smeared his shirt, and then Hector and two of his men were carrying him to a waiting SUV. Alejandro moved to Jet's door. "Let's go. Leave the damned thing here."

She studied the temperature gauge. "How far are we from the ocean?"

Alejandro gave her a puzzled look. "Why?"

"If I don't take off and lead the helo away from here, you're dead meat. Seconds count."

"Too far. Maybe eighty kilometers."

"Damn. Can you think of anywhere else I can ditch this?"

Alejandro's brow furrowed as he thought. "There's a river about ten kilometers due west of here. It's pretty secluded."

She shook her head. "They'll be able to recover it in a river."

"There's a lake twenty-five kilometers south."

"Same problem."

"What's the alternative?"

Jet paused. "You wouldn't happen to have any grenades in your car, would you?"

Alejandro turned and yelled at Hector's men. One of them ran to a black sedan, opened the trunk, and then sprinted to the helicopter, a bag in hand.

"Will a satchel charge do?" Alejandro asked.

"Even better. How do I detonate it?" she asked, taking it from him and setting it in the cabin.

"There's a digital timer in the pocket. We weren't sure how many we'd need for the transformers..."

"All right. Can you get someone to pick me up at the river?"

"Of course. Take the cell phone, and call when you're ready. I'll leave now and pick you up. But it'll take me at least fifteen or twenty minutes to get there."

"What about your father?"

"He's tough as shoe leather. There's nothing I can do while he's in surgery." Alejandro paused. "Are you sure you want to do this?"

"Might as well finish out the inning in style. Now get out of here."

Alejandro spun and sprinted for the vehicles. Jet juiced the throttle and lifted off, continuing to rise until she was sure that she'd appear on the chase helicopter's radar. If Alejandro was lucky, the police would think that she'd just dipped too low for them to differentiate from the surroundings, and would continue to follow her once she was back on their screen. She turned her radar on and veered west, praying that the oil pressure would hold sufficiently for her to make it another six minutes.

Jet leveled off at two hundred feet, not daring to go higher, and returned to the GPS, checking for an indication of where the river lay. She quickly found it – nine kilometers away – and saw there was a bridge that spanned it, but no other nearby roads that she could see further north along its course. She entered a waypoint and then shifted her attention to the radar screen's soft glow, spotting a blip moving fast from the northeast. Jet watched it for several moments and plotted the speed – it would be close. They'd be no more than two or so minutes behind her by the time she reached the river, if that.

The only answer was to push her speed. It was a tradeoff: the risk that the engine would seize and she'd have to land without power versus the risk of being gunned down by police snipers once she was on the ground. The temperature gauge climbed into the red as the helicopter accelerated through a hundred thirty knots, and she white-knuckled the joystick as the aircraft began to vibrate ominously.

Jet only needed the damned thing to hold together another two minutes, tops. Two lousy minutes at that clip and she'd be in the clear. She began gradually reducing her altitude as she neared the river – and realized that she hadn't breathed for the last half minute.

An alarm sounded, a klaxon wail, and she roared over the rooftops of a community near the river. She took a final glance at the GPS. She was only a half kilometer away and closing fast.

Jet reduced her speed, trying to eke out a little more life from the straining engine, and then the lights disappeared below her and she was facing a cottony bank of fog drifting over the water. She realized that she had no idea how wide the river was just as another red light began blinking on the instrument panel. Whether she liked it or not, she'd run out of time, and she slowed to a hover and descended the final hundred feet into the fog.

All the panel lights illuminated when the altimeter said she was thirty feet off the ground, and the rotor automatically disengaged from the transmission, spinning freely. Her drop accelerated, and she steeled herself for the crash she knew would follow, pulling as much collective as she could before the crash. When the bird hit the riverbed, the impact threw her forward against the harness. The helicopter bounced and then came to rest on its side.

Jet shook herself, checking to ensure that nothing was broken, and then hit the belt release while groping beneath her for the satchel charge. Her fingers found it along with the night vision goggles. She grabbed both and pulled herself to the pilot-side door.

Jammed.

She cursed and clambered into the rear passenger compartment and tried that door, which opened with a creak. Confident that she could now get clear, she opened the satchel and felt for the timer.

There.

She armed it, set the delay for sixty seconds, and pressed the red activation button. The green LED numbers began counting down, and she placed it in the front of the cockpit and pulled herself up and out of the helicopter into a ghostly riparian Neverland of thick fog.

The thump of rotor blades approached as she fumbled with the night vision headset and pulled it on. She activated it, but it was of little use – all she could see was gravel by her feet, with visibility no more than a few meters due to the dense fog. After a last quick look at the mangled helicopter, she bolted away, determined to put as much distance as she could between herself and the aircraft before it blew.

The police helo neared. She could feel the downdraft as she ran, her rubber soles slipping and sliding on the gravel bank. The blades seemed like they were only scant meters overhead, and then the satchel charge detonated, followed instantly by the fuel tank. The fog glowed orange from the fireball's flash, and she felt a concussive shockwave on her back as she poured on the speed, her breathing coming in ragged gasps as she ran with all her might.

Three minutes later, the shape of concrete pilings materialized out of the dense white haze. She'd reached the bridge. She slowed and retrieved the cell phone from her pocket and called Alejandro.

"I'm at the bridge."

"I'm still a few minutes away. I'll call you when I'm there. How did it go?"

She heard voices through the fog. "Can't talk. I've got company. I'll call when I'm clear," she whispered and then hung up, frozen in place, listening for a hint of pursuit.

The sound of water lapping at the bank greeted her from her left. Jet turned, head cocked. The fog made it difficult to make out where the voices were coming from, blunting any sense of distance or direction, while the police helicopter's thumping back by the wreckage masked any nearby noise. She slid the soldier's pistol from her jacket pocket, flipped the safety off, and then took cautious steps along the base of the bridge.

Another snatch of discussion floated up from down the river. She ducked under the overpass and worked her way to the opposite side, and after a pause, hurried up the bank to where the road curved into the foothills. Once on the shoulder, she called Alejandro again.

"Where are you?" she asked.

"Coming up on the bridge now. I can't see squat. Fog's too thick."

"I'm on the west side, just after the bridge."

"I'll pick you up in a minute. Watch for my lights."

She saw the glow of approaching headlights before she heard him. Alejandro's tires thumped across the bridge, and then he was pulling to the shoulder so she could get in. She swung the door open and slipped onto the passenger seat, still clutching her pistol.

"You probably don't need that. I promise I won't attack you," Alejandro said, his tone dry.

She put the gun back in her pocket. "Let's go. The police copter landed down the river. I blew our helo to bits, but I'd expect every cop within shouting distance to be on their way. I hope you know this area – we'd be well advised to stick to back roads."

"I've got something better." He tapped his navigation system to life, and she found herself looking at a roadmap of the area. As Alejandro swung around and recrossed the bridge, they saw the blue and red glow of emergency lights approaching in the fog.

"Shut off your lights and make a right up ahead," Jet warned.

He complied, twisting the wheel and pulling onto a smaller road.

She activated the night vision goggles again as he slowed. "Keep going straight. Looks like you'll curve to the left in about fifteen meters."

"Wouldn't it be easier if I had those instead of you?"

"Here." She handed him the headset.

He slowed to pull the headband on and then smiled. "That's better." He picked up his speed, and soon they were driving past rows of tiny identical homes. Several minutes later she checked the GPS.

"We should be in the clear. Can't see them getting roadblocks in place this quick, can you?"

"Never happen." He removed the goggles and turned on the car's headlights.

"What's the news about your father?"

"He should be in surgery by now. We have a doctor who handles these types of situations for our men. He's very good – probably has more experience with gunshot wounds by now than any doctor in Chile. We're headed there. Hector said that it looked ugly, but the doctor thought he could patch him up. Cross your fingers."

She sighed and shook her head. "What a night, huh?"

"You said it. By the way, thank you. We're all in your debt."

She eyed him, his face glowing faintly from the dashboard lights. "You'll get a chance to repay it soon enough. Now tell me what you've learned about my daughter."

CHAPTER 32

San Felipe, Chile

A dog barked somewhere down the gloomy street from where Drago had parked, likely prowling behind a warehouse fence in what passed for the industrial district of town. Drago darted from shadow to shadow on crepe soles. He carried a black backpack with some tools inside. The six-inch blade of a bread knife protruded from the top, gleaming in the dull moonlight that streamed between the gathering clouds.

A brick façade loomed on his right as he crept along. A weathered aluminum sign in front of it announced the headquarters of AARAM mine equipment and supplies, the lettering only slightly faded by the last winter's snow. Drago studied the iron fence on the left side of the building and the gate that spanned the width of the driveway that stretched to the loading docks at the rear of the long building.

He'd been watching the building for almost three hours and was satisfied that there was only a single security guard on duty, who emerged from a doorway at the back every forty-five minutes or so to have a cigarette and stretch his legs. The guard had last made an appearance a half hour earlier, and Drago checked the time before making a run for the gate and vaulting up its side. He cringed at the rattle as his body hit the metal, and then he pulled himself over the top, the obstruction child's play for a man of his talents.

Drago landed in a crouch on the pavement and edged to the nearest dock. His gaze roved over the roofline, looking for security cameras or motion detectors, but he didn't see any. Confident that the building's precautions were amateurish, he ran along the loading area until he arrived at the door the security guard used. A bucket half-filled with sand and several hundred stinking cigarette butts rested beside a folding metal chair. Drago flattened himself against the wall and waited for the guard's final appointment with his addiction.

Nine minutes later, the door groaned open on rusty hinges, and the guard stepped out, already raising a lit match to the cigarette in his mouth. Drago waited until the door had swung closed to make his move. The man must have sensed him at the last moment because he dropped the match, but too late – the blade's point sliced through his spine at the base of his skull, and he crumpled like a sack of wet dirt, dead by the time he hit the ground. Drago withdrew the knife and wiped it on the man's shirt, and then knelt beside him and removed his pistol – a Browning HP .40 caliber – as well as the spare clips in the man's belt compartment, and then dropped them into his backpack. He eyed the dead guard and considered dragging him inside, but then decided to leave him where he'd fallen, which was what an opportunistic thief would have done. After another glance around, Drago slid the guard's flashlight from his belt and entered the building.

The interior was black as pitch except for a small office near the front, where the faint melody of a radio song echoed from the metal ceiling. Drago snapped the flashlight on and shined the beam on the neatly stacked pallets in the center of the floor. He moved farther into the space. In one corner of the warehouse, the light reflected off stainless steel chain link that stretched to the ceiling – a security cage and the probable location of his objective.

The lock proved impossible to pick, but the chain link was no match for the bolt-cutters he'd brought. He snipped an access way through the fencing and stepped through, unconcerned with keeping his profile low – the workers would know soon enough what had been stolen, so there was no point in subterfuge.

Drago scanned the crates until he found several with "Tovex" stamped on them. All of the crates were stenciled with high explosive warnings, but he knew exactly what he was after. He removed the backpack and then pried one of the crates open and extracted several bundles, which he slipped inside the bag before continuing down the racks. Another crate held blasting caps, still another various ammonium nitrate-based explosives. When the backpack was bulging, he moved to a gray steel cabinet and opened it. There, on the second shelf from the top, were row after row of radio-transmitter-controlled detonators – a common item in metals mining, as were the explosives.

His backpack now stuffed to the brim, he returned to the gap in the cage and stepped through it, eager to be on his way. Drago's primitive research earlier that evening had proven illuminating. A half hour spent at an Internet café had enabled him to locate the military outpost on a satellite map, and he had a good feel for the topography now: a single gated dirt road led to its three buildings from the highway, a relatively sheer mountain facing skirted the far side, and a taller peak loomed over it to the south. If he was going to try to get into the compound, it would be from the adjacent summit – the cliff looked far too steep for him to tackle without an overwhelming reason, and the road would no doubt be fortified.

Once he'd seen the layout, he knew his instinct to use explosives had been correct. He was good – the best, he thought immodestly – but even so he wasn't about to take on a group of heavily armed combat soldiers with a frontal attack. No, what he had in mind was something different, and a strategy had taken form as he'd studied the photo. He'd use nature against the outpost, and if he did it right, there would be very little left of it by the time he was through.

When he returned to his car and drove out of the industrial park, his cell phone vibrated in his pocket.

"Yes?" he answered.

"Have you seen the news?" the agent asked.

"Uh, no, I've been busy. Why?"

"The local news just covered your story."

"What?"

"Yes. The official version is that terrorists were captured in a mine near San Felipe and are being held at the outpost you asked about."

"Terrorists?"

"Probably a catch-all term to give them the authority to arrest whoever they like." The agent hesitated. "Is that going to create a problem?"

Drago considered the question carefully. "I hope not. But it does make me wonder why they'd say anything about it at all."

"I got the sense that it was journalistic digging. Apparently the army presence is all that the locals have been talking about today. I'm guessing there were too many questions, and somebody felt compelled to issue a statement. Either that or a good old-fashioned leak."

"Any more chatter from your source?"

"More of the same. Two prisoners. That's it."

"I don't like surprises, and this is a big one. Now it's on the radar. If I didn't know better, I'd say it was a setup. Why would they broadcast their operation otherwise?"

"A setup? For what? Nobody knows you're after him."

"I don't know. It just feels wrong. Too weird."

"Look, you caught a break. Enjoy it. Although how you're going to get at him now beats me."

"That makes two of us."

When Drago hung up, his mind was working at warp speed. It had been a reasonable bet that his target was one of the two prisoners, but to have it on the news…something shifted in his guts, a stir of anxiety. There were forces at work he wasn't aware of, and that's how you got crushed if you weren't careful. That his target was at the outpost, or at least had been, was a safe bet. Whether he still was couldn't be verified until Drago saw it with his own eyes.

Of course, to do that meant taking on the Chilean military.

Then again, he'd had tougher assignments.

He patted the backpack on the seat beside him and smiled to himself. He had enough explosives to blow the outpost to Mars, and had managed to acquire a gun – an unexpected bonus. Naturally, he'd have preferred to have a couple of machine guns and a tank, but beggars couldn't be choosers. And for half a million bucks, he could make what he had work.

Upon reflection, Drago against an army battalion seemed like a massively uneven match. He pitied the parents of the soldiers who would die tonight.

It was always roughest on the survivors.

~ ~ ~

Fernanda's cell phone screeched from the night table, and she fumbled for it in the dark hotel room. She glanced at the bedside clock and sat up as Igor shifted beside her and pulled more covers onto his side of the bed.

"Yes?"

"We got a hit. In Chile. One of our intelligence agency sources confirmed it via a computer match on some police footage from last night. She was involved in a shoot-out at a hotel."

Fernanda was instantly wide awake. "A shoot-out?"

"Yes. It's all over the news. A hotel in the middle of nowhere was shot to pieces, and apparently our girl was caught on tape by a hidden camera used to ensure the employees weren't robbing the till. At least that's the report."

"Where is this hotel, and what else can you tell us?"

"San Felipe. Makes sense – it's on the way from Mendoza to Santiago. So if they drove…"

"They?"

"Yes. Apparently the footage has her, a man, and a child. It's hard to say for sure, but based on body language, it's possible the child is hers."

"Hit Mom? Are you serious?"

"I'm just telling you what I was told. I'm waiting for more information."

"What's the fastest way to get to San Felipe from here?"

"I had a feeling you'd ask."

CHAPTER 33

Santiago, Chile

Tendrils of fog crept like ghostly fingers between the wooden houses lining the residential street down which Alejandro turned. Jet had been silent for the last half of the trip. The revelation Alejandro had delivered about her daughter's whereabouts was more alarming than any news she could have gotten besides that she'd been hurt or killed. He'd pulled out all the stops with his military contacts, and one had verified that Colonel Campos from Valparaíso, a known ally of the Verdugos, had conducted an unsanctioned operation around San Felipe, ostensibly related to smuggling and possible terrorism in the port he oversaw, and that the upper command was looking into. The news broadcast had raised the stakes on getting to the bottom of it, Alejandro assured her. The last word was that Campos had taken over a base in the mountains and was holding prisoners there.

"Explain that to me. How can a rogue officer mount an offensive and take captives? Is that how this country is run? Where are the police in all this?" Jet fumed.

"Things aren't as simple as you might think. There are many factions in the military, constantly shifting allegiances, and this wouldn't be the first time that troops have been used for less than appropriate purposes. Much like in other countries, if the pretense of terrorism is used, virtually anything can be excused. At least for short bursts."

"But surely with your clout you can cut this Campos off at the knees? We both know the attack on the mine had nothing to do with smuggling or terrorism and everything to do with your enemies trying to gut you."

"Once my father is back at the helm, you can rest assured the action will be swift."

"That's fine and good, but does nothing for my daughter right now."

Alejandro pulled into the driveway of a stately home and honked twice, and two men with submachine guns pulled the wrought-iron gate open. He followed the drive along the side of the house until it widened in the rear, where six vehicles were gathered, mostly big SUVs. Lights seeped from beneath the curtained windows of a guesthouse where a small crowd of armed men gathered, smoking and talking. Jet recognized Hector in the group as she stepped from Alejandro's vehicle and approached him.

"How is he?"

"Not bad, all things considered. I have to admit I'm impressed, young lady. That was a hell of a stunt you pulled. Never seen anything like it."

"Well, the good news is it worked, and he's free."

"Yes, although he's not out of the woods yet."

Alejandro joined her. "Can we go in?"

"The doc's still cutting," Hector said. "The wound was worse than I originally thought. But your father's made of stern stuff, Alejandro. He'll pull through."

"I want to see him," Alejandro said.

Hector frowned. "Maybe you should wait out here with the rest of us. Right now the important thing is for the doctor to be able to concentrate. I'm not sure barging in during surgery's the best idea, no disrespect intended."

Alejandro began pacing. Jet moved to his side. "Another few minutes won't make a difference."

"Assuming it's only a few minutes."

Jet nodded. "I can understand your impatience. And not to change the subject, but I've done everything I said I would – I got your father out of prison, led the cops on a chase so he could get clear, destroyed the helicopter so you had deniability – all of which involved me risking my life over and over. And now I need you to focus on my problem. There's nothing we can do for your father right now, but there's a lot you can do for me."

Alejandro stopped walking and took in her determined expression. "You're right. I've been so wrapped up in getting my father out…"

Jet cut him off. "He's out. And it sounds like everything that can be done is being done."

Alejandro nodded. "Let's go into the main house. I'm sure the doctor won't mind us having a seat while he works." He turned to Hector. "You should probably come along."

They climbed the stairs to the back door and found themselves in the kitchen. Hector led them into the dining room, and then they sat at the circular table. Alejandro flipped open a tablet, tapped the screen several times, and then handed it to Jet. On it was a satellite image of the mountains northwest of San Felipe.

"The area I've zoomed in on is the base. You can see that there's only one road leading to it."

Jet studied the image and enlarged it, poring over the surrounding landscape with a seasoned eye. Alejandro and Hector watched her in silence, not wanting to break her concentration. When she looked up, her expression was pinched and her stare hard.

"That hillside looks extremely steep. Almost impassable. You can see from the altitude readings – it's almost two hundred meters of sheer drop," she said.

Alejandro nodded. "I know. I already looked at it."

She continued studying the image for several moments. "Which is why that's where they'd least expect an approach. Anyone in their right mind would come up the road or drop in by parachute or helicopter. I suppose it's silly to ask whether you have access to paratroopers?"

Hector shook his head once. "There are limits to even what we can do."

"That's what I figured. And they'd hear a helicopter from a long way away. Assuming the airspace in the entire region isn't locked down about now, which I'd expect after our escapade."

"So there's no way in. That's why I'm counseling waiting for progress through official channels."

Jet eyed him grimly. "You didn't take that approach when it was your father in prison, though, did you? Official channels didn't do much for him, did they?"

Alejandro didn't have a rejoinder to that. Hector took a cigarette out of his crumpled package but returned it to the pack when he caught Jet's glare.

"Gentlemen, my daughter and my husband are in that camp. We have no idea what's being done to them, but my little girl is two and a half years old, and I'm not going to let her spend one more minute in the hands of your enemies than I have to. Which means, with all due respect, that waiting for something to shake loose on your end isn't an option. We need to go in hard, be smart about it, and rescue them. Tonight. Or I should say, this morning. While they least expect it."

Alejandro and Hector exchanged a glance.

"We obviously can't just go in shooting," Alejandro said. "We need a plan that's feasible. Otherwise it's suicide."

Jet nodded. "Of course. But if you haven't noticed by now, I've got some experience at this. Give me a little time to think." She frowned at Hector. "Go have your cigarette. Just leave me alone for a while."

Hector stood. Alejandro pushed back his chair and accompanied the older man to the rear door and exchanged a few words before he returned. Jet ignored him as she fiddled with the image, rotating it, zooming in and out. Alejandro disappeared into the living room and reappeared a few moments later with a bottle of expensive Scotch and two glasses.

"Drink?" he offered.

"No. I want to be sharp." She gave him a flat look. "You could learn from that."

Color flushed his face, but he didn't say anything. He went back to the other room and reappeared with a bottle of Coke. "Is this better?"

"The caffeine and sugar might help," she conceded as he poured some into the two glasses and went in search of some ice.

She was sitting back, staring at the tablet, when he returned with an ice tray. "What?" he asked.

"You're not going to like it. We're going to have to go up the side of the cliff there," she said, tapping the image.

"Are you insane?" He tempered his remark. "I mean, you really believe that can be done?"

She smiled for the first time since he'd picked her up on the bridge. "You have to ask that after what I just pulled off?"

"Perhaps a poor choice of words," he agreed.

"Anything can be done if you have the motivation and the skill. You mentioned that you have ex-commandos in your group?"

"Yes. We hire only the best."

"I need three men with good climbing skills who are highly competent with weapons."

"I can arrange that."

"We'll need climbing gear – rappelling rope, pitons, carabiners, the works. And compact assault rifles with night scopes, noise and flash suppressors…and grenades. Oh, and transmission-jamming gear."

Alejandro didn't blink. "Why only four of you?"

"Any more and we increase the risk of detection. And frankly, if we can't do this with four, we won't be able to do it with ten." She thought for a moment. "On the rifles, we'll want fully automatic weapons."

"Of course."

"Preferably with high accuracy. That rules out burp guns. Figure we'll want weapons that are good for at least four hundred yards."

"No tracers?"

She cocked an eyebrow. "Can you get some?"

"I'm kidding. Although yes, I probably could. We have access to everything that gets lost on bases all over Chile. You'd be surprised how much goes missing."

"We don't need tracers. Although a few RPGs might come in handy, as well as some smoke grenades, too."

"Should I be making a list?"

"How soon can you have it ready?"

"I'll ask Hector. My guess is a couple of hours. Somebody is going to have to round it all up from the safe houses we use as armories."

She checked the time. "That would be, what, around one thirty a.m.?"

"Something like that."

"What about the men?"

"Hector will select them. He knows everyone in my father's organization. I'll make it clear we want the very best."

"Good. We'll want to roll out of here no later than two, and that will put us up there by, what…three thirty or four?"

"That sounds right. But you haven't told me what the plan is."

She pointed at the base of the cliff. "See that path? It's faint, but it looks to me like a game trail. Maybe more goats. The nearest intersecting road is this one." She zoomed out and tapped a finger against the screen. "That ground could be covered in fifteen minutes. My thinking is that we go in by foot, scale the cliff, and then kill anything that moves."

His expression didn't change. "Not really a cliff, is it? More like a series of steep slopes."

"Close enough. It's not going to be easy to climb, if that's what you're thinking."

It was his turn to smile. "I've done worse."

She appraised him. "How much of that whiskey did you drink?"

He toasted her with his cola. "None. You were right. I need my wits about me. What you don't know is that in my misspent youth I was an avid climber. I'd climbed half the Andes by the time I was out of school. And that's nothing by the looks of it." He considered the image again. "Maybe not nothing, but it's certainly achievable. Look, up by the top it's a gradual drop, then there are those trees, and then a steeper drop. It's just a matter of which area we decide to climb."

She took a long sip of her drink and set the glass down carefully. "We?"

"You don't think that after everything you've done tonight I'd let you do this on your own, do you?"

"But your father—"

"Assuming he pulls through, which we should know for sure soon enough, there's no reason I can't spare the rest of my night to go on an outing with you. After the mine, this will be like a vacation."

"I wouldn't quite say that."

He slapped his hand down on the table. "Then it's decided. Rifles, subsonic ammo, smoke and regular grenades, RPGs…anything else?"

"Pistols and night vision goggles."

"Ah, right."

He stood. "I'll go make our requirements known. Hector's too old for this, but I have a feeling I'm going to have to have him tied up to stop him from coming."

Jet's voice grew quiet. "Alejandro, what about your brother?"

"I'll let my father deal with that. Thank God I don't have to. I'll give him all the information and let him make the call."

She watched him exit the rear door and walk down the steps. It would be risky, there was no doubt, but in her operational days she'd done far more difficult. Then again, she'd also been considerably younger and hyper-fit, her training ongoing and as demanding as any in the world.

But this time it was Matt and her daughter she was fighting for, not some anonymous target or nameless objective.

Which made all the difference in the world.

CHAPTER 34

Mountains northwest of San Felipe, Chile

"How can you be sure she'll come?" Bastian asked Leonid, who was sitting at a rough-hewn wooden table inside the main outpost building, cleaning the Kalashnikov rifle Bastian had provided.

Leonid cleared his throat. "Oh, she'll come. She won't let anything stop her. We have her daughter and her man."

"But she doesn't know that. Not for sure. Even the news bit we planted didn't specify exactly who had been captured."

Leonid looked down the rifle barrel with approval and set it down on the table. "She'll read between the lines. There aren't that many possibilities. I don't think it's likely that she'll ignore it. There was a reason I wanted their capture to be broadcast far and wide." He shook his head. "She'll come for them. The only question is when."

"At least we'll have plenty of warning. Did your men deploy the motion detectors?"

"Of course. But it would be best to get the soldiers out of here and let my group handle this. We're specialists, and I don't need distractions."

Taking his cue from the Russian, Colonel Campos finished placing a sheaf of documents in his satchel and turned to face them. "Gentlemen, now that my part in this is done, I'll be on my way. I've already spoken with Franco. I need to get my troops back to the port and deal with the fallout from this little escapade. I hope it was worth it. Three men wounded – which, of course, can be swept under the rug with the right financial incentives – but still, difficult to explain away."

206

"Thank you, Colonel. I'm sure the Verdugos will be very appreciative," Bastian said.

"They'd better be. My neck's out a lot farther than I'd bargained for."

Rodrigo stubbed out the cigarette he'd been smoking. "I'm getting out of here, too. I've got no dog in this fight, and I'm thirsty. Colonel, could I trouble you for a lift?"

Campos appeared uncomfortable and looked to Bastian, who shrugged. Campos nodded. "Certainly. But I'm headed to Valparaíso."

Rodrigo smiled grimly. "I have unfinished business with Franco, so that would be perfect. I'll find somewhere to hole up and see him in the morning."

Bastian cleared his throat. "Valparaíso has some intriguing nightspots that might be able to accommodate you. I'm sure the colonel is familiar with some of the more diverting and can point you in the right direction." Bastian approached Rodrigo and shook his hand. "We're all on the same team now. I'm sure I'll be seeing a lot more of you."

"Let's hope so. The news of my father's breakout was more than a little troubling."

"Yes, and again, my condolences. Apparently there was little left of the helicopter after the crash. A sad day."

Rodrigo shrugged. "He should have stayed in prison. But let's not forget that Alejandro is still out there somewhere."

Bastian sighed. "Antonio is attending to that personally. With your father out of the picture, the organization will be in disarray."

"Yes, and many of my men are loyal only to me. Once the smoke clears, I'll announce that I've negotiated a merger with your group, and everyone will be happy to see the long feud finally over. The combined entity will be much stronger than two battling families. It's for the best."

"A visionary realization," Bastian agreed.

Rodrigo's eyes narrowed. He didn't like the Verdugo lieutenant much, and couldn't decide whether he was subtly mocking him.

"Come, young man," Campos said, checking his watch. "It will be a long drive over the mountains to Valparaíso."

Rodrigo ignored the Russian – his dealings with Bastian were none of his concern. He was just glad to be rid of them all. All he could think of was his increased power now that he would run the organization, with his father and brother out of the way. A historical juncture, to be sure, and one deserving of being celebrated properly, starting with several tall whiskies, a taste of cocaine to compensate for the fatigue and a nubile young thing who could relieve the tension that had been accumulating all day as he'd been virtually trapped in the primitive outpost.

The collected Jeeps and personnel carriers roared to life and filed slowly down the dirt road to the highway, leaving a cloud of dust in their wake. The wounded had been airlifted out earlier which, combined with a series of hard questions from Campos's command office, had decided his withdrawal. His story – that he'd pursued a group of smugglers – was as flimsy as any, but as long as he stuck to it he was sure he'd be able to bluster through. Franco and he had discussed it that evening by phone, and the gangster had agreed to contribute generously to making the entire episode go away.

Bastian watched their taillights through the window and then returned his gaze to the Russian.

"You feel like your six men will be sufficient?" Bastian asked.

"More than sufficient. Just keep yours out of our way and we'll be good," Leonid warned.

"As you wish." Bastian had ten gunmen at the outpost, so he wasn't intimidated by Leonid. He wanted to get paid, and he wasn't about to allow the man to eliminate the girl and then disappear, which was the primary reason for his show of force. He'd have been just as happy to have been rid of the camp, but Antonio's instructions had been clear: keep his eye on the Russian, play along, but don't let him out of sight.

More troubling was that so far Alejandro hadn't surfaced. While Antonio had sounded confident, if not delighted, at the elder Soto's untimely demise while making his ill-advised escape, Bastian wasn't so sure. From all accounts Alejandro was almost as dangerous as his father – nothing like the vain show horse Rodrigo. And having an adversary like that unaccounted for was troubling, even if Antonio was convinced that he'd be eliminated within a matter of hours.

His men had returned that afternoon with the equipment the Russian had requested – weapons, motion detectors, grenades. Bastian had been impressed with the Russians' demeanors, their quiet competence and the methodical way they'd gone about laying their trap. A part of him thought the ambush overkill, but all he had to do was consider the pile of dead men the girl had left for him to clean up at the hotel to rethink that position. If hardened men like the Russians thought the situation serious, he wouldn't allow his prejudices to color his actions, and he'd warned his men to be on the alert.

Two of the Russians had been deployed to watch the road, accompanied by two of Bastian's in an uneasy alliance, and the remaining three were outside waiting patiently for the assault Leonid was sure was coming. How one girl could think she'd overwhelm an army outpost was beyond Bastian's ability to grasp, but it wasn't his fight. He was there to ensure they got paid, nothing more; his job was to watch the watchers.

Bastian glanced at Leonid, who was now inspecting the night vision scope on the AK-47, and shook his head. Overkill, he thought again, but if it made the man happy, it was none of his concern. Antonio would charge him top dollar for the specialized equipment, no doubt tacking on an additional ten percent to the already large fee.

This all assumed that the Russian was correct and the girl was bent on committing suicide.

CHAPTER 35

Santiago, Chile

The doctor was a smallish man with sparse gray hair and thick glasses, his pot belly bulging under his surgical smock. Alejandro, Hector, and Jet entered the guesthouse, which turned out to contain a fully equipped surgical suite and recovery room complete with vital signs monitors, air purification system, anesthesia machine, autoclave for sterilization and a full array of surgical equipment that would have been the envy of most mid-sized hospitals.

"How is he?" Alejandro asked as he looked over at his father, who was lying with his eyes shut in a newish hospital bed.

"He'll be fine. The damned bullet tore some of his intestines up when it fragmented, but I patched him up. In a week he'll be good as new," the doctor said, slipping off the smock and handing it to an assistant likewise garbed in scrubs.

"When will he be able to talk?"

"The anesthesia should wear off within another half hour. I'll have him on morphine and antibiotics for the next couple of days, but beyond that, just no pole vaulting or wrestling till he's healed."

"Can we move him?" Hector asked.

"I'd rather you wait for at least twenty-four hours, so I can ensure there are no complications. I won't take responsibility for him if he's moved sooner."

"Voids the warranty?" Alejandro said, smiling.

"Exactly. It's all in the fine print, young man."

Another physician's assistant moved to Gaspar's side and hooked up an IV. The doctor glanced back at him and gestured to the door as he felt in his shirt pocket for a pack of cigarettes. The irony of a doctor smoking wasn't lost on Jet, but it seemed that, like the Argentines, most of the men here smoked, so she didn't comment.

Outside he and Hector lit up. Alejandro waved away the offer of a smoke, and the doctor continued. "He was actually lucky. The slug glanced off a rib. If it had gone the other direction, his liver or, worse yet, his lung would have been involved."

"That's a positive, I suppose. But if he was really lucky, the shot would have missed entirely," Hector observed.

The doctor offered a wan smile. "Still. He lost a fair amount of blood, but he's stable now. I really think he'll fully recover."

"There are a number of important decisions he'll need to make pretty soon. Do you think he'll be up for it?" Alejandro asked.

"You'll have to be the judge of that. I just stop the bleeding." He took another drag on his cigarette and blew smoke at the overcast night sky. "Seriously, though, he might be a little out of it from the anesthesia and the morphine, but there was nothing wrong with his cognitive function I could see. He was swearing like a sailor when they brought him in and had a few well-chosen words for me. Something about cutting my manhood off and forcing me to eat it if I didn't do a good job." The doctor shrugged. "That's one way to discourage malpractice. Very effective."

"My father can be quite the kidder, as you know," Alejandro said.

"Yes, he's a regular comedian," the doctor acceded, suddenly less interested in the discussion.

Jet and Alejandro moved away, leaving Hector and the doctor to discuss the price of morphine in China. Alejandro seemed concerned, but Jet had no words of comfort to offer him. His father would either make it or not.

"Sounds like you're going to be running things for a while," she said.

"I don't have a problem with that. I'm going to call a summit of all the lieutenants tomorrow and map out a response to the Verdugos. Obviously this is full-scale war, and I see no reason to pull any punches. I didn't ask for it, but I'll sure as hell finish it."

"And your brother?"

"That's one of the calls my father will have to make. I want no part of it. But I do think he needs to be given a chance to explain."

"Like you were given in the mine?"

"We don't know he isn't one of the captives. It's entirely possible he is."

"Sure it is. But how did the shooters know we were at the mine?"

"Maybe a tracking device in his clothes or his wallet? I don't know. I just know I'm not going to have him…dealt with…without a chance to clear himself. But in the end, it will be my father, not me. He built this business from the ground up."

Jet frowned. "Not exactly something fun to wake up to, is it?"

"Not a lot about this business is fun."

She decided to change the subject. "Any luck on the list?"

Alejandro nodded. "We're getting it all. Hector has sent for the two men he feels are best equipped for this. Both were in the Chilean army's Lautaro Special Operations Brigade before joining our organization, so they've received the best training available. He has complete confidence in them."

"Do you know them personally?"

"I've met them. They look like what you'd expect. Seasoned. No-nonsense."

"Good. Will they have any problem taking direction from a woman?"

"That won't be an issue."

Thirty minutes later Alejandro entered the guesthouse and, after spending ten minutes with his father, emerged and waved Jet down. "He wants to see you."

"Me? What for?"

"Let's find out."

Jet accompanied him to the elder Soto's bedside. Gaspar looked pale but alert.

"My son told me about all you've done. It appears we owe you a considerable debt."

Jet didn't say anything.

Gaspar studied her, his gaze lingering on her bottle-green eyes. "He also tells me that you're not done yet."

"They've got my daughter. She's two and a half years old. What would you do?"

Gaspar nodded. "I'd scorch the earth to get her back and crush whoever had taken her."

"That's a good description of my plan."

"Alejandro insists on going with you."

"It's his choice. I'd just as soon he didn't. Maybe you can talk him out of it."

Alejandro rolled his eyes.

Gaspar shook his head. "He feels that going is important. I don't have the strength to argue with him." Gaspar coughed and flinched, his color graying. "He also tells me you met Rodrigo."

"Yes."

"Give me your impression."

"I wasn't around him much."

"You feel that he is behind the attack on the mine?"

"It's the only logical explanation. He was at all three attack points and refused to join us inside the mine for no reason. There was nowhere to hide outside." Jet shrugged. "But there are ways to know for sure."

"Such as?"

"Whenever you find him, check his cell phone for calls. I'd bet money you'll find some to the Verdugos."

"And if there are none?"

"Then I'm overly suspicious. Just one of my many character defects."

Gaspar grimaced and looked to Alejandro. "Put out the word that whenever Rodrigo surfaces, I'm to be contacted immediately. No action is to be taken. I'll deal with it."

Alejandro nodded.

"And now, if you don't mind, this old man needs his rest. Good luck with your daughter. My experience has been that coming between a mama bear and her cub is a risky proposition. Based on your performance tonight, I almost feel a little sorry for the men who took her."

Jet's expression was blank, but her jade eyes flashed dangerously. "I don't."

CHAPTER 36

The fog that hung over the Santiago valley dissipated as Jet, Alejandro, and the two Soto gunmen drove into the foothills from San Felipe. Xavier and Simon were around Jet's age and not particularly gregarious, preferring to sit in silence on the trip north. They were both dressed head to toe in black, as was Alejandro. He'd done his best for Jet and gotten her a black long-sleeved shirt and combat jacket, which would easily fit over the ceramic-plated bulletproof vests that lay in the back of the SUV next to the cache of weapons.

Jet had explained the approach they'd take as the driver, who they'd agreed would remain with the vehicle, concentrated on the road. When she finished, she passed Alejandro's tablet to the men so they could study the terrain. Both had substantial climbing experience as part of their training, and as they asked short, on-point questions, her confidence in their chances improved.

The Soto watcher Alejandro had arranged for, who was monitoring the access road, had called earlier to alert them that the soldiers seemed to have largely vacated the base. Alejandro had placed a flurry of calls to his army contacts and gotten word back that no prisoners were being transported back to Valparaíso, so it was likely that the offensive on the mine was deemed over and the personnel were being redeployed, except for a guard contingent at the base, which the watcher said was still well lit and obviously occupied.

"This Colonel Campos caved to the pressure my contacts brought and pulled most of his men out. Hopefully that will mean far fewer soldiers and improve our odds," he'd said.

Jet hadn't been as sure, but didn't voice her reservations. They wouldn't know how stiff the resistance they'd be facing would be until they were in the heat of it, but she wasn't inclined to assume anything but the worst – which so far had been the appropriate philosophy since hitting the Chilean border.

They made good time, and it wasn't quite four a.m. when they rolled onto the gravel track that led into the hills, terminating near the trail that meandered to the base of the slope. Jet rolled down the window and let the mountain breeze caress her face, carrying with it the smell of grass and moist dirt, a welcome break after Santiago's exhaust and asphalt. The driver ran out of road several minutes later and shut off the engine, and they piled out of the vehicle and moved to the rear to get their gear. Each would carry an American-manufactured M4 carbine with M68 CCO laser scope, which was designed to work with night vision goggles like those Alejandro had sourced. He handed out six thirty-round box magazines to each of them, which they fitted into their jackets and pants, and the now-familiar FN-750 pistols with three extra magazines of 9mm ammo. Four fragmentation grenades apiece, one RPG each for Xavier and Simon, and a satchel of smoke grenades completed their equipment, along with four bundles of climbing gear.

Jet gave them a hushed last-minute summary, reiterated that her orders were to be followed to the letter, and then moved out, her stride fluid as she led them along the game trail, night vision goggles illuminating the dark with a neon glow.

~ ~ ~

Drago climbed the final fifteen meters to the top of the peak adjacent to the outpost and stared down at it. He was surprised to see no military vehicles – only five SUVs arranged in a semicircle in front of the main building, which was lit up like a Christmas tree. He gazed down the twist of road and spotted the guards halfway to the bottom, no larger than ants from his vantage point, and then shifted his attention back to the center structure. A group of men in civilian clothes loitered around the front entrance, smoking and talking, their weapons hanging from shoulder straps or leaning against walls.

He didn't spend time dwelling on why there were no soldiers. It was immaterial to him. Perhaps the Chilean intelligence service had taken over the duty. What mattered was that his target was somewhere inside.

He glanced around at the hillside, which was mostly rock with occasional scrub that had managed a toehold on the inhospitable slope. Perfect for his purposes. He'd been unsure that his plan would work until he'd arrived and seen the terrain, but it more than surpassed his expectations. There were plentiful boulders and evidence of prior rockslides. With a little help from his explosive friends, he could arrange for half the mountain to tumble down onto the camp, and in the ensuing chaos pick off any of the defenders who weren't crushed in the avalanche.

Drago slipped the backpack off his shoulders and went to work, carefully placing the explosives into three piles as he surveyed the rocks for the most likely candidates to start the landslide. It took him ten minutes to get all the charges situated, and he was catching his breath and calculating how to move to a safe position on the hill from where he could be in the camp moments after the rocks hit when the door of the main building flew open, and four men carrying assault rifles burst through the entry and made for the cliff on the far side of the camp.

He wasn't sure what was happening, but whatever it was wouldn't alter his strategy. What was important to his plan was that the camp's occupants had no idea he was there, enabling him to find a safe spot and then rain destruction down upon them like the wrath of a Biblical God.

~ ~ ~

Leonid stiffened at the sound of a low beep from one of the motion alarms he'd set up – six different receivers for the six different zones of the cliff slope. It was the far one, which corresponded to the detector on the steepest section. His men were already on their feet gathering their weapons as he stood and moved to the little box. He shut it off, its purpose served, and waited several moments to confirm that none of the others had been tripped. When he was satisfied that it was only the far sector he needed to be concerned with, he turned to his men. "You know what to do. She's going to try to scale the cliff. Smart. It's the least appealing, so likely to be unguarded."

"We'll wait until she's halfway up and pick her off. Almost too easy."

"Don't underestimate her. Nothing is likely to be easy." He nodded and adjusted the holstered pistol on his belt. "All right. Let's go. Absolute silence from here on. Watch for my hand signals."

Leonid led them out the door. Bastian's idiots were gathered in plain view, making enough noise to wake the dead. Leonid trotted past them, and when Bastian approached him, Leonid shook his head. Bastian nodded – it was going to be showtime soon, and he was to stay out of it, as agreed. Fine by him. Let the Russians take all the risk. They seemed adamant about doing so, and after all, the customer was always right…

~ ~ ~

At the bottom of the wash, Jet paused and looked up the slope. The satellite imagery had been deceptive – this section was steeper than it had looked, whereas the area to their left was easily scalable, probably with a minimum of trouble. She turned to Alejandro, who was behind her, and pointed forty meters away at where the cliff became a series of rises strewn with boulders and trees for cover.

"The terrain's different than I thought," she said in a low voice. "But that area seems like a better bet. I didn't see anyone guarding the perimeter, so there's no reason to take the hard route unless you want to practice your climbing skills."

"I'd say I've had enough adventure over the last day to last me a lifetime. How do you want to do this?"

"You and the boys follow me. Once we're on that section, let's spread out so if anyone spots us, we're not easy targets." She waved Xavier and Simon over. "Alejandro and I will go up the middle. You flank us. We're going to go up that part instead." She nodded toward the series of tiers on the slope.

They moved left, skirting the base of the hill, picking their way through the rocks and trees as silently as the goats that called the inhospitable mountains home.

~ ~ ~

A second motion detector alarm sounded inside the outpost's main building, beeping softly at the uncaring walls, but there was nobody left inside to hear. Leonid and his men had departed, and Bastian stood out front smoking with his men.

~ ~ ~

Jet was halfway up the slope, taking a break behind a rock outcropping, when she heard something above her position. She glanced over at Alejandro, five meters away, and held her finger to her lips. The others were too far from her to warn – she could see Xavier on her right scrambling higher and Simon a little further down on her left.

She peered up at the top of the ridge and froze when she saw the outline of two men silhouetted against the cloudy night sky, weapons pointed down the cliff that she'd originally planned as their ascension point. They hadn't spotted her, but with Xavier moving, it was just a matter of time.

Another man appeared next to the two she'd seen. She motioned to Alejandro and then brought her M4 rifle around and sighted on the closer of the two. The distinctive shape of a night vision scope had decided her next move – if they were equipped with NV gear, she was at a serious disadvantage, being fired upon from an elevated position. One of the first rules of engagement was, whenever possible, to use the terrain to your advantage, and taking higher ground was rudimentary.

Her initial burst shattered the night and caught the first gunman in the chest. His body tumbled down the cliff, slamming against the rocks as he dropped before sprawling at the base, head cocked at an unnatural angle. Alejandro fired, and she saw him hit the second man, and she was drawing a bead on the third when the distinctive lower-pitched chatter of an AK-47 barked from the ridge, and Xavier cried out in pain before sliding a few meters down the slope and lying still.

Simon and Jet kept firing, but they'd lost the element of surprise, and a hail of rounds rained down on their positions. Jet was shielded from the bullets by the rocks, but Alejandro and Simon were out in the open, and all she could do was to lay down covering fire while they took whatever cover they could. She emptied her magazine at the ridge, hoping to buy them some time, and was slapping a full one home when the gunmen above opened back up. Alejandro had managed to scurry to a small boulder, but Simon was still exposed. He'd flattened himself against the slope and was returning fire when a line of divots tore from the earth around him, and then a stream of rounds shredded his torso, the bulletproof vest offering insufficient protection against fully jacketed rifle rounds from less than a hundred meters.

Alejandro squeezed off some more shots in measured bursts, but it was worse than useless – they were pinned down, gravity working against them, the ridge too far for them to be able to reliably toss any grenades, and the RPGs now lying out of reach next to their dead companions.

Jet felt on her vest and found the cylindrical shape of a smoke grenade and, after pulling the pin, tossed it as far as she could. A stream of terephthalic acid fog spewed from the canister. Alejandro followed her lead and threw one of his own, creating a curtain of smoke above them. When she couldn't see the ridge any longer, she scuttled to Xavier's body and recovered the satchel with the rest of the grenades as well as his RPG. Alejandro kept firing into the smoke, hoping to make it unappetizing for the men on the ridge to poke their heads up, but the answering volleys and whining of ricochets off the slope told her that they were professional and weren't going to let up.

A slug tore a chunk off a rock only a foot from her head, and she rolled and began military crawling back to the rock outcropping as rounds peppered the ground around her. Alejandro tried lobbing a grenade to the top of the ridge, but it fell short and detonated as it rolled back down, momentarily blinding them both. The smoke was thinning, blown by the breeze, and Jet had barely made it behind the shelter of the rocks when more shooting erupted from above, this time almost directly overhead – the defending gunmen had pinned them down by moving into a more favorable spot from where they could inflict maximum damage.

Alejandro cringed as bullets tore into the slope, blasting rock chips from the outcropping. Jet held her weapon up one-handed and fired over the small boulder behind which she'd taken cover, unwilling to raise her head and offer a target for the shooters. Her prudence was validated when another burst of rifle fire hit the outcropping – the gunmen were good and, with their night vision scopes at that distance, would be able to easily take them out whenever they showed themselves.

The shooting waned and then stopped.

A man's voice called out from above. "You're surrounded and have nowhere to go. Throw down your weapons and stand up with your hands in the air. This will be your only chance."

Jet's pulse thrummed in her ears. The man was speaking English with a Russian accent. He repeated the order in Russian and then tried it in poor Spanish.

What are Russians doing in the middle of the Chilean mountains, at a Chilean army base?

There was no point engaging with the Russian in an effort to pinpoint his exact location. If he was smart, he would be moving, anticipating her ploy, so it wouldn't do any good.

Jet looked over at Alejandro, and even behind his goggles she could tell by his expression that he understood there was no way out. She tapped the RPG and pointed, and he nodded. They may have been screwed, but she could still inflict some real damage with the rocket-propelled grenade if she got lucky. She readied the launcher, waiting for an opportunity, and Alejandro seated another full magazine into his rifle so he could provide maximum cover for her in the hopes that she could fire the RPG without being cut to pieces.

Doing so was at best a fifty-fifty proposition with the shooters where they were. She drew a deep breath and prepared to fire, aware that it was the last she might ever take. Shooting from the ridge started again, and a brief vision flashed through her mind, Hannah running delightedly after a laughing Matt in a Mendoza park, the sun shining on her innocent face as he pretended to stumble so she could catch him, and then the image dissolved into the grim reality of the killing field the slope had become.

CHAPTER 37

Drago saw muzzle flashes from the ridge as the night erupted with gunfire, followed by explosions. Grenades, he thought absently as he tried to discern what was happening. Someone appeared to be attacking the camp – or trying, he thought. He didn't like their odds against the gunmen who'd run from the main building. He'd evaluated and discarded that approach as too risky, even if an ambush hadn't been lying in wait. Better to take the much longer route he had, he thought as he shifted in his hiding place.

The gunmen by the SUVs made no move to help the ones by the ridge, but rather ambled around aimlessly with their weapons pointed at the perimeter, prompting Drago to use the confusion arising from the shooting to unleash his little surprise. He depressed the transmitter buttons in series, smiling to himself as the *whump* of the explosives detonated up the hillside, followed by a rumble as hundreds of tons of rubble dislodged and rolled down the mountain, straight at the camp.

He watched as the wave of rocks and dust washed over the main building like a tsunami, catching the gunmen there by surprise as they tried to run in all directions, and then he was sprinting down the hill, pistol drawn, his eyes on the concrete bunker where two men had been standing guard.

~ ~ ~

The massive blast on the mountainside above the camp took Jet by surprise, as it apparently did the Russians, because the shooting stopped for a brief moment – just long enough for her to rise in a crouch, aim the RPG at the approximate position the Russian's voice had sounded from, and fire.

The grenade detonated, and Jet pushed herself to her feet, satchel over her shoulder and M4 clutched in front of her. She saw the blurred form of a body blown into the air as she charged sideways up the hillside. Alejandro's boots slid on the loose rocks behind her as he forced himself to his feet, and then the ground trembled as the avalanche hit the camp in a blinding cloud of dust.

She kept moving even as rocks skittered over the ridge and down the cliff. The angle of the main building had blocked most of the landslide, but enough made it past to still pose a danger. The firing from above had stopped, and she willed herself to vault up the remaining three meters of slope, and then she was rolling after throwing herself over the crest, her rifle in her hands.

Bullets pocked the dirt near her head, and she snapped off a burst, the dust haze so thick she could taste the displaced earth. Another shot from near a tree went wide, and she squeezed off a long volley from her position on the ground as Alejandro's head poked over the rim. She waited, afraid to move, but there was no more shooting, only the last of the avalanche's dull roar.

She caught a blur of motion on the periphery of her night vision and thought she was seeing things – a man running full speed down the mountain in the wake of the avalanche – and then he was gone on the other side of the main building. She returned her attention to the crater the RPG had created as she rose, leading with her M4 as she took cautious steps toward the surviving shooter, who was lying beside a tree.

Jet made a hand signal to Alejandro to stay back as she neared the gunman, and saw a bloody stump where his right leg had been. That he'd still been firing at her after an injury like that said much about his determination, as did the pistol by his hand, which he was feebly groping for even as she stood over him. He seemed to only just register her as he turned his head toward her, and she frowned – half his face was a raw wound, shredded to hamburger by the grenade blast, the other half as intact as though he'd just woken up. His shirt was dark with blood, and she was surprised he was still conscious, much less trying for a final shot as his life spurted out of him.

She toed the pistol out of reach and leaned toward him.

"Who are you?" she asked in flawless Russian.

His voice was a rasp, barely audible. "More…will come. You…will never…be…safe."

"Where's my daughter?"

"See…you…in…hell…"

The death rattle was the same as all the others she'd heard, unremarkable, more a groan than anything, finishing with a burble. He shuddered and lay still. Alejandro moved alongside her, eyeing the nearby buildings for more threats. She handed him her rifle, quickly searched the dead Russian, and after finding nothing but an iPhone and a wad of cash, pocketed them for later inspection. Alejandro returned the rifle to her, and she loaded a fresh magazine before pointing with two fingers at the partially buried main building.

Three pistol shots rang out from the other side of the compound, and they both ducked, but there were no ricochets. More gunfire echoed through the dust cloud, and it became obvious that they weren't the targets. Jet leapt to her feet and ran to the corner of the building. She peered around the corner, and a burst of automatic rifle fire ripped into the wall just in front of her head. Dropping to the ground, she felt for her final smoke grenade, which she tossed a few meters from the building's edge, hoping the wind would comply and the smoke would drift toward the shooter, providing her cover.

It did, and she used the opportunity to duck around the corner and spray lead at the faint shapes of approaching gunmen. One went down hard, and the other threw himself to the side, firing as he did, but his aim was off and the shots went wide. The power had gone out when the landslide had washed across the camp, which told her that these were more night scope-equipped shooters, probably Russian ex-Spetsnaz mercenaries like the dead one behind her. That was both a negative given their experience level, but also a positive, because she was familiar enough with their training to guess what this one would do next.

She fired another burst at the man's position, knowing her chances of hitting him behind the rubble were slim, and then pitched a fragmentation grenade after counting off a few seconds so it would explode close to him. Her effort was rewarded with a blast near the rock he'd taken cover behind, and she followed through by charging toward his position at a run, Alejandro behind her.

When she arrived, the shooter's dead eyes were staring at the sky, a gash in the center of his temple where a piece of shrapnel had penetrated. Alejandro crouched next to the man and repeated Jet's earlier search, but found nothing till he pushed the man's head aside and spotted the telltale form of an earbud on the ground. He retrieved it and handed it to Jet, and she slid it into her ear. Nothing. Only the faint buzz of static.

More shooting from the darkened hulks of the SUVs startled them: the staccato rattle of submachine guns. The pop of a pistol answered, and after another exchange the submachine guns fell silent.

Alejandro leaned into her. "What's going on?"

"I don't know. Seems like nothing's as we expected. These guys are Russian and seriously pro."

"Russian?"

"Does the Chilean military have Russians on an exchange basis or something?"

Alejandro shook his head. "I've never heard of it."

"Then this is something else."

"Who's doing the shooting over there?"

"Beats me. But I saw someone running down the mountain. Whoever it is started the avalanche…" Jet's voice trailed off. Why would another player be on the game board, trying to cripple the camp so he could assault it? Single-handedly?

The possible answers chilled her blood.

"What now?"

"We find my daughter. Let's check the main building first."

Alejandro looked over at it. "Good luck. It's half buried."

"I'll go in through that window," she said. "Cover me."

Jet zigzagged through the dust cloud and acid smoke until she reached the building. She hesitated by the window, its glass blown out from the landslide and the grenade, listening for any sounds from inside, and when there were none, she heaved herself up and through the opening.

She landed on the wooden planks and was immediately up, shaking off glass shards from the floor as she swept the room with her rifle barrel. It was obvious to her within seconds that the area was empty, and she was turning back to the window when an engine revved outside. Jet ran to the window as Alejandro arrived.

"What was that?"

"One of the trucks."

They watched as a black SUV accelerated down the dirt road. Jet climbed out the window and landed on the rocks outside. Alejandro indicated one of the two remaining outbuildings, where the doorway was open and two dead men lay nearby, their machine guns by their sides. She was torn between going after the SUV in case someone had taken the prisoners, or finishing her search of the compound. The doorway seemed to beckon to her, and she edged toward it, rifle in her hands, ready to fire at anything that moved.

Shots rang out from down the road as the SUV passed the gunmen there, and then the night fell silent again, the only sound the low howl of the wind as it blew through the camp, carrying with it the smell of gunfire and death.

CHAPTER 38

Jet motioned to Alejandro to take the left side of the door and threw herself against the wall on the right. She increased the sensitivity of her night vision goggles and peered into the dark space, leading with her M4. The red laser dot bounced along the wall, and then Jet gasped. Hannah was crouched in the far corner of the room, cowering in fear.

"Hannah!" Jet whispered, entering the room. "It's Mommy."

Hannah didn't seem to register the words, and Jet realized that she either couldn't see at all in the darkness, or what she did see looked like an alien – Jet in a combat jacket, night vision goggles covering most of her face.

"Sweetheart, don't be scared. It's Mommy. I came for you."

"Mama?" Hannah asked, her voice tentative.

Jet could see her looking around, so her first guess was correct – it was too dark for her daughter to see her. "I'm right here. Stay where you are. I'm wearing a special mask so I can see you. I'm coming to you right now, okay?"

Jet moved to her daughter and called out to Alejandro. "Keep an eye out. My daughter's here."

"Mama!" Hannah cried as Jet picked her up with her left arm, holding the rifle with her right hand.

"Oh, baby, I love you so much," Jet said, her eyes welling with tears.

"Love you too."

"It's scary in the dark, huh?"

Hannah nodded.

"Was Matt here?"

Another nod.

"Do you know where he went?"

Hannah's face scrunched as she struggled for a word. "Man come."

"A man came for Matt?"

"Yeth."

"How long ago, do you know? Just now, or a while ago?"

Hannah was confused by the question, having no concept of time. "Just now?" she said, sounding unsure.

Jet carried Hannah to the door. "You see anything else, Alejandro?"

"No. No movement. Looks like between the avalanche and the shooter you saw, everyone's dead."

"Crap. I think the gunman took Doug. Come on," she said. "You remember Hannah, don't you?"

"Of course."

They bolted for the only SUV in sight that hadn't been crushed by the falling rocks, an anthracite Ford Expedition. After glancing around to ensure they weren't about to get shot, Jet strapped Hannah into the back seat. Alejandro was already in the passenger seat when she climbed behind the wheel. The keys were in the car, and she twisted the ignition. Relief flooded her when the big motor roared to life.

Jet pulled away, the Ford's all-terrain tires throwing a shower of grit behind them, and she used the wipers to remove the film of dust that coated the windshield. "Hannah, I want you to scrunch down and make yourself as tiny as possible, okay? This is super important, do you understand?"

Hannah nodded. Jet was driving without headlights to buy them an edge over the waiting gunmen – without lights to aim at, all they'd be likely to see was a dark blur blowing by. She increased her speed until the tires began to lose their grip on the dirt. Alejandro rolled down his window and stuck out his M4, watching for any shooters in front of them.

The gunfire, when it came, was haphazard and largely missed them, only a few rounds punching into the rear quarter panel as they tore past. Jet floored the gas pedal and focused on keeping the big SUV on the narrow dirt road as it careened around a bend, drifting as all four tires lost purchase. For an instant the vehicle seemed to be floating, skidding as if on ice, and then the tires gripped again just as they were nearing the edge where the mountain dropped down five stories into a ravine.

"I'm sorry. I couldn't see anything to shoot," Alejandro said, rolling the window back up.

"No worries. Everybody okay?" She looked in the rearview mirror at where Hannah was still doing her best to make herself small. "You can sit up now, honey. All done."

Hannah did so, and Jet's heart broke when she saw that her little girl was crying again, but another part of her burned with rage.

Alejandro shifted next to her and spoke softly. "Uh-oh."

Jet looked over at him.

Alejandro touched his side, and his hand came away with bright red blood. "I'm hit. Didn't even feel it there for a few moments."

"Where?" Jet said, concentrating on keeping them from running off the road.

"Nicked the inside of my arm. Bastard. Now it hurts…"

"Grazed or worse?"

"Grazed. I'll live."

They hit the bottom of the road, and she twisted the wheel left. Far down the mountain she could just make out brake lights.

"Hold on," she said. "We're going to set some records here."

Alejandro nodded, and she flattened the accelerator to the floor.

~ ~ ~

Drago held the submachine gun he'd lifted from one of the dead gunmen on Matt as he followed the road down the pass, the vehicle leaning as he cut the curves too fast.

"Where are the diamonds?" Drago demanded again.

"I have no idea what you're talking about."

"Then I'll just kill you now and call it a day," Drago said, slowing and leaning away so as to not get blood all over himself.

"Fine. They're hidden in my car."

"Which is where?"

"At a hotel in San Felipe."

"Ah. And how many diamonds are we talking? What's the value?"

"I don't know. Maybe ten, twenty million?"

"That's a big difference," Drago observed.

"I have no way of knowing exactly how much. That's all I've got left. But it's a lot." Matt appraised him. "Enough so that if we split them, no matter what you're being paid, it'll be ten or twenty times as much. We go our separate ways, you retire rich, and it's all good."

Drago grinned. "Wouldn't that be nice?" His eyes narrowed as he slowed and pulled over at the turnout where he'd left his rental car.

"Why are we stopping?"

"Change of vehicles. You'll want to be on your best behavior, because I'll gladly shoot pieces off you if you aren't. It doesn't much matter to me whether we do it that way or not. Understand?"

"I do. Look, think about the diamonds for a second. You're a freelancer, aren't you?" Drago didn't respond, so Matt continued. "Which means you don't know the whole story. What did they tell you?"

"You stole the wrong person's diamonds."

"Not exactly. I was running ops for the CIA in Thailand. The diamonds were payment for heroin that was bound for the U.S. I decided I didn't want to work for drug traffickers, so I took them and disappeared. You're being used by a faction in the CIA, which means once you're done, there's nowhere in the world you'll be safe. They can't afford to have you around, so one night you'll be offed, and you'll never know when or where."

"Says you."

"That's how they do things. You serve your purpose and they wipe you. The only way you stand a chance is with enough money to vanish forever, without leaving any trail. The diamonds will more than do that. Think about it. Anywhere in the world, a new life. Never having to worry."

"Nice pitch, but wrong guy." Drago rolled to a stop next to his car. "Open your door and get out, slowly, and put your hands on the car, where I can see them."

Matt held up the cast. "In case I have a Tommy gun in this?"

"I'm glad you've kept your sense of humor. Now do it, and if you make a move I don't like, I'll put a bullet in you."

Matt nodded and eased out of the SUV, Drago's weapon trained on him, and put both hands on the roof of the car. Drago opened his door and was out in a second, the submachine gun unwavering in his hand. He neared Matt and tilted his head for a moment, listening. The only sound was the rushing river winding its way at the bottom of the ravine far below, and his breathing.

Except.

He closed his eyes for a moment. *There.* The thrum and high whine of tires from up the hill. He opened his eyes and glanced at the road – no lights. Which was impossible. It was almost pitch black out, with only occasional flashes of moonlight between the clouds.

And yet now he could hear it drawing closer. Tires on asphalt coming fast and a big motor. A V-8, by the sound of it.

Drago hissed at Matt. "Stay where you are or you're dead, do you understand?"

"I'm dead anyway, aren't I?"

"You want to be dead right this second or live a while longer?"

Matt didn't answer, which Drago interpreted as a vote for life. He moved to the opposite side of the SUV and waited for whatever was coming at him to show itself on the bend. It looked like a hundred yards, maybe a little more, before the vehicle would come into view, which was fairly close to the limit of the submachine gun's effective range.

He saw a glint of something in the night and then could just make out the big SUV bearing down on him. Drago forced himself to wait, counting one second, then another, and then fired a long burst at the vehicle, hoping to hit it. Contrary to movies, hitting a moving target was difficult, much less at relatively long range with a weapon whose accuracy was unknown, and so his strategy was to spray enough lead in the vehicle's general vicinity that at least a few of the rounds might hit it.

His luck had run out. The big truck kept coming, and he had to make a lightning decision: shoot it out in the road or run for cover and draw his pursuers after him.

Drago glanced down the ravine – it wasn't particularly steep, and there was plentiful scrub and trees he could use as cover. Staying up on the road would mean a swift exchange, with him the likely loser. He'd grabbed the submachine gun out of convenience as he'd pushed Matt by one of the dead gunmen, and he hadn't stopped to get extra magazines, which meant that he only had whatever rounds were still in the gun, and his pistol, which wouldn't do much good in an open shootout – but could work in the brush if he could ambush his hunters.

Drago spun and snarled at Matt. "Get going. Now. Over the side." He motioned with the submachine gun.

Matt raised his hands over his head, his cast gleaming white, and nodded. "Okay. Where?"

Drago jabbed with the weapon at a gap in the dense bushes by the edge of the turnout. "There."

~ ~ ~

Jet swerved as bullets punched into the hood and windshield. Hannah screamed and ducked down again in the back seat. Jet avoided locking up the brakes and putting the SUV into a skid by downshifting and allowing the motor to slow it.

"Can you shoot?" she yelled at Alejandro.

He brought his weapon up and rolled the window down again. "I'm not hurt that badly. But good luck hitting anything while we're moving."

Jet caught a better look at the turnoff as she steadied the SUV. "Hold off. That's Doug leaning against the car. See the cast?"

"You're right. What do you want to do?"

They watched as the gunman moved to Matt and then disappeared.

"Don't shoot," Jet warned.

The engine was making an ominous clanking. Jet cursed – one of the bullets had hit something and done real damage. She could still see through the windshield – the bullets that had drilled through it had done so in the center, leaving neat holes without much starring around them. But there was no telling how long the motor would keep running.

"I'm going after them. Looks like he's making a run for it. With the NV goggles, that's advantage, me," she said.

"Unless he's got a night scope on his weapon."

Jet's jaw muscles clenched as she ground her teeth. "I'll take my chances."

"Park behind them."

Jet coasted to a stop on the cusp of gravel, and steam hissed from beneath the hood. She shut off the ignition, and the clanking stopped.

"Sounds like the rounds bent something. Maybe the fan or a pulley. They definitely hit the radiator," Alejandro whispered.

"That doesn't matter. Stay with Hannah."

Alejandro shook his head. "You can't do this alone."

"You're wounded."

"I'm grazed. But you go one-on-one with this guy, your chances of walking away drop significantly. He took out the gunmen at the camp and started an avalanche, for Christ's sake. This isn't some Verdugo stooge."

"What about Hannah?"

"You're not going to be much good to her dead. Lock the car up. She'll be fine for a few minutes on her own."

"No."

Alejandro exhaled noisily. "Think. We're running out of time. Why did he run for the brush? Either to escape or to draw us in. If the former, we got his ass. If the latter, if we spread out, his odds of nailing either one of us go way down."

Jet checked her magazine and scowled as she eyed Hannah in the mirror. She didn't want to leave her alone, but Alejandro was right. With two of them, they had a better chance.

"Damn. Okay." Jet spoke to Hannah. "Honey, I'll be right back, okay? You'll be safe here. Stay in the car, all right, sweetheart? I'll lock it so nobody can get you."

Hannah's eyes looked panicked, but she nodded.

"And be quiet, okay? No matter what, stay down inside the car, stay quiet, and Mommy will be back for you before you know it."

~ ~ ~

Matt crashed through the brush, making as much noise as possible without being obvious, taking care to stumble regularly, slowing their progress as much as he could. Drago prodded him along impatiently, and they heard a clatter from up at the turnoff.

"What's your plan? We can't outrun anyone," Matt said.

"One more noise and I'll drill you," Drago warned, his murmured threat all the more ominous for how flat his tone was.

Matt didn't want to test him. His captor was clearly as lethal as they came. If it was Jet behind them, she'd need every bit of luck she could summon, because Matt had watched this guy gun down three of Bastian's crew without blinking after killing the two men guarding the storeroom entrance. He had the demeanor of a true sociopath and was more than good, and Matt had seen enough to realize that whoever was following them had their work cut out for them.

~ ~ ~

The hiss from the radiator sounded like a freight train as Jet jogged to the gap in the vegetation. Alejandro trailed her, a length of cord cinched around his left arm to slow the bleeding, his M4 gripped in his right. At the edge of the turnout she stopped and listened, her ears straining for any hint of movement, and she heard crashing from halfway down the hill. She eased herself over the side and followed the trail down the slope.

When she arrived at a small clearing, she studied her surroundings and then whispered to Alejandro, "It looks like they're headed down to the river. You can see where the grass is flattened. I'm going to take the trail they took, and you take the other one. With any luck you'll come up behind them. If you get a clear shot, don't hesitate – take him down."

Alejandro nodded understanding and moved down the track she'd indicated as she pushed forward through the bushes, pausing occasionally to listen. The trail was almost nonexistent after the clearing, where discarded beer bottles and garbage pointed to youthful gatherings away from prying eyes. The one she was now following looked more like a true game path used by goats and small deer making their way to the river rather than young lovers looking to steal a few moments of privacy.

A thump sounded from ahead of her, and she slowed, aware that if she suddenly burst from the underbrush she'd be a sitting duck. Her leg muscles ached from the effort of moving silently down the slope after the breakneck climb by the camp.

The snap of a twig to her right brought her up short, and she froze. It might have been Alejandro. Or someone waiting in ambush by the river. She could see the plants thin out ahead, and she decided to err on the side of caution and complete the final meters on her stomach. Putting aside any thoughts of snakes, she inched forward, weapon in hand, and was poking the rifle barrel through the final layer of vines when gunfire erupted from the riverbank.

Alejandro cried out ten meters to her right, but Jet was focused on the flash. There. The gunman was also on his stomach, a submachine gun with a night vision scope on it clearly visible, and Matt was lying to one side. It would be a difficult shot, but not impossible at that range, and she slowed her breathing in preparation to fire as she flipped the selector switch to single shot.

As if he could sense the danger, the man leapt from his position with the grace of a panther. Jet resisted the urge to pull the trigger – he had his weapon trained on Matt now, who was struggling to his feet. Her entire awareness narrowed to a dark tunnel, the only object in existence the shooter. The river was only a few meters behind them, and they'd disappear from view in seconds, leaving her fully exposed when she had to cross the ground.

Her shot caught the gunman in the chest and spun him halfway around. Matt must have seen the tiny red dot on the man's shirt just before she fired because he hurled himself to the side, leaving his captor in full view for an instant – just long enough. She squeezed off another shot and saw the impact as it slammed the man backward and out of her field of vision, and then she was up and sprinting for the rise before her conscious mind had caught up to what instinct had driven her to do. She switched her fire selector to burst as she neared the spot where Matt had dived and threw herself onto the hard gravel, ignoring the pain as she landed, her gun at the ready.

On the other side of the rise, Matt was lying on his back, the wind knocked out of him. There was no sign of the shooter, but she swept the surface of the water with her weapon as she leaned toward him.

"Did you see where he landed?" she asked.

Matt coughed and grimaced. "Over there." He pointed with his good hand. "In the water. You hit him."

The surface of the river undulated like a black serpent as she forced herself to her feet and approached it. Watching for any irregularity in the streaming water, she thought she saw something and fired, again and again, to no obvious effect.

Matt called out to her. "You can only kill a man once."

"I like to make sure they're dead."

"The water's got to be freezing. I saw him fall in. Probably pretty deep through this ravine – cuts straight through the rock."

Jet continued her vigil for a half minute and then turned to Matt. "Who was he?"

"The people who sent Tara must have hired him. Freelancer. But…I don't know. Different. Like a machine or something – he was about the best I've seen."

"There's always someone better."

Matt struggled to his feet. "I guessed that was you shooting your way in before the avalanche."

"You know me well."

"I knew there was no way you would leave Hannah to her fate."

"Or you." She moved to Matt and hugged him, then pushed her goggles away from her face and gave him a long kiss. His arms moved around her waist, and he pulled her close, and then they froze when a voice hissed at them from the river.

"How touching," Drago said, rising from the water, pistol in hand. "You almost had me, you know. But you didn't figure for a Type IV vest, did you? I liberated it from one of the guards after I blew his brains against the wall. I'll admit I've never been a fan of ceramic plates until now."

Matt released her, and Jet slowly turned, her M4 pointed at the ground. Drago's pistol was aimed at her head, the barrel unwavering.

"Drop the pop gun, sister."

She locked eyes with Drago as the moon came from behind a cloud and saw the intent in his dead pupils. Her moment of hesitation only lasted until he cocked the hammer on his pistol and smiled.

A burst of gunfire blasted from the bushes and knocked Drago backward into the river. Jet was swinging her rifle up when he sank beneath the surface and disappeared. She emptied her rifle at the area where he'd sunk and was still squeezing the trigger, the bolt locked open and the weapon empty, when Matt approached and put his hand on her shoulder.

"It's over."

She pulled her pistol from her belt and shook her head. "No, it isn't. My rounds didn't stop him the first time. There's no reason to believe Alejandro's did any better."

Matt shook his head. "Not necessarily. Each shot weakens the vest, as does age. You have no idea how old that thing was or how many bullets it's stopped. Looked to me like those punched through it."

Alejandro approached carrying his rifle. "It was a good thing that submachine gun was a 9mm. My vest stopped them, although it feels like somebody used me for a punching bag."

Matt glanced at him. "You're lucky. A few inches higher and they would have hit above the armor."

Alejandro adjusted his NV goggles and offered a pained smile. "That's about how my whole day's gone." He looked at Jet. "Are you okay?"

She was still staring at the river, having lowered her goggles back into place, her pistol clenched in her hand, watching for any sign of Drago in the swirling eddies and currents.

It took ten minutes without any signs of life for Matt to convince her that the assassin was really gone this time.

They walked together back up the hill to where Hannah was waiting, Matt stiff from the interrogation beating and Alejandro limping from a slightly sprained ankle. Only Jet strode seemingly effortlessly, occasionally stopping to look back at the river snaking through the ravine as though at any moment the phantom hit man might rise up for a final reckoning – an impossibility after being underwater that long, but a lingering fear in the part of her mind where her nightmares brooded like starving wolves.

CHAPTER 39

Santiago, Chile

The driver who had been waiting for Jet and Alejandro's return from the camp picked everyone up at the turnout after Alejandro called him; the cell signal was faint but fortunately usable, the line of sight to the San Felipe valley through the pass clear. The group was quiet on the long drive back to Santiago, and Alejandro drank several liter bottles of water on the way. Jet had contrived a dressing for Alejandro's wound from the first aid kit in the back of the SUV, and he dozed the final half hour of the trip.

Jet went through the contacts and messages on the Russian's phone, and her heart skipped several beats when she came to one from someone named Filipov, written in Russian. She reread it three times as the vehicle bounced down the road, Hannah cradled in her arms, asleep. When she was sure she hadn't misinterpreted the missive, she elbowed Matt, who was slumbering beside her, head leaned against the window, her jacket rolled up as his pillow.

"What?"

"There's a message on the Russian's phone."

"And?"

"It's from an attorney in Moscow, asking for a progress report on the contract and responding to a question about what would constitute proof that I was the person in question and was dead. This Filipov answered back that a DNA match would be optimal, and reminded him that anything less would result in nonpayment of the ten-million-dollar contract price," she whispered, not wanting Alejandro or the driver to hear.

Matt let out a soft whistle. "Ten million. Who would want you dead badly enough to be willing to take out a contract on you?" he whispered back.

"I have no idea. Unless it's somehow connected to one of the jobs I did there. Or Grigenko."

"Hmm. I suppose it's conceivable that he had a failsafe policy in the event he was killed. I've heard of that before – you set aside enough money to ensure that whoever killed you would be signing their own death warrant in doing so. A kind of mutually assured destruction. But like most doomsday weapons, it only works if everyone knows about it, so it should be fairly straightforward to check."

"If there's an open contract on me…" She didn't have to finish the thought, her expression grim.

"For that kind of money, you can expect a constant string of aspirants." He took her hand and squeezed. "It's not good news. Trust me, I know how it feels."

"But…that kind of an arrangement would have to be dependent upon the attorney, right? I mean, it's not like it could be assigned – even in Russia, I'd imagine it's illegal to engage in murder for hire, so it's not like there's an actual written document that's enforceable."

Matt thought about it. "Right. The term 'contract' is a euphemism. Call it a hit."

"So if the attorney were to meet with an accident…"

Matt's eyes narrowed. "Moscow can be a dangerous place."

"Exactly. I have no sympathy for him if he's hiring mercenaries. Live by the sword, and all that."

"What are you thinking?"

She squeezed his hand back. "Guess."

When they arrived at the doctor's home, there were even more gunmen than before. Hector met them outside the guesthouse, his usual dour expression on his face, and hustled Alejandro into the operating suite after a brief nod to Jet. The doctor was able to patch up Alejandro in a matter of minutes, the entire procedure consisting of cleaning the wound, suturing it, and giving him a bottle of orange juice to drink. Alejandro refused anything for the pain and, once he was through with the doctor, sat with his father in quiet discussion for a half hour, occasionally interrupting the dialogue to make a phone call.

Jet waited with Matt and Hannah in the doctor's house at his invitation. Jet sat next to her daughter's sleeping form on the sofa as Matt slumbered in an overstuffed chair. Her body had been pushed to its limits, but her mind was still racing, formulating a strategy in response to the new information she'd acquired from the dead Russian's phone. By the time Hector entered the kitchen through the back door, she'd made several difficult decisions, and she joined him there, leaving Matt and Hannah to their dreams.

"Gaspar and Alejandro would like a word with you if you could spare a few minutes," Hector said.

She nodded. "Sorry about your men."

Hector shrugged. "They knew what they were getting into. Their families will be looked after."

Jet took a final look at Matt and Hannah and followed Hector to the guesthouse. Alejandro was standing by Gaspar's bed, and he motioned to a chair.

"Have a seat."

Jet did as asked and waited.

Alejandro cleared his throat. "My father and I have been discussing your situation. I told him about your desire to leave Chile without having to deal with customs formalities. But I wanted you to lay things out for him so he understands exactly how we can help you."

Jet shifted her gaze to Gaspar. "I have a couple of things in mind. First, I'd like to get my daughter and Doug out of Chile as soon as possible. Alejandro suggested by ship, which I'm fine with. Most of them go by Panama, if I'm not mistaken, so that would be as good a place as any for a destination."

Alejandro nodded. "That can be easily arranged, out of San Antonio, which is smaller than Valparaíso and under our control. It's a busy port."

"What kind of pull do you have with the Chilean government?" Jet asked.

Gaspar cleared his throat. "What do you need?"

"Three Chilean passports would come in handy. With new names. The genuine article, so if they're checked, they'll show up in the system as legitimate."

Gaspar appeared to consider it. "That will take several days, but it can be done. Political asylum, or perhaps newly recovered birth certificates – many records were destroyed in the last earthquake. I know the person to call."

She smiled at his response. "Finally, I need to get to Moscow as soon as possible."

Alejandro's stoic composure cracked. "Moscow! Russia?"

"Exactly. But I first need to get across the border into either Peru or Bolivia without going through immigration." She could feel the weight of Gaspar's stare. "I have my reasons."

Gaspar exchanged a glance with Alejandro, and then looked at Jet. "Using your own passport or a new Chilean one?"

"Time is of the essence. If you can get a passport in twenty-four hours, I'd say on the Chilean. If it would take longer, I'll use my current one."

Gaspar adjusted the bed control, trying to get comfortable. "You're in a hurry, are you?"

Jet's expression was unreadable. "I need to attend to an errand as soon as possible."

"I see. Alejandro, can you arrange for someone to meet our guest near the border?" Gaspar's eyes bored into her. "I am deeply appreciative of your actions today. I owe my son's life, and probably my own, to you. That makes you…if not family, someone I cannot say no to." He hesitated. "I have a jet – an old man's vanity, but one that comes in useful from time to time. A Lear. It can take you north, and we'll have one of our people drive you across the border to La Paz, Bolivia, where we can arrange for a larger charter to get you to Europe."

"That would be wonderful. I have some money…"

Gaspar waved her offer away. "Consider it my pleasure. I would have paid many, many times that to be out of that hellhole, much less have my son safe."

Alejandro glanced at his watch. "The government offices won't open for another four hours. I'll put everything into motion first thing. We'll need to get photographs of you all this morning so there are no delays."

Jet nodded. "I can't tell you how much I appreciate this."

Gaspar smiled, a somewhat pained expression. "As I said, the pleasure is mine. Good luck with your 'errand,' young lady. Although I'm quite sure you won't need any."

Alejandro led her out of the guesthouse. "I'll have Hector take you to a photographer at nine. I'd attend to it myself, but my hands are full at the moment."

"I can only imagine. Any decision on your brother? Has he surfaced?"

Alejandro didn't answer. "I want to add my own thanks to my father's. Once you're finished in Moscow, you can always call on me if you need something. I have a long memory, and the offer's sincere."

"Let's hope I never have to."

Alejandro's phone rang. He checked the screen and held it to his ear. "Will you excuse me?"

"Of course."

Jet returned to the house, where the two loves of her life were blissfully unaware of the arrangements she'd just put into motion, sleeping peacefully after thirty-six hours of hell on earth. Hannah shifted as Jet sat beside her, and Jet eyed her daughter, thumb in her mouth, eyes screwed shut, breathing easily, and wondered whether there would ever come a time when there wouldn't be danger lurking just over the horizon, threatening their lives and happiness.

She closed her eyes as the first faint rays of a new dawn filtered through the curtains, exhaustion catching up with her, the manic adrenaline jitters finally calmed now that, at least for a few hours, they were safe.

CHAPTER 40

Valparaíso, Chile

One of the two young women, barely out of her teens, pulled the sheet over her naked body as the other smirked at Rodrigo and lit a cigarette. Rodrigo had taken a shower and fortified himself with another couple of lines of cocaine, and was feeling eerily sober considering he'd gotten no sleep for two nights and had drunk a half bottle of top-shelf Scotch in the last few hours. He studied his reflection in the dresser mirror with blurry red eyes – the four days' dusting of beard looked good on him, he thought. Maybe he'd keep it for a while.

Now that he was the effective head of the Soto empire, he could say or do anything he wanted. He had absolutely no doubt that Antonio and Franco would make short work of Alejandro – for all his brother's airs, he wasn't the leader their father had been, and the men wouldn't follow him into battle the same way. With the empire in disarray, a swift strike would sever that head, leaving Rodrigo at the helm.

As it should be. He was the smartest of the pair, as proved by his negotiating this deal with the Verdugos from a position of strength. He'd be able to enjoy all the financial benefits of the business with none of the risks. Franco and his group would do all the heavy lifting, and Rodrigo could live like royalty, spending half his year in Europe and the other half in South America, perhaps racing a sailing yacht in different events around the globe, or maybe living in Beverly Hills and producing films. His talents were squandered in Chile – he was a renaissance man, bigger than their provincial country, and he couldn't wait to get clear of it.

His father had never understood him. It had gotten so that Rodrigo didn't even try to reason with the old man, who was obsessed with the organization he'd built and had failed to see the path it would have to follow to prosper. Merging the two gangs was not only brilliant, but necessary. As things in the narco-trafficking business changed, the organization had to change with them – wisdom his father was blind to.

No matter. What was done was done.

He extracted a wad of bills from his pocket and disdainfully flipped several onto the dresser. He'd had his fun and the girls had served their purpose, and now he needed to get things straight with Franco. The smoking girl pulled the sheet back to give him a view of her perfectly sculpted thighs and flat stomach, the smile on her face as knowing as a judge's. He felt a stirring but shook it off. It was time to get something to eat and then see Franco.

"*Ciao*, darlings. See you around, eh?" he said as he pulled on his jacket.

"You don't like us anymore?" the smoker said, affecting a pout.

"It's not that. Things to do. Maybe I'll be back tomorrow."

"You have other girls?"

He grinned. "Of course."

"But not like us."

He winked at her. "Nothing like you."

The brothel was in a large colonial home near the La Matriz del Salvador church, its green shutters clashing with the garish pink exterior. Rodrigo looked through the window at the surrounding buildings and shook his head – it would be a miracle if there was a decent restaurant anywhere nearby. He went to the bathroom and blew his nose, ignoring the blood, and then sauntered to the bedroom door.

"You come back soon, okay, *El Toro*? I need more of that crazy love you got," the smoker said, her tone professionally flirtatious.

"We'll see."

He pulled the door closed behind him, ready to be rid of the whores, and then moved to the darkened stairway. A radio crooned a plaintive song downstairs, where a cleaning woman was scrubbing away the prior night's debauchery from the lounge area. He was just about to take the first step when two iron hands gripped his arms from behind and a black cloth sack descended over his head. He screamed and struggled, and then a sharp stab of pain shrieked from his neck. His legs turned to jelly and he drifted away, his last thought that somebody had made a mistake.

~ ~ ~

Colonel Campos took a final swig of black coffee from a china cup and placed it on its saucer, finished with his meal and ready to face the new day. The paper had been filled with the story of Gaspar Soto's daring prison break and subsequent crash, as it no doubt would be for many weeks. Those kinds of headlines rarely happened and were a dream come true for the news outlets, which sensationalized and distorted as well as any of their North American brethren.

The planted piece about an antiterrorism offensive in the mountains north of San Felipe was below the fold on the front page, where it would ensure visibility. As intended, it was long on speculation and short on detail, other than getting across that there were prisoners being held at a nearby military outpost.

He pushed back from the table and rose. His housekeeper stood by the kitchen entry, waiting to clear the table.

"Will you be home for dinner, sir?" she asked.

"Yes, I expect so."

"Very good. Shall I make your favorite? I can pick up some fresh fish this afternoon."

"That would be wonderful, Mari. Expect me by seven."

He strode to the living room and collected his things – his briefcase, a stack of reports he'd brought home to study several days before, his overcoat. It would take the rest of the week for him to feel completely normal after the sleep deprivation of the last few days, but he could manage, and it had certainly been worth it. Franco would have to be extraordinarily generous this time, and Campos knew exactly what he was going to demand – an additional percentage of the take from the smuggling activity through the port. Franco would bitch and moan, but in the end he'd concede. At this point it was purely ceremonial; Franco was about to become far richer, and Campos saw no reason he shouldn't share some of that wealth. After all, it had been his soldiers who'd done the dirty work, and without Campos's help Franco would have still been losing men at the mouth of the mine.

Campos swung the heavy front door open and walked down the steps, but stopped near the bottom when he saw the four armed military policemen on the sidewalk, their expressions stern. He recognized the officer with them – a particularly hateful prick from Santiago whom Campos had always considered a meddler and a fool. Major Ariana, he remembered, as the man approached.

"Colonel Campos, you are under arrest." Ariana turned to the nearest soldier. "Place him in restraints."

"What is the meaning of this? This is preposterous," Campos protested as the MPs wrenched his briefcase away from him and twisted his arms behind him as they cuffed him. "I'll have you broken, Major," Campos spat, his tone as menacing as an attack dog's growl.

"I'd keep your mouth shut, Colonel. Just some advice. Save it for your trial."

"You have no right—"

The major stepped nearer, his voice quiet. "I said shut up."

"Under whose authority are you acting? I want to know. It will go very badly for you, Major, and I want to know who else to ruin for this outrage."

"Not that it's any of your concern, but my orders are signed by the commander-in-chief of the army. So you can start your ruining at the top."

Campos seemed to deflate as he absorbed the information, and his complexion turned gray as he glared at Ariana and saw nothing but confidence. Something had gone very wrong if the charges had come from the commander-in-chief, and Campos smelled Soto all over it.

But it was only a matter of hours until Franco found out, and then the tables would be turned. If Alejandro had managed to get to the higher-ups, they'd soon be swayed by reality once they fully understood the new lay of the land.

Campos squared his shoulders as the detail led him to a van, his dignity intact even under the difficult conditions. Irritants like Ariana were ants in the scheme of things, and now that the elder Soto, with whom all the personal relationships and power rested, was out of the way, this was nothing more than a road bump by some fools who would be very sorry for their impudence by day's end.

~ ~ ~

Antonio could barely sit still as he listened to the report on the speakerphone in his father's office. Franco's face had aged ten years through the morning as bulletins had arrived from the field – his strongholds in Santiago had gone dark an hour and a half ago, and he suddenly couldn't get anyone that mattered in the police department or with the government to accept his calls.

The voice of one of Franco's lieutenants sounded panicked. "Two of the ships that we're loading weapons on in Valparaíso have been seized by the military and the cargo searched."

"Get Campos involved. That's his backyard."

"I tried. He's not picking up. And my contact on the dock says he doesn't recognize any of the officers directing the raid, so they aren't his men."

"What do you mean he's not picking up? I'll ask him myself. We have a meeting at my club in half an hour."

"I tried calling Arturo in Santiago earlier to check through his channels, but he also didn't answer," the lieutenant said. Arturo was one of their most influential fixers in the capital.

"Stay where you are. This will be resolved within the hour," Franco snapped and stabbed the call off.

"Any word from Bastian?" Antonio asked, a tremor in his voice.

"No."

"What about that buffoon Rodrigo? Perhaps he can get some useful information from his network?"

"I expected him to call by now, but he's probably sleeping it off somewhere. You know what he's like. Worse than useless. Hard to believe he shares the old man's genetic material." Franco shook his head. "And the other one? Alejandro? If they're mounting a counterattack, it's got to be him pulling the strings now that Gaspar's toast."

"I've had my men looking everywhere. Some have yet to check back in, but all reported a substantial increase in the number of Soto enforcers on the streets. They couldn't get near his usual haunts. Too dangerous."

Franco looked at Antonio disgustedly and then eyed his wristwatch. "You can stay here and use my office as your base until I return. I need to sort out this idiocy at the wharf with Campos. There's no way he knows about it," he said, rising. He smoothed his oxford shirt and Hermès tie and angled to the coat rack where his blue blazer was hanging. "I want you to talk to the men you can get in touch with and have them plan to move on Alejandro's likely headquarters. He's no fool, but he's got to be running this from somewhere." Antonio began to speak, but Franco cut him off. "Saying you don't know for sure where he is isn't good enough, Antonio. You've had eighteen hours. Start producing results and not excuses. Do I make myself clear?"

Antonio nodded glumly at his father's words. The rebuke was all the more painful since Antonio had assured him that he'd have Alejandro neutralized by morning – which had come and gone.

"Now, if you need to reach me, I'll be at the club for brunch and then at the boat. I've got one of the engines being overhauled, and it's taking twice as long as it should."

"Don't you think–"

"What I think is that I need people around me who can do their jobs, because if I have to do it for them, I don't need them taking a cut," Franco interrupted, not about to be scolded by his impudent offspring. "Now if you don't have any objections, I'm off."

Franco was seething as he made his way to the elevator, accompanied by two somber bodyguards in dark suits. His mood wasn't improved by the realization that his son didn't have the grit to lead the organization when he retired. Antonio was fine dealing with the day-to-day, but in this, the first real time of crisis where Franco had needed to rely on him, he'd failed. There was no other word for his lack of performance with Alejandro. If he hadn't been Franco's son, Antonio would have already been floating in the harbor.

The underground parking lot was quiet, cars just beginning to arrive as the nearby offices came to life. Their footsteps reverberated off the polished concrete slab as they walked to his platinum Mercedes sedan, its chrome rims glinting in the fluorescent light. He normally maintained a low profile, but there were some things that warranted splurging for: his yacht, his car, his villa and vacation homes, his platinum A. Lange & Sohne perpetual calendar watch. The things that confirmed to him that the sacrifices he'd made had all been worth it.

The bodyguards stood on either side of Franco as he opened the car door, their eyes roving over the few surrounding cars, shielding him with their bodies. A uniformed security guard at the entrance waved at them, and one of the men nodded, preoccupied by monitoring the area for threats.

Franco's cell phone rang as he slid behind the wheel, the AMG leather interior still exuding the rarefied aroma of new car. He waved his men away and looked at the number, but it was blocked. When he thumbed the call to life, all he heard was the sound of breathing on the other end.

"Who is this?" he demanded, his voice cracking on the last syllable.

Silence. Only the hum of the phone line.

Franco hung up and twisted the ignition, disturbed by the call. The Mercedes seemed to plump like a frank on a hot grill before it exploded in a fireball, and the doors blew off and hit the wall with enough force to gash a deep chunk in the reinforced concrete. Car alarms sounded throughout the space as flames belched from the vehicle, the thick clouds of black smoke billowing from the burning chassis creating a toxic fog in the garage that would prevent the fire department from putting out the fire for half an hour.

The security guard hurried from his position at the gate and dropped his red peaked uniform cap in a trash can as he made his way from the area, rushing against the pedestrians gravitating toward the blaze. A van skidded to a stop at the corner, and he hopped into the passenger seat, offering Hector a grin as the older man pulled away. He looked into the cargo bed, where two of Hector's men were sitting, Rodrigo's hooded unconscious form prone on the steel floor next to a large roll of heavy chain, and shook his head.

"You'd think he would have at least tried to scrub his call log."

"Not the smartest. He really believed he'd get away with it," Hector said. "But look at the bright side. It's a lovely day for a boat ride."

CHAPTER 41

Santiago, Chile

Jet hugged Hannah tight and then held her at arm's length and looked her in the eyes. "You need to promise to listen to Matt. Just like it's me, okay?"

"Otay."

Jet rose to her feet and gave Matt a long kiss. "I'm going to miss you. Try to stay out of trouble on that luxury cruise. I've heard about how those cougars get."

"With a broken wing, I'm not much danger."

"You did all right."

A single tear leaked from the corner of her eye. Matt wiped it away. She hugged him and whispered in his ear, "I'm so tired of this. I just want it all to be over."

Matt stroked her hair and nodded. "Don't worry. Everything will work out. Just be careful and take care of yourself. Don't do anything stupid. Hannah and I are depending on your coming back soon."

She sighed and cleared her throat. "Count on it."

~ ~ ~

San Antonio, Chile

Alejandro gazed out over the water at the black and red hull of the cargo ship inching toward the harbor mouth, the tops of the cranes on the massive jetty beside it hidden by low-hanging fog. He'd personally arranged for Matt and Hannah's departure two days after he'd officially taken over the Soto organization, refusing to allow subordinates to see them off. He'd given the woman his word that they'd make it onto the ship safely. Now that he'd discharged his obligation, he was free to focus on more pressing matters.

Gaspar was recovering nicely and would be smuggled out of the country later in the week, having chosen to remain dead in the eyes of the Chilean authorities and thus free to enjoy his remaining years and considerable fortune incognito in Spain, where one of his untraceable shell companies had invested in an oceanfront home southwest of Málaga.

Alejandro and Gaspar had never spoken of Rodrigo, and Alejandro preferred not to know how his father had handled the difficult matter of determining his guilt and meting out punishment. He had other issues vying for his attention, not the least of which was dealing with the army of attorneys that were already battling the government for Gaspar's sprawling estate, more for symbolic reasons than anything else – "To keep it out of the clutches of the thieves," Gaspar had said. And of course, cleaning up the remainder of the mess the Verdugos had left behind in Valparaíso.

Antonio had disappeared, which was just as well, Alejandro thought. There had already been too much killing. It was better to build bridges and incorporate the Verdugo crew into his organization than to continue on a vendetta. His father had preferred a scorched-earth policy, but had relented when Alejandro had argued the wisdom of allowing even those who had once been enemies to find prosperity under the Soto mantle.

Alejandro walked slowly back to the car, silently wishing the voyagers well, intuiting that the road ahead of them would be more difficult than for most. He hoped he'd never get a call from the woman, but knew in his heart that if he did, he'd move the earth to help her, just as his father would have – just as she'd done for them both.

~ ~ ~

"Where Mama?" Hannah asked Matt, her tiny hand nestled in his as they watched the port fade into the fog bank behind them. They were standing on the stern of the ship, the steady rumble of the engines beneath their feet reassuring, the black and blue bruises on Matt's face already fading to yellow and orange.

"Mama is going to join us in our new home. In a little while. Like she told you this morning."

"Why no Mama?"

"She has something very important to take care of." Apparently Hannah's selective two-and-a-half-year-old's memory was hard at work.

"I want Mama."

Matt's jaw clenched as the big vessel's bow swung north on its long journey up the Pacific coast of South America, ultimately bound for Long Beach, with an unscheduled stop off the coast of Panama to rendezvous with a local fishing boat that would take them to Panama City.

"Me too, Hannah. Me too."

~ ~ ~

Jet stepped onto the tarmac at Chacalluta International Airport in the northernmost reaches of Chile and shielded her eyes from the sun. Gaspar's plane had made the trip in two hours and would take off moments after landing for the return trip to Santiago, where it would become Alejandro's toy. As Gaspar had suspected, the authorities had made a last minute inspection of the plane. Finding no Sotos on board and assured that it was a private charter, they'd disembarked, leaving her to her business.

A forest green Toyota 4Runner was waiting in the small parking lot next to the passenger terminal, just as she'd been told it would be. A pudgy man, badly in need of a shave, was sitting inside reading the paper, munching from a bag of chips. Jet approached and leaned into the passenger-side window.

"Estefan?"

The driver looked up with hungover Bassett hound eyes. "Ah. You must be…my fare." He squeezed out of the Toyota and opened the rear cargo door. "You can throw your bag back here."

Jet did so, wondering how the rusting conveyance was going to make it over the Andes – a route that would exceed sixteen thousand feet at its highest point. Estefan smiled as if anticipating her skepticism.

"Don't worry. It has the heart of a condor and the soul of an eagle."

She eyed the vehicle. "I'm more worried about the tires of a jalopy and the engine of a lawn mower."

"I've done the trip many times."

"In this?"

"Don't worry, be happy."

The road to Bolivia was largely empty and in far better condition than she'd expected. At one of the two volcanic lakes near the summit, Estefan pulled over next to a waiting semi-rig. "This is your ride across the border."

She looked at the sad truck, which was easily older than she was. "Really?"

"Don't worry. I'll be right ahead of you. Going into Bolivia doesn't take that long, so no more than an hour."

They got out, and the driver of the semi-rig greeted Estefan like a long-lost relative, and then showed Jet her berth – a slot barely a half meter high by two deep, with little more width than could accommodate her shoulders.

"I hope you don't get claustrophobic," Estefan said as the driver helped her inside the compartment, her bag wedged by her feet.

"Let's get it over with."

The ride, even though not long, was excruciating due to the truck's poor suspension, and by the time she saw the sun again on the other side of the border, she felt as though every one of her fillings had been jarred loose, and she badly needed a shower.

Estefan was waiting when she crawled out, a wide grin on his meaty face, and she couldn't help but laugh. The rest of the trip was anticlimactic after that save for herds of alpaca in the high plains and a breathtaking view of the twin snow-capped volcanoes, Parinacota and Pomerape, in the distance. The road stretched to the far mountains like a runway to the stars, the air crisp at the high altitude and clean in a way Jet couldn't remember. True to his promise, the 4Runner chugged along valiantly, and they arrived in La Paz as twilight shadowed the sky.

Gaspar had arranged for a Falcon 7X charter, with a flight plan to Lisbon, Portugal, and from there to Moscow. When Jet arrived at the airport, the plane was waiting, the crew alerted by a call from Estefan. Jet gratefully stepped aboard and strapped herself in as a perky young flight attendant announced that she'd be available for anything Jet wanted, and had dinner and breakfast loaded and ready to be served whenever she wished.

The flight to Lisbon took twelve hours, and after an hour on the ground for refueling and replenishing, she was hurtling east, where an attorney who believed that you could erase people from the insulated safety of an office would soon be getting the last rude awakening of his life.

CHAPTER 42

Moscow, Russia

The broad boulevards of Moscow were already icing over, the sidewalks knee-deep in snow from the storm that had blown through overnight and continued all through the miserable day. Anatoly Filipov stood at his office window, staring down at the pedestrians slogging through the freezing slush, and shivered as he turned back to his desk, to consider the pile of documents that had accumulated throughout the day, a blizzard of paper that matched the one outside for its intensity.

A French antique clock on the wall chimed softly – it was seven in the evening, several hours after his offices normally closed, but he'd had a lunch that had run long with a pair of up-and-coming players in the petroleum industry who wanted to upgrade their legal counsel, and had hoped to catch up on the work that hadn't gotten done while he'd been pressing the flesh. Unfortunately, circumstances had conspired against him, and he'd have to come in early if he was going to have any shot at climbing from under the pile.

As one of the top legal minds in Moscow, Filipov was always in demand, and because of the amount of power and influence he wielded as the right-hand man to a number of oligarchs, his firm had more business than it could handle. His brother, who was his partner, specialized in structuring deals, whereas Filipov loved making them. It was a good fit, and the firm was successful beyond any of his aspirations, now with over thirty employees.

But there were some things that had to be handled personally, and much as he'd have liked to pass them on to a subordinate, anything that made it into his inner sanctum required his, and nobody else's, attention.

Filipov sat back in his executive chair and rubbed a tired hand across his face. He felt older than his years, no doubt because of the constant stress of his position. And his mood hadn't improved when for days now Leonid hadn't responded to his messages. He'd gone from cautiously optimistic after the last missive when Leonid had requested clarification on what Filipov would accept for identification of the target to despondency after Leonid had gone dark. Two follow-up requests from Filipov had gone unanswered, and in spite of his distance from the operation, Filipov felt anxious.

He sighed and yawned. Tomorrow would bring its own set of challenges, and possibly news from Leonid. There was no point to dwelling on that which he couldn't influence. Filipov placed a quick call to the garage to alert them he was on his way down so they could pull his car around, and then grouped the documents on his desk into three piles: critical, urgent, and to-do ASAP. He'd be in earlier than usual in the morning and hit the ground running – the downside of having the rich for clients was that they, like spoiled children, expected their needs to be attended to instantly, and they didn't care for excuses.

He moved to the door, turned off his office light, and then walked down the marble hall to the lobby, noting with approval that over half his staff was working late. They would likely remain in the office until the wee hours, billing insane amounts for their time. It was a good business, but on days like this one, retirement seemed far more appealing than usual. It wasn't like he still needed money – he had enough to last him ten lifetimes no matter how lavish a lifestyle he indulged himself in. It was that he thrived in the game, immersed in the corridors of power, making moves that would make or break whole companies and change lives. While the prospect of rest was appealing, he couldn't see himself relegated to a life of brunches and soirees.

The uniformed attendant all but saluted when Filipov descended the stairs and approached his car, which was purring at the curb, the heater warming the interior. An icy wind blew a flurry of snow as he climbed behind the wheel, but the attendant didn't seem to notice.

The short drive home was annoying, traffic coagulated at a major intersection where a truck and motorcycle had intersected in a grisly fashion, and Filipov tapped his fingers on the steering wheel as he waited for the police to wave him around the grim scene. His sense of impatience was unwarranted – he was divorced, his two children grown, and he lived alone, so there was nobody waiting for him to get home. Dinner would consist of whatever delicacy his housekeeper had prepared and left for him in the refrigerator, washed down with a half liter of excellent vodka while watching the international news stations distort world events.

He immediately sensed something off when he stepped into the foyer and placed his briefcase and keys on a long side table. It was subtle, but there, as if the atmosphere was electrically charged. Filipov flipped on the light switch and the hallway illuminated, the polished wood floors glistening, nothing different from when he'd left that morning. As he made his way to the kitchen, he shrugged off the feeling of unease; his nerves were overly sensitive, a function of the stress he was under.

Filipov swung the refrigerator door open and looked inside, and then froze when he heard a click behind him from the dining room. Not so much a click as a *snick* – metal on metal, some mechanism snapping into place. He straightened and turned slowly, his face gray, and peered into the darkness. A figure sat at the dining room table, unmoving, facing him. Holding a pistol.

"Come in, have a seat. Anatoly Filipov, I presume?" a woman's voice said, her tone even, her words measured, her Russian that of a native speaker.

He took several cautious steps, and his eyes darted to the wooden block on the counter, its array of Swiss knife handles holding slim promise against a gun. The woman snapped her fingers.

"Don't even think about it. Walk this way, pull up a chair, and sit down."

"Why should I do anything you ask?"

"Because I'll splatter your brains against the wall if you don't. Consider this your only warning. Now sit."

Filipov approached the dining room table. As he neared it, he could see the intruder better – short black hair, Asian features, the pistol steady in her hand, her expression as calm as though she were in church. His gaze drifted to the tabletop, and he saw a bottle of his favorite vodka there, a tumbler poured three-quarters full next to it, a prescription medicine container beside it.

The woman motioned with the gun. "Sit."

He did as instructed, wondering whether he could make it to the bottle and somehow evade being shot while he broke it across her face. Another look at the woman's alert emerald eyes dispelled that idea.

"So, Anatoly, here we are, just the two of us."

"Not for long. I'm expecting company any minute."

"Oh, well, then, we'd better make this quick. You contracted a group of killers to hunt me down and eliminate me. That didn't go so well. I'm here to stop you from ever doing that again." She eyed the gun for a moment and then smiled. He realized she was an extraordinary beauty even in the dim light, the thought incongruent with the situation. "It was considerate that you had a Makarov handy," she said. "Not a bad pistol. One of the few things the Soviet Union did well."

"I have no idea what you're talking about. I'm an attorney. I don't hire killers."

She ignored his denial. "I have messages from you to someone named Leonid. Ring any bells?" She placed a cell phone on the table and tapped it with her finger. "Let's spare each other the effort of pretending you're innocent. I'm here to make you an offer."

Filipov's pulse quickened. Perhaps this was to be a negotiation. His specialty. Maybe there was hope after all. He slowly reached toward his coat pocket. "Do you mind if I smoke?"

"If anything comes out of your pocket but a pack of cigarettes, you'll be dead before you can blink."

"I believe you." He slid his hand into his pocket, felt around, and then slowly removed a package of Marlboro reds and placed them on the table. He tapped out a cigarette and lit it, all the time studying her. "You mentioned an offer. You're sitting here, holding my own gun on me, and you have an offer for me?"

She nodded. "It's the best one you're going to get."

He took another puff and blew a stream of smoke at the ceiling. "Let's hear it."

"You have two choices. The first is that you can enjoy your cigarette while sipping your favorite vodka, washing down that bottle of valium with it, and slip into oblivion with no pain or suffering. The second is I shoot you."

His eyes narrowed. "That's the offer?"

"If you like, I can waterboard you and then dismember you with one of your knives." She smiled for the first time. "You sent men around the world to execute me like they would a dog. They didn't give me as civilized an option. That's the only offer on the table. Decide which it's going to be. Apparently we don't have all night."

"If you shoot me, the police will be all over this place within seconds. You'll never get away with it."

"I'll take my chances. Does that mean you want the bullet?"

A bead of sweat ran down his face. "Please. We can come to an arrangement. This is nothing personal, I assure you."

"Really? I take being murdered rather personally."

"It…it's a mistake. I had no choice. It was…I don't want to insult your intelligence by saying it was only business, but it was. Grigenko's estate set aside funds to…well, you can imagine."

"And you put the contract into motion. That makes you the problem. The contract dies with you."

"No. Others will see that it's carried out. I'm nobody in this."

She shook her head. "I don't believe you. You were his attorney. His confidant. There's no way anyone else knows about this. He'd have never committed it to writing, and even if he did, there are few stupid enough to pursue it." She paused. "What's it going to be? Pills or bullet?"

He sighed. "You don't have to do this."

"Neither did you. But I intend to finish it. Decide. Or I'll decide for you."

He reached for the pills and shook several out. "You're really going to make me do this?"

"Stop talking and start swallowing. I counted twenty. I want the bottle empty in the next two minutes."

He placed three pills under his tongue and took a burning sip of vodka. His eyes watered as he swallowed, and he considered hurling the tumbler at her but realized it would do no good.

"Now some more. Hurry up. Remember, your guests will be here any minute," Jet said.

"I lied. There are no guests."

"Probably the first honest words you've spoken this year."

"I have a lot of money. You can have it all. Many millions."

She waggled the gun at him. "More pills."

"You'd be rich," he said. "Unimaginably so."

"Didn't do you any good, did it? Swallow."

He gulped down three more pills and took another pull of the vodka. She stood and picked up a small glass ashtray in her gloved hand and slid it across the table to him. "Hate to see a beautiful piece of furniture get scarred because of your filthy habit."

Filipov tapped the ash into the glass disk and nodded, his eyes beginning to droop. "Thank you."

"All right. Enough. Down the rest. Now."

He spilled the pills onto the table as his hands fumbled for the bottle. She sat back down and aimed the gun at his head. "Pick them up. You have ten seconds. Pick them up and put them in your mouth, or this ends now."

Seeing no way out, and beginning to drift from the first effects of the Valium, he clumsily gathered the pills and stuffed five more into his mouth, and then drained all but the last inch of the vodka. He tried a defiant stare, but his face seemed to be melting like it was made out of hot wax, the muscles liquefied, his will no longer his own. The woman stood again and circled the table. Standing far enough away from him so that he couldn't make a move on her, she poured the glass full again.

He stared at her, his vision blurry. "The angel of death. You're beautiful. Deadly, but beautiful."

"Now the rest of the pills. It will all be over soon."

He nodded, her wisdom suddenly making perfect sense. It was so clear. He managed to get another handful into his mouth and chugged a few more gulps of vodka before he coughed the pills onto the table in a pool of liquid.

"Pick them up before they melt. Swallow them," she ordered, steel in her voice.

He did the best he could, got about half down before his neck muscles refused to support his head and he fell face first onto the table.

Jet rose and circled over to him, picked his cigarette up, and placed it gently in the ashtray. She knocked the vodka bottle over, spilling the contents over the table and floor, and then hurried to the bedroom and replaced the pistol in Filipov's night table drawer. When she returned to the dining room, she removed a glove and felt Filipov's neck for his pulse. Faint as a butterfly's trembling wings. She replaced the glove and pressed against Filipov's carotid artery for a minute, and then felt for his pulse again. Nothing.

Another alcoholic suicide in a city with the highest alcoholism rate in the world wouldn't raise eyebrows, and the attorney's passing would be a nonevent. The contract died with him, and the madness that had been Grigenko's legacy expired there, in a lavishly expensive dining room, on a cold Moscow night.

Jet studied the empty street before she walked down the steps to the sidewalk, the townhouse dark behind her. A dusting of snow drifted from the sky as she turned and made her way toward the large boulevard three blocks away, the sound of her boots muffled, the danger to herself and her family eradicated in a way that would arouse no suspicion, ending the pointless vendetta for good and leaving them safe at last.

CHAPTER 43

Santiago, Chile

The afternoon sun was blindingly bright, streaming through the hotel windows with the intensity of a laser. After four overcast days in San Felipe, and then the nation's capital, the glow was a welcome relief from the seemingly unending drab gray – a color that perfectly reflected Igor and Fernanda's mood after running into a brick wall on locating their quarry.

Igor was packing his satchel when Fernanda's cell phone rang.

"Tell me you have some good news," she said.

"I think I might. Or rather I will. Soon," the agent promised.

"It's taken long enough. The trail's worse than cold."

"Maybe not."

"Explain," she said.

"It's delicate. But by this evening, at the latest, I'll have information for you."

"Why is it taking so long?"

"Haggling over price. We don't want to overpay, do we?"

Igor was watching her when she hung up and slipped the phone into the back pocket of her jeans. She moved to him and kissed him on the lips, and she leaned into him as his hands moved to her breasts.

"He says we'll be in play by tonight. Which gives us a little more vacation time."

"I wonder what the late charge on the room will be?"

She pulled him by his leather jacket to the bed. "Whatever it is, let's make sure it was worth it."

~ ~ ~

Moscow, Russia

Jet stood near a sad collection of atrocious Russian art mounted along a wall adjacent to the departure gates of Sheremetyevo International Airport, waiting for her cell phone call to go through. The warbling in her ear was replaced with a series of pops and clicks, and then Matt's voice came on the line.

"Sorry about that. These satellite phones aren't the greatest," he said.

"No problem. How's the cruise going?"

"Good. Relatively calm seas. We should be in Panama in another day and a half or so."

"I'll be there right around the same time. I'll come meet the fishing boat at the wharf. Alejandro gave me pretty decent directions. Said any cab driver would know it."

"How did everything go?"

"Never better. How's Hannah?"

"She's behaving herself. Misses her mother." Matt paused. "Same here."

"I miss you too."

"You believe your problem's solved now?"

"Yes. Definitively."

"That's great. You want to talk to Hannah?"

"Of course. How's the hand?"

"I'll be up to my old tricks in no time."

"Let's hope so."

Matt called to Hannah, and Jet's throat tightened at the sound of his voice. The flights back would take a full day, with connections – now that she was on her own dime, she was flying commercial. She missed them both with a dull ache in her stomach, and couldn't wait for her plane to take off, winging her back to her daughter and the man with whom she'd finally found peace, if the world would only let them alone. She heard Hannah squeal with happiness when Matt announced that Mama was on the phone, and Jet closed her eyes, marveling that the sound of a little girl's voice could cause the earth she was standing on to shift as profoundly as a realignment of the poles.

"Mama!" Hannah cried delightedly, and for a brief moment, everything in the world was exactly as it should be.

<<<<>>>>

ABOUT THE AUTHOR

A *Wall Street Journal* and *The Times* featured author, Russell Blake lives full time on the Pacific coast of Mexico. He is the acclaimed author of many thrillers, including the Assassin series, the JET series, and the BLACK series. He has also co-authored *The Eye of Heaven* with Clive Cussler for Penguin Books.

"Capt." Russell enjoys writing, fishing, playing with his dogs, collecting and sampling tequila, and waging an ongoing battle against world domination by clowns.

☼

Visit RussellBlake.com for updates
or subscribe to: RussellBlake.com/contact/mailing-list

Co-authored with Clive Cussler

THE EYE OF HEAVEN

Thrillers by Russell Blake

FATAL EXCHANGE

THE GERONIMO BREACH

ZERO SUM

THE DELPHI CHRONICLE TRILOGY

THE VOYNICH CYPHER

SILVER JUSTICE

UPON A PALE HORSE

The Assassin Series by Russell Blake

KING OF SWORDS

NIGHT OF THE ASSASSIN

RETURN OF THE ASSASSIN

REVENGE OF THE ASSASSIN

BLOOD OF THE ASSASSIN

REQUIEM FOR THE ASSASSIN

The JET Series by Russell Blake

JET

JET II – BETRAYAL

JET III – VENGEANCE

JET IV – RECKONING

JET V – LEGACY

JET VI – JUSTICE

JET VII – SANCTUARY

JET – OPS FILES (prequel)

The BLACK Series by Russell Blake

BLACK

BLACK IS BACK

BLACK IS THE NEW BLACK

BLACK TO REALITY

Non Fiction by Russell Blake

AN ANGEL WITH FUR

HOW TO SELL A GAZILLION EBOOKS

(while drunk, high or incarcerated)